UNSEEN BONDS

THE DEIFORM FELLOWSHIP THREE

SARAH ETTRITCH

NORN PUBLISHING
TORONTO, CANADA

Copyright © 2014 Sarah Ettritch

All rights reserved. No part of this book may be reproduced, except for brief quotations in articles or reviews, without written permission from the author.

This is a work of fiction. Names, characters, places, and incidents are the product of the author's imagination or are used fictitiously, and any resemblance to actual persons, living or dead, business establishments, events, or locales is entirely coincidental.

All Scripture quotations are taken from THE HOLY BIBLE, NEW INTERNATIONAL VERSION®, NIV® Copyright © 1973, 1978, 1984, 2011 by Biblica, Inc.® Used by permission. All rights reserved worldwide.

Library and Archives Canada Cataloguing in Publication

Ettritch, Sarah, 1963–, author
Unseen bonds : the deiform fellowship three / Sarah Ettritch.

ISBN 978-1-927369-21-0 (pbk.)

I. Title.

PS8609.T87U57 2014   C813'.6   C2014-907519-7

v1

Published by Norn Publishing
www.NornPublishing.com

For Kath and Jim

Acknowledgements

My thanks to Jennifer Brinkman (my lovely partner and beta reader extraordinaire), Debbie Stevens (my good friend and fantastic beta reader) and Marg Gilks (my fabulous editor).

Chapter One

JILLIAN UNCLENCHED HER hands and resisted the urge to snap, "You must know more than that!" If she wanted certainties and large flashing signs, she'd joined the wrong group. She gazed at the conference room's blank monitor, then refocused on Roberta. "So it's a church that caters to the rich, and it has cushioned pews and an organ?"

Roberta nodded. "I believe the minister is white."

Well, that narrowed it down.

"You don't have any idea where it's located?" Sam asked, her tone milder than Jillian's. "Any clue would help. Could you see out a window?"

"No. The congregation is English-speaking. I do remember seeing . . ." Roberta's brow furrowed. "One of the children was wearing a blue sports jersey."

"That helps." Sam made a note on the pad in front of her.

"Someone mentioned a farmer's market," Roberta added.

"Those two hints will definitely shorten the list. Anything else?" Sam asked.

Roberta clasped her hands on her lap and closed her eyes. If it had been anyone else, Jillian would have snorted and labelled them a charlatan. She was beginning to trust Roberta's ability to identify situations that called for the Fellowship's intervention. In the two months since the Fellowship had shut down the soul healers, Roberta had directed Jillian and Sam on four other investigations. Okay, there had been a fifth case that hadn't led anywhere, but according to Sam, that sometimes happened. Jillian couldn't scoff at an eighty percent success rate.

The problems they'd resolved hadn't been anything on the scale of the soul healers case. Two were hypocrites claiming they could heal; one, a clergyman with a weakness for the race track; another was protecting a fraudster from having his day in court. All were quick in and out jobs—cowards quickly caved when presented with solid proof and the threat of exposure. Two were ousted from their jobs; the two others would be monitored.

"Snow and cold in the winters," Roberta murmured. "Oh, and the team name, the one on the jersey, starts with T-E-R."

Now that does help, Jillian thought as Sam smiled and wrote down the information.

Roberta opened her eyes. "If I see anything else, I'll let you know."

"We have enough to start searching." Sam picked up her pad. "I'll get Jeremy on this." She strode from the room.

For once, Jillian didn't mind that Sam had left without giving her a second thought. "Can—can I talk to you for a minute?" she said when Roberta rolled back her chair.

"Of course." Roberta crossed her legs and waited.

Jillian forced herself to meet Roberta's eyes. The long preamble she'd rehearsed flew out the window. "Maybe it's time for me and Sam to part ways. I think—I'm ready to work on my own."

Roberta studied her. "Is that what you want?"

No. She was doing what was best for her, for both of them, even though she hated the idea. "Yes."

"Why?"

"Because I'm ready," Jillian repeated lamely. "Because Sam doesn't have to protect me anymore. The Beguilers have given up on me. We haven't seen them since they grabbed me at the cemetery."

Roberta's gaze sharpened. "Is Sam being a problem?"

"No." Well, yes, but not in the sense that Roberta was asking about. "But we both know she wants to work on her own. Our partnership was only a temporary arrangement, until I was ready to go solo—which I am." Maybe Roberta disagreed. "Right?"

"You didn't use your gifts during the last few investigations."

Blood pounded in Jillian's ears. She jabbed her finger toward herself. "I'm trained. I can use the gifts. I see them differently than you do, but that doesn't mean they'll fail me."

"I never said it did," Roberta said calmly. "When I said 'you,' I meant both of you."

"Oh." Jillian felt like a petulant child, especially since she worried that the gifts would fail her at the worst possible time. There were several she'd never used in the field. Lock picking, bugging residences, surveillance, perusing social media accounts, and eavesdropping on phone conversations usually did the trick. Sam had astral-projected a few times, but Roberta wasn't concerned about Sam. "If you don't doubt my gifts, why does it matter that I haven't used them?"

"It's not using them per se, but knowing when best to use them. After you've received more guidance in that from Sam, I'll consider sending you out on your own."

Give me a freaking break! Consider sending me out on my own? Had Roberta required the same of the others? Probably not. Was it Jim's death, or was she lying about her confidence in Jillian's gifts? Jillian wouldn't press her, because she'd asked for something she didn't want and was relieved that Roberta had said no. "We don't know what this case is about yet." If there *was* one. The jury was still out. "We might not use our gifts."

Roberta nodded. "We don't know the scope of it, either, another reason to keep you with Sam for now."

Bullshit. Jillian was working her way through past cases and becoming more familiar with how the Fellowship operated. Deiforms usually worked alone. When they needed help, Supporters became involved. There were exceptions. *Exceptions*, not the rule. Wasn't everyone always wishing there were more Deiforms? She was ready! And conflicted, damn it. "If that's what you want, okay."

Roberta frowned. "Are you sure there isn't a problem?"

Nothing she couldn't handle, or at least she kept telling herself that. It would blow over. It had to. "Positive. I just want to pull my weight."

"You are pulling your weight." Roberta paused. "Is there anything else?"

"No. I'll go help with the search." She quickly left the conference room, disappointed with herself for being pleased that Roberta had denied her request. It made it difficult to pat herself on the back for trying to do the sensible thing.

Time to focus on finding the church in Roberta's vision and figuring out what, if anything, was amiss.

When she stepped inside Jeremy's cave, as she called it, Sam was sitting next to him. Jillian listened as they discussed the meagre information Roberta had provided. "I'll look at all the professional sports teams, and the university ones." Jeremy pursed his lips. "I'll try searching for sports teams with blue jerseys in places with snowy winters, but I doubt it'll help." He twisted to face his keyboard.

Jillian looked over his shoulder as he typed the phrase into a search engine. She skimmed the results. Yep, it wasn't going to be that easy. "Don't forget the farmer's market."

"I'll use that to narrow down the list I get from the jersey clue."

"The team's name begins with T-E-R."

"Or the town's," Sam pointed out.

"I'll explore both avenues." Jeremy flexed his fingers. "I'll start by compiling a list of teams that match the criteria. Then I'll move on to towns." He bent over his keyboard, then glanced at Sam and Jillian. "This could take a while."

"Talk to you later," Jillian murmured.

"I guess there isn't anything we can do," she said when Sam joined her in the hallway.

"We can pack. We could be gone for a while. Knowing Jeremy, we'll have a preliminary list in no time. We'll leave tomorrow."

"There could be a lot of churches on that list."

Sam shrugged. "If we're lucky, Roberta will come up with more to narrow it down." When they reached the stairway, Sam gave her a tight smile. "I know you're reading cases. Look up the Anderson case. It started like this one. Church hunting."

"I will," Jillian said, knowing she was being dismissed, so she wasn't surprised when Sam said, "See you later," and climbed the stairs. Whether Jillian would see her later was an open question. Sometimes they had dinner together—with others—and sometimes they didn't. Well, she had a case to read. The sooner she absorbed herself in it, the sooner she'd stop thinking about how she wouldn't mind if the church hunt took a while—although she also hoped they found the church quickly. *Yep, conflicted. Con-freaking-flicted.*

With a groan, Jillian threw her blanket aside and swung her legs off the bed. She'd had a feeling that trying to fall back asleep would be futile. At least it was after six. Not exactly the middle of the night, but earlier than she usually rose. She could read, but a brisk walk in the dawn light appealed. Jeremy's list contained churches in over seventy cities and towns. Who knew when she'd walk the island's paths again?

After dressing, she crept past Sam's room and down the stairs. The dogs were nowhere to be seen; she wouldn't risk waking someone by calling for them. Outside, the crisp air chased away her lethargy. She strode down the path that would take her past the chapel and her favourite rock, then loop back to the house.

A minute later, she slowed and listened. Was that music? It had to be coming from the chapel. As she approached its entrance, she recognized the organ's distinctive sound. Her curiosity grew. Who would be playing at this time in the morning? Did they play at the twice-weekly services? She stayed well away from the chapel while those were taking place, but lately her thoughts were with those who attended. Maybe, just maybe, she'd sneak in and sit in the back sometime.

In university, she'd known an atheist who regularly attended church. She'd thought he was nuts, but now she understood. People went to church for all sorts of reasons: to belong to a community, to get to know their neighbours, to find a date, to introduce their children to Christianity, to please their spouses, for the music . . . hell, there were probably as many reasons as there were people who went to church. She wished she'd asked her friend why he attended, but she'd been too close-minded and arrogant and had railed on about hypocrisy and stupid believers. Was it any wonder that he'd suddenly been busy every time she suggested they study together or take in a movie?

She swung open the chapel door and stepped inside. Of course, she'd make it clear to everyone that she was sitting in on the services because her stubborn refusal to attend no longer sat well. The services were important to those she lived with, and she wasn't only thinking about Sam. She'd started to feel excluded and a bit selfish. She knew them well enough that she wouldn't fear being dragged to the altar, so yeah, maybe—

Her mouth dropped open when she peered into the sanctuary. *What the hell?* She whirled and marched from the chapel. All those times she'd prattled on about her guitar, and Sam hadn't once said,

"Oh, by the way, I play the organ." Jesus! Why the hell did she bother trying to get through to the woman? If Sam wanted to be Ms. Mysterious Loner, let her. Jillian didn't give a crap!

She stopped and blew out a sigh. If only that were true. She shoved her hands into her pockets and stomped down the path. She didn't want this damn crush, or whatever it was. She'd been oblivious to that side of life for years, too caught up in work, and too wrapped up in herself, to give a shit about anyone. When it had dawned on her that she had feelings for Sam, she couldn't have been more shocked, mortified, surprised . . . and pissed off. She'd tried to convince herself that she was drawn to Sam because Sam had trained her and seen her at her most vulnerable. They'd spent months working together. Jillian had left everyone and everything she knew. It was natural that she'd gravitate toward the one person who'd guided her as she'd transformed her life, and had remained with her since. She'd awakened from her slumber and mistaken trust and respect for something more.

Uh-huh.

She was good at lying to herself; she'd done it for years. But when it came to Sam, her intellect refused to buy its own fabricated story.

All those sappy songs could go jump in a lake. There was nothing enjoyable about having thoughts of Sam intrude whenever she wasn't there, searching Sam's words and actions for signs of interest, and experiencing the occasional burst of sanity that allowed her to see how stupid and futile and pathetic it was to feel the way she did. Crushes sucked, especially when the object of one's desire was such a mismatch. It would be a disaster. It would be insane. It would ruin everything. But none of that stopped her from wanting it.

Why should she care about someone who couldn't even share that she played the freaking organ, and why should she defend Sam by admitting that she was partly to blame for not knowing? She could read Sam's file anytime she liked, but she continued to resist the temptation. One night she'd gone so far as to bring up the file on her laptop. *The Deiform Sam (Samantha)* had graced the first page, taunting her. She'd turned away and closed the file, because she wanted Sam to trust her enough to tell her. What a freaking moron she was! Maybe she should go back to Roberta and plead with her to split them up. Maybe—

She stopped short. Ruth regarded her with amused eyes. "I thought you were going to run me over."

"Sorry. I was somewhere else." In moron-land.

"I don't normally see you at this time," Ruth said.

"I usually get up around 8:00." And apparently missed half of what went on around here while she slept. "Are you heading to the chapel? Sam's in there playing the organ." She managed to keep her voice even.

Ruth's eyes lit up. "Oh, good. That always makes my morning contemplations more pleasant."

"Does she play it during the services, too?"

"Sometimes, but she usually plays the piano."

Jillian blinked at her. Okay, time for a change of subject, because every mention of an instrument was raising her blood pressure by twenty points. The next one would have steam blasting from her ears. It didn't help that the music was the one aspect of church services she'd always enjoyed and sometimes missed. "Do you know how Jane's doing?" After recuperating on the island, Jane had returned to the UK.

"She's all right. She's settling back into her old life and turning her attention to other cults." Ruth squinted at Jillian. "You'll be off today, and maybe for a while. It's always challenging when Roberta's information is sparse. The last time we had so little to go on was when we were looking for you."

They'd lost a Deiform and Supporter as a result. "It didn't turn out very well."

"We suffered terrible losses, yes. But you're here. It's what Jim wanted to see."

If the Beguilers hadn't murdered him, he'd be here, too, and so would Joanna, who'd been in the wrong place at the wrong time and hadn't had a special interest in Jillian. The familiar guilt stirred, even though she knew everyone would have hung up on him if he'd called and told them they were a Deiform. "I'll let you get to the chapel."

Ruth patted her arm. "Be patient, and careful."

She gave Ruth a small smile. "I will."

Chapter Two

On the plane, Jillian studied the map Jeremy had prepared. The red dots marking churches stretched from one side of the country to the other. Yeah, it could take a while, so she'd better snap out of her surly mood. She was thirty-seven, not fourteen. If she only communicated by grunting, as she had when she and Sam had decided on a route, this would be a long investigation. She set the tablet on the empty seat next to her and met Sam's eyes. "It will seem weird staying in hotels and motels." They'd stay in safe houses too, as they would for their first stop, but most of the churches were located too far from a major city for them to bunk in a Fellowship house.

"You can take care of yourself now, but we'll have to insist that our rooms are next door to each other."

"Have you been to any of the more far-flung towns?"

"Just two." Sam pointed to one dot, then to another. "Fortunately they were cases I worked on over ten years ago. I didn't attend church for one, and there's new clergy at the other."

"We might not have to go to church there, anyway." Supporters would help them narrow down the list based on the cushioned pews requirement. It would be great if Roberta could give them more, but so far, nothing.

She was about to ask Sam whether the church she'd attended had cushioned pews, but then she realized that anything could have changed over the past ten years. "When we show up for a service, what should we look for? If there's anything untoward going on, it won't be obvious to a visitor."

"No, it won't. We'll have to gain each congregation's trust, which will mean attending for a while." Sam jutted her chin toward the tablet. "That route is preliminary. We won't go to all the churches, and we could end up jumping around."

"So, we'll attend a church until we find something or eliminate it." Jillian had better practice her smile. *Be patient.* Yeah.

Two hours later, she dropped her bag on the floor of a safe house bedroom and did what she usually did first: wandered into the kitchen. For some reason, she always wanted to snack after flying. Today she was out of luck: empty cupboards, sour milk in the fridge.

"Nothing?" Sam asked behind her.

Jillian turned and shook her head. "Not even a crumb."

Sam glanced at her watch. "It's almost dinnertime. How about I go to the grocery store, then pick up dinner?"

"That sounds like a good idea," Jillian said, wanting to suggest they go together. Not so long ago, Sam would have insisted that Jillian go with her, but she'd been trying to trust that Jillian would be okay on her own. If only Sam would trust her in other ways. "I'm easy. Get whatever you want. Oh, but get chocolate chip cookies. We'll take them with us when we leave."

Sam's mouth turned up at the corners.

"You sure you don't want company?" *Damn it!*

Sam shook her head. "I won't be long. See you in a bit."

Jillian wanted to kick herself. To keep herself busy, she unpacked what she'd need for their short stay, then went back into the kitchen and looked for a glass—her throat was dry. Water would have to do. She ran the tap until the water was ice cold, then filled the glass and gulped down half its contents. She'd flick on the news, find out what was going on in this city. As she strolled into the living room, her thoughts wandered to Sam. Had she found a grocery st—

She was hurtling through space! Her heart raced. She threw out her arms to balance herself. Glass shattered. Breathing raggedly, she swayed for a moment, then glanced around in confusion. Her surroundings came into focus.

She wasn't moving. She was standing just inside the living room, her arms outstretched. Worried that her knees would buckle even though she didn't feel weak, she carefully avoided the puddle and broken glass on the hardwood floor and sank into the nearest chair.

She pressed her hand against her forehead. *What the hell was that?* A dizzy spell? She'd never experienced one out of the blue. Was it low blood sugar? She *was* hungry, but she hadn't felt light-headed. She'd felt as if she were moving at high speed, about to blast through the living room wall. "Hello, my name is Jillian," she said, on the off chance she was having a stroke. She sounded okay—no garbled speech—but if she *was* having a stroke, would she be able to tell?

Chill. She was getting carried away. She flexed her fingers and toes. Everything worked. She felt normal. She hadn't fainted. Whatever it was had quickly passed, and she had a mess to clean up before Sam returned. With a wry shake of her head, she went in search of a rag, broom, and dustpan.

SAM SMILED AT a passing parishioner and continued to flip through the devotional magazine she'd taken from one of the tables in the church hall. She peeked over the top of the magazine, watching Jillian chat with the three elderly women who'd quickly surrounded the more sociable of the two newcomers. If embracing one's fellow human beings was required to be a good Christian, Sam would be a failure. But she believed that the Lord acted through people in different ways, and hers wasn't to pretend that she cared about people she didn't care about. She was better at caring about her neighbours in broad strokes, working against injustices and protecting people from those who didn't care on any level. When spending time with a congregation was required, Sam gritted her teeth or, more commonly, worked with a Supporter.

She lowered her eyes back to the magazine. Teaming with Jillian was different. Supporters were sometimes deferential to Sam, which she hated. The Lord had blessed her with the gifts, nothing more. Everyone could be His agent and enjoy a relationship with Him. There was no need for Supporters to set her apart and treat her like an alien. Jillian, on the other hand, made her feel like a regular human being. Sam inwardly chuckled. Deferential didn't remotely describe Jillian's attitude toward her, and it wasn't because Jillian was an atheist and a Deiform. She just wasn't into bullshit, though she worked a room really well. Jillian wasn't exactly thrilled with having to be Ms. Congeniality, but she was good at it. Sam understood how she'd managed to wheedle her way into her co-workers' lives when she was a white-collar crime investigator.

"I'm not picking up anything suspicious," Jillian said, breaking into Sam's thoughts and demonstrating another advantage to working with her.

"One visit won't do it." Sam glanced at her watch. *"But I think you can wrap it up now."* They had a long drive ahead of them.

Sam set the devotional magazine back on the stack and murmured good-byes to those who smiled at her as she made her way to the exit. Five minutes later, she pulled on her seatbelt, started the car, and drove onto the road that would take them to the highway.

"There are still a lot of churches on the list," Jillian said with a weary sigh.

"I'm still hoping Roberta will come up with more hints."

"That would be nice."

Sam could hear her frustration, and shared it. "Nothing alarming at all this morning?"

"Nope. But then, nobody's going to tell a stranger the juicy gossip right off the bat." Jillian paused. "The ladies I spoke to this morning were very interested in my professional life. I was thinking that maybe I shouldn't be an accountant for this one. It was okay for the soul healers. Everyone was indoctrinated and they figured I was, too. But for a regular church, if anyone's stealing money, the last thing they'll want to do is befriend an accountant."

"We don't know if it's that." When Jillian didn't reply, Sam noticed her stiff shoulders and the tension around her mouth. She didn't have to be a mind reader to know that Jillian was thinking about her father. "What do you want to be, then?" she asked.

"I don't know. A math teacher?"

Sam chuckled. "It has to be something you could actually do, in case someone checks."

Jillian snorted. "Not that, then. I don't have the training, or the patience. Five minutes in a classroom and I'd want to slap the beggars silly. I don't know how teachers do it. They all deserve medals."

Sam silently agreed. "The best jobs are those that are done in a private office, or from home or on the road, so it's not easy for someone to confirm that it's your actual job."

"I can't be a consultant, like you. Well, I could, but that might be a bit much. Sisters, both consultants . . ." She fell silent for a moment. "I know. I'll be a virtual assistant."

"A what?"

"A virtual assistant. You do stuff for people over the Internet. You can find jobs on freelancing sites or hang out your own shingle. I'll ask Jeremy to put a site up for me with all sorts of glowing testimonials from Supporters." In her peripheral vision, Sam saw Jillian pull out her phone. "I'll have to stay an accountant for the church this morning, but I don't think anything's going on there, anyway."

"You're probably right." Sam stopped at a red light and tapped the steering wheel while she listened to Jillian chat with Jeremy. Too bad he couldn't keep her on the phone until they reached their next destination, but it was a three hour trip. When Jillian hung up, Sam would turn on the radio and hope that Jillian got the hint. They could talk when they stopped to eat. *Would You consider giving Roberta another hint?* Working with Jillian had its advantages, but it also meant having someone around all the time. The sooner they found the church or exhausted the list, the sooner Sam would be back to working on her own.

A month later

Jillian sipped the weak, lukewarm tea a parishioner had pressed into her hand and nodded when Linda, the woman she was chatting with, said, "You work with people all over the world?"

"I do things like data entry, proofreading, research, basically whatever the client needs."

"How do you get paid?" Linda asked.

"It depends on the client. Sometimes I get paid through PayPal, sometimes—"

"What's PayPal?" The elderly woman who'd joined them leaned on her cane.

"It's a way to pay for things on the Internet," Linda explained. "This is my mother, Jean," she added.

"I wouldn't trust my money on the Internet," Jean growled. "How do you know where it's going?"

Linda smiled stiffly. "If it was up to you, we'd all have our money stuffed between our mattresses."

"You don't see it anymore!"

"See what?" Jillian asked curiously.

Jean gave her a withering look. "Money. You don't see it. It's all funny money. Electronic. Easy for them to steal."

Linda caught Jillian's eye and raised her brows. "Nobody's stealing your money."

Jean's mouth pinched. "Don't be so naive."

"Do you think Leanne's stealing my money?"

Jillian perked up her ears. "Leanne?"

Linda looked around, then pointed at a dark-haired woman across the church's basement hall. "She's a financial advisor. She offers her services to the congregation at a reduced rate."

"No, I don't think Leanne is stealing your money." Jean's eyes narrowed. "I think people on the Internet steal money."

"Well, I'm glad you don't think Leanne is a thief," Linda said, her irritation evident in her voice, "because since I closed my accounts at the bank and gave the money to her, she's more than doubled it."

Jillian didn't have to feign interest. "Really?" *"I might have something,"* she said to Sam, who was lurking on the fringes of the gathering, as usual. "So you closed your accounts at the bank and gave everything to Leanne to invest?"

"Just my investment accounts. GICs, bonds, mutual funds, that sort of thing."

"My eyes glaze over when it comes to finances and investments," Jillian murmured.

Linda grinned in sympathy. "So do mine. That's why I'm glad I don't have to worry about it. Leanne keeps me up to date. It's great getting statements with positive numbers in the columns. The banks tell you that if you invest young, your money will grow exponentially. Mine only bounced like a yo-yo, up when the markets were up, then down when the markets crashed. One step forward, two steps back. I'm glad I finally found someone who knows what they're doing."

Jillian took another sip of her tea and eyed Leanne over the rim of her cup. Was she looking at a con-woman?

She expressed the same question to Sam as they drove from the church's parking lot. "We definitely have to come back here next

Sunday. This is the first time I've thought that we need to dig deeper."

"Are you sure you're not jumping at shadows?"

Jillian straightened. "I know this is frustrating, but—"

Sam shook her head. "I mean because it's the sort of thing you used to look into when you worked for the agency."

And because her father had dipped his hand into the offering plate? "I didn't look into individual citizens being ripped off, but yes, maybe it is," she said, through clenched teeth. "Or maybe alarm bells are sounding because I know what sounds fishy when it comes to finances." Deep breath. She softened her voice. "It could be nothing. But after god knows how many freaking gallons of tea I've had to drink at coffee hours, someone finally said something that raised a red flag."

"Then we need to investigate Leanne. Let's get Jeremy and Emma on it. They can put together a file. Did you get a last name?"

"Hartley. I told Linda that if we end up moving here, I'll give Leanne a call. She offered to introduce me to her, but I said it could wait until next time." Jillian reached into her pocket for her phone. "I'll call Jeremy."

JILLIAN STEPPED OFF the elevator and crossed the hotel lobby to the restaurant. Another city, another church . . . after attending a service tomorrow, they'd head back to Linda's church and make contact with Leanne. The file she'd received from Jeremy hadn't contained anything suspicious, but many of the rats she'd investigated during her agency days had appeared lily-white on the surface, too.

Inside the restaurant she searched for Sam, then checked the time. When they'd checked in, they'd agreed to meet here for dinner in half an hour. Jillian headed for an empty table tucked away in a corner. Sam should be down—

The floor disappeared! Darkness engulfed her. She plunged through the air, her arms flailing. *Help me!* Her stomach roiling, she squeezed her eyes shut. Someone gasped. Her knuckles hit something cold and solid.

"Are you all right, ma'am?" an anxious voice asked.

She opened her eyes and stared down at the floor in confusion. Someone touched her elbow. "Ma'am? Are you all right?" She lifted her head. A busboy peered down at her, his brow furrowed. "Let me help you up." She didn't protest when he gripped her arm and pulled her to her feet. Blood rushed to her face. Everyone at the nearby tables had stopped eating.

One diner had risen from her table and hovered anxiously nearby. "Are you okay?" she said softly.

"I'm fine," Jillian said, as it slowly dawned on her that she'd collapsed to her hands and knees, right here in the restaurant in front of everyone. *What the hell happened?* "I—I tripped." She forced a smile to mask her mortification and shock, then turned to the busboy, who still had a firm grip on her arm. "Thank you. I'm fine," she said, pulling her arm from his grasp.

"Let me walk you to your table," he offered.

Not wanting to make a fuss, she said, "Thanks. I was going to the corner table over there."

When he pulled the chair out for her and gave her a reassuring smile, she thanked him again, feeling like a first-class dolt. "Are you sure you're okay?" he said.

"I'm fine. You'd better get back to work." *Don't worry, I won't sue.* Good, her spunk was returning, but it hadn't calmed her fear. Something was wrong with her. She'd been falling, dropping like a lead balloon through nothingness, with no awareness of where she actually was and what she was doing. It had felt so real, and it wasn't the first time she'd experienced a sensation that didn't jibe with reality.

"Enjoy your meal."

He'd only been gone ten seconds when the waitress arrived and handed Jillian a menu. "Are you okay?" she asked.

Jillian bit back a snitty, "I'm fine, already!" and said, "I'm okay. No harm done." She looked down at the menu in her hands, then up at the waitress. "I'm meeting someone. In fact, she's here," she added, spotting Sam strolling toward her.

"I'll bring another menu." The waitress bustled off.

Sam pulled out the chair across from Jillian and sat. "She's getting another menu." Jillian met Sam's eyes and fought the urge to tell her about what had just happened. What would she say—I'm having weird turns; I'm hallucinating? She wanted to review every second of her falling episode and do some research before she told anyone. Sam was already putting up with her. Jillian didn't want to be a pain in the ass.

"Here you go," the waitress said, setting another menu on the table.

Sam murmured a thank you, then looked at Jillian and frowned. "Are you feeling all right?"

"Yeah, I'm fine." *Fine, fine, fine!* She opened her menu and hid behind it.

Chapter Three

Jillian shut her hotel room's door and headed for her bag. Tonight she'd been grateful that Sam wasn't the chatty type and had declined an after-dinner tea. All Jillian could think about was getting back to her room and researching whether any other Deiforms had experienced what she'd decided to call "breaks from reality." She pulled out her laptop and flicked it on, then sat on the bed and called home. Emma answered.

"Hi," Jillian chirped. "I need to look up a few things. Can I have a code?" As Emma recited one, Jillian punched it into the appropriate field, then typed in another code that was displayed on the security device in her hand. "Thanks."

After hanging up, she typed *Deiform break from reality* into the Fellowship's search interface and requested that only Deiform files be returned. She blinked at the single search result: *The Deiform Sam (Samantha)*. Nope, she wasn't opening the file, and she didn't have to; the result snippet was all she needed. She already knew about Sam's involuntary shifting problem and understood why Sam would have described it as breaking from reality. When Jillian shifted, she was fully aware and could see her surroundings, but events were sped up, and she was never sure if she was seeing her environment through her eyes, or in her mind. If she'd shifted without knowing what was happening, yeah, it would have been damn frightening. She would have thought she was nuts and losing touch with reality. *Try another search term.*

Deiform falling sensation. Her heart skipped a beat. She looked into the seven results, but they were all about Deiforms literally falling. *Deiform losing touch with reality.* Sam again. *Deiform hallucinating.* The two new results—and Sam—didn't describe her experience. After trying two dozen other phrases, she wanted to scream. Nothing, at least in the digital records. Even if relevant information existed in the earlier records, she could conclude that breaking from reality wasn't a common experience.

She lay back on the bed and closed her eyes. Could she be ill? She felt okay, but what if her turns were an early warning sign for a medical condition? She reached for her centre, probed . . . and didn't detect anything. But if she were sick, could her ability to identify problems and heal herself be impaired, especially if her brain was involved? If she assumed that she wasn't ill, then what could it be?

Had using the gifts somehow upset her inner equilibrium? Probably not. She'd experienced her first episode right after leaving the island, and when she was training, Sam had never said anything about the gifts adversely affecting the body. But then, Sam believed the gifts came from without, and Jillian believed they originated within her. Could that be it? Was reaching into herself causing some type of problem? Or . . .

If she assumed, to cover all the possibilities, that God existed and the gifts did indeed come from Him, was He punishing her because she didn't believe in Him but used the gifts? No, that wouldn't make sense. She hadn't asked for this! If He did bestow the gifts, He'd chosen her and given them to her, so He couldn't turn around and be angry about it. She snorted. Why would she expect it to make sense? When one thought about it, nothing associated with God made sense. A benevolent God who loved his creations but never showed Himself and did nothing while millions suffered and horrors abounded? Yeah, and she was Mary freaking Poppins riding around on a freaking rainbow unicorn. But she'd had to hypothetically consider it, because she needed to get to the bottom of whatever was going on.

So far, she'd been lucky. Her turns had taken place indoors. What would happen if she broke from reality when she was crossing the street, or driving, or facing down a Beguiler? Maybe she should speak to Sam. Jillian didn't want to bother her with this, but she also didn't want to let her down at the worst possible moment. How would she open the conversation? "I seem to be hallucinating." She wasn't seeing things, though; she was feeling as if she were moving, when she wasn't. She'd also lost touch with her surroundings for a second or two.

She suddenly realized that she was overcomplicating her situation. If she wasn't a Deiform, an illness was the only cause she'd consider, so why the hell was she sitting here searching through Fellowship records and considering supernatural explanations? Jesus! Maybe there *was* something wrong with her brain. Irritated with herself, she grabbed her phone off the nightstand and called Emma again. "I'd like to see a doctor."

"Just a second." Jillian could hear typing. "Someone can be there in a few hours."

"It's not that urgent," Jillian said. "Tomorrow morning would be fine. We'll be leaving the hotel around nine."

"Are you sure you want to wait until then?"

"Yes." She cleared her throat. "My throat's a little scratchy. It might not be anything, but in case it is, I'd rather nip it in the bud."

"For sure. All right, expect Peter around 8:00. What room are you in?"

Peter? Last time they'd spoken, she'd been adamant that she wouldn't join the Fellowship. "Room 1806. Thanks, Emma." She hung up before the compulsion to swear Emma to secrecy got the better of her, then called Sam. "I've got a scratchy throat, and I want to keep it that way. Peter's coming tomorrow morning at 8:00 to look me over."

"If you're not feeling well, we can stay an extra day."

"I'll see what Peter says," Jillian said, not surprised that Sam hadn't suggested she heal herself. Probing herself for a potentially serious health problem was one thing. Curing herself of a sore throat would be quite another. Frivolous use of the gifts was a no-no.

"I thought something was bothering you at dinner," Sam said, shocking Jillian. "Are you sure it's just a sore throat?"

"Yeah, and I wouldn't even say it's sore. Look, I don't know how long I'll be with Peter, so go down for breakfast without me."

"If you're coming down with something, you don't want to skip breakfast. I haven't seen Peter in a while. We can go down together when you're done."

"He'll probably have eaten already."

Sam chuckled. "I'm sure he'll have room for more."

"Big appetite?"

"Yeah. Anyway, go to bed and get some rest. I'll see you tomorrow."

They disconnected. Jillian stared down at her phone, then at the wall that separated her room from Sam's. Would curing herself of a crush be frivolous? If only.

Perched on the edge of the bed, Jillian rolled down her sleeve and looked up at Peter. "Any ideas?"

Peter lifted the two test tubes of blood he'd just drawn. "We'll see what these have to say."

"When will you have the results?"

"Tomorrow." He labelled the tubes and slipped them into a refrigerator bag. "I didn't pick up anything from my exam. Now, don't take this the wrong way, but could it be stress?"

"I don't think so. I've been under tremendous stress before, but I've never broken from reality."

"Did you break from reality, though? From what you told me, it sounds like you were disoriented, but you knew where you were."

Jillian thought back to her latest episode. "I'm not sure. Last night I was falling through darkness, but only for a second or two. As soon as the sensation stopped, I knew I was in the restaurant." Being gawked at.

"So when you were falling, the restaurant was completely gone?"

"Yes."

His brow furrowed. "And you didn't detect a health problem when you examined yourself?"

She shook her head. "But I'm new at this. My gifts are still in their infancy."

"Let's ask Sam—"

"No!"

Peter frowned.

"I don't want anyone to know unless they have to." She heaved a sigh. "Sam resents working with me as it is." The amused glint in Peter's eyes encouraged her. "You know how she is. I don't want her to think I'm nuts, on top of everything else."

"Why does she think I'm here?"

"Because I have a sore throat."

Peter's brows shot up. "Do you think she believes you?"

"Why wouldn't she?"

"Because you're not the sort of woman who calls a doctor because you have a sore throat."

She stared at him. He was right, but did Sam know that about her? She had the distinct impression that Sam didn't care what sort of woman she was. "If she knows I'm lying, she hasn't let on."

"She probably figures you don't want to make a fuss unless you know for sure that it's something serious." Peter patted her on the shoulder. "If your blood work is normal and you believe that you're breaking from reality, I'd talk to her and Roberta about it. I can treat your physical body. I can't do anything for problems of a . . . Deiformic nature."

Jillian almost hoped the blood work would turn up a problem

The next day, she was disappointed. "It's Peter," she said to Sam when her phone rang. "Hi, Peter. What's the verdict?"

"Your test results were normal."

She forced a smile. "Good. I'm sorry for making a mountain out of a molehill. I'm still new," she said, mainly for Sam's benefit. "I didn't want to slow us down by ending up in bed with something I could have treated."

Silence, then, "If you don't want to tell Sam, tell Roberta."

"I'll think about it," she said, knowing she wouldn't. "Thanks."

"Call me if you need me. You've got my number now."

"I will. Bye." She disconnected. Results were normal. She should be pleased. Nothing was wrong with her! She'd panicked, blown two fleeting episodes out of proportion. The fall in the restaurant had simply shocked her. At the safe house, she'd been hungry—low blood sugar wasn't out of the question, and the blood work wouldn't have picked up a transient drop that had occurred weeks earlier.

"Everything okay?" Sam asked.

"Yeah." She slid her phone back into her pocket. "Everything within normal range."

Sam slowed to stop at a light. "Weird that he took blood for a scratchy throat."

Jillian kept her eyes on the road. "Well, I also mentioned that I'd been feeling tired. I guess he wanted to be thorough."

Sam grunted.

"So you're thinking of settling down here?" Linda bit into one of the biscuits she'd picked up from the refreshment table.

Jillian nodded. "We've had an interesting time, visiting the different towns in the area. Now we're giving our shortlist another look."

"It must be nice, being able to work from anywhere."

"That's the great thing about having an Internet business." She sipped her tea. "What do you do?"

Linda smiled. "I'm a teacher."

Really? How could she afford this affluent neighbourhood? "What grade?"

"Two right now."

Jillian raised her brows. "I don't know how you do it. I wouldn't have the patience."

Linda's eyes danced. "I do have my moments, believe me. But I'd rather have my students than deal with patients, like my husband does. He's a cardiologist."

"Oh," Jillian said, chiding herself for missing the obvious. She'd noticed Linda's wedding band the first time they'd met. Apparently Mr. Linda didn't attend church.

Linda gazed to Jillian's left at the same time Jillian sensed Sam beside her. "Your sister was just telling me that you might settle here."

"We're thinking about it," Sam said. *"I think we should stick around here for a while. I just overheard an intriguing snatch of conversation about the regular minister, and there's also the potentially bogus financial advisor."*

"What's it like, working together?"

Sam turned to Jillian. "We'll find out."

Linda's brow puckered. "You mean, you haven't before?"

"I've been a virtual assistant for a while," Jillian explained. "When Sam told me she wanted to quit her job and work for herself, I decided to go in with her. If things don't work out, I have a list of satisfied clients I can go back to." *"I agree. Call it a gut feeling, but I think there's something here."*

Sam gave her an indulgent look. "It'll work out."

"It's a web design business, right?" Linda said.

"It's a little more than that. We'll also do custom coding."

Linda chuckled and brushed her hand across the top of her head. "You've already lost me. I don't think I could work with one of my siblings. We'd be at each other's throats."

"I think we'll do okay. We've always been close," Sam said.

If only that were true. Jillian swallowed some tea.

"And you're moving because you want a change?" Linda asked.

"That, and so we can work in the same physical space." Jillian set her empty cup on the table behind her. "We could work together over the Net, but we discussed it, and we figure it'll be easier if we're in the same room."

"We don't live in the same city right now," Sam added. *"Let's make our exit."*

Linda's face lit up with comprehension. "I see."

"Anyway, we should go." Jillian patted Linda's arm. "I hope your mother feels better."

"Me too. She's not the easiest patient. Maybe we'll see you next week?"

"You just might."

They said their good-byes.

As soon as they were in the car, Jillian turned to Sam. "What did you hear about the minister?"

"Some people are actively scheming to get rid of her."

Jillian barked a laugh. "That's normal."

"Yeah, but they want to get rid of her because they don't like her priorities when it comes to the budget."

Christ, it always came down to money. "Why? What's she spending it on?"

"I don't know, and I don't know if everyone has a problem with her, or just those huddled together in the corner. They petitioned the Diocese to move her somewhere else. They just received a response. It wasn't what they wanted."

"Okay, so we definitely want to stick around. According to Linda, their usual minister," she peered at the program for that morning, "Reverend Patrice, will be back in a couple of weeks." While the reverend was on a sabbatical, some in her flock had taken the opportunity to stage a coup. Anyone who thought politicians were the most ruthless, scheming hypocrites on earth had never belonged to a congregation.

"We need somewhere to live, and we need to be out and about in the community because people are more likely to talk away from coffee hour." Sam pulled into a restaurant parking lot and swung into a spot. She turned to Jillian. "That'll be your job."

"What will you be doing?"

"I'll be attending Bible study and helping out at the church." Sam's eyes glinted. "Unless you'd prefer to do that."

"No, no, I'll be Ms. Out and About in the Neighbourhood," Jillian said with a grin. "We've got to be in business, too."

"Yeah, well, Jeremy and Emma will help us with that."

"Next coffee hour, I'll start making noises about wanting financial advice."

"Good."

Jillian's step was light as they strolled to the restaurant's entrance. They'd finally stay in one place for a while, and her gut told her it was the right place. Best of all, she felt great. Grounded. Clear-headed. She shouldn't have panicked and called for a doctor. There was nothing wrong with her.

Chapter Four

Sam gazed across the wooden table at Angela and half-listened to her explain what Matthew 6:19–21 meant to her. The eight people around the table—nine including Reverend Dougherty, who was filling in for Reverend Patrice—were participating in a typical Bible study, which suited Sam fine. She'd attended countless gatherings like this one over the years. Most people quietly expressed their views and deferred to the minister, but there was usually one person who interpreted the verses differently. This group was no exception. Thomas, a gruff old guy with a bushy moustache, kept things interesting. If Sam were to express her interpretation of some verses, she'd likely raise eyebrows too, but she was here to fit in, not to provoke. Then there was Jean, Linda's mother, who managed to somehow relate every Bible passage to the deteriorating state of society and the rude people within it.

When Angela finished speaking, Dougherty said, "Thank you for sharing that, Angela. You've given us all something to ponder." He closed his Bible and clasped his hands on it. "I think we've all gained better insight into Jesus' words. Thank you all for a lively discussion."

As Sam hoped, everyone quickly rose and filed from the room, eager to get home. She slowly pushed in her chair. Now on his feet, Dougherty smiled at her. "I'm very pleased that you joined us tonight. I hope it won't be the last time."

"We're moving here, so I'll be coming again."

"Ah, are you the one who's moving here with your sister?"

Sam nodded.

"Your sister, uh . . ."

"Jillian," Sam said, not considering it a lie. She'd normally think of a Deiform in her cell as a sister or brother in Christ, and maybe the same was true of Jillian. She had the gifts. At the very least, she was a sister in the Fellowship.

"Jillian," Dougherty repeated. "Is she wrapping things up in . . . Calgary?"

"No, she's here, but . . ."

"She's not the Bible study type," Dougherty guessed.

That was putting it mildly. Sam forced a chuckle. "No. I've persuaded her to come to church with me. I think she just fell out of the habit. I'm hoping she'll get back into it."

"She's lucky to have you, and so are we." His eyes narrowed; he wagged his finger at her. "You must also be the one Sandra mentioned. You want to help out with the fundraising for the new appliances."

"At my old church, I was on the fundraising committee for the new carpeting and furniture for the church hall." Now that was a lie she didn't like telling. She couldn't care less about carpets, furniture, and appliances. "Do you always fill in for Reverend Patrice?" she asked, wanting to change the subject for two reasons.

"Usually. I used to be the minister here."

"I haven't met her yet."

Dougherty's mouth pressed into a thin line. "I probably shouldn't gossip, but I recognize a kindred spirit, and I feel I should warn you. She has some weird ideas. The congregation has asked for a new minister, but the administration," his tone turned mocking, "feels that it's important for the membership to be exposed to a range of preaching styles and viewpoints."

Sam could hardly wait to meet her. "Why did you leave this church?"

"I'd been here for a while and wanted a change."

Or was pushed out? Sam wouldn't pry. She was interested in Patrice, not him. "I won't keep you. It was nice meeting you. Thank you for the interesting study."

"You're very welcome. I hope to see you next time I'm filling in for Reverend Patrice."

Sam smiled and left.

At the hotel, she tapped on Jillian's room door. *"It's me. It's safe to open the door."*

When it swung open, Sam stepped into the room. With her arms folded, Jillian faced her. "How was the Bible study?"

"Typical."

"Did you manage to stay awake?"

"Yes, I managed to stay awake." Sam eyed the open laptop on the desk and the notepad sitting next to it.

"I'm looking over Emma's notes. I have to sound like I know what I'm talking about, and we might have to take on a client or two from around here."

"That's not a good idea. We don't know when we'll be leaving."

"It doesn't matter if we leave. We—well, Jeremy and Emma—can work with clients over the Net." Jillian dropped her arms to her sides. "Why don't you join the choir?"

"What?"

"The choir. The rag-tag group they have isn't bad, but they could use a few more voices."

"Why don't *you* join the choir?"

Jillian snickered. "Trust me, you don't want me joining the choir. Cats in heat sound better than I do."

Was that why Jillian always mouthed the words? Sam had assumed Jillian didn't sing because she didn't want to be hypocritical. "Why should I join the choir?"

Jillian tutted and rolled her eyes. "Oh, come on. You have a fantastic voice."

Sam blinked at her.

"Of course, you could also fill in for the organist. Not that I would have known about that if I hadn't been up earlier than usual one morning and wondered who was playing. Ruth told me it makes her morning contemplation more enjoyable." Jillian's face tightened. "I guess I was the only one who didn't know." She sounded bitter.

Didn't Jillian get it? There was no point in growing close to people. When she finally worked on her own, she'd rarely see anyone more than once, except for Roberta and the others who called the island their permanent home. She might cross paths with Deiforms and Supporters every once in a while, as she had with Peter a couple of weeks ago . . . after not seeing him for months. She'd occasionally work with a Supporter. But that was it. She'd spend her life alone. The congregation at the church would soon be a distant memory. Becoming attached to someone was to travel a road littered with broken glass.

Sam had learned to remain distant the hard way. She'd grown close to Brian when he was bringing her in, only to see him abruptly disappear from her life. Ruth had trained her, then left her behind. Only when Ruth had retired from the world had Sam opened up to her again. She'd brought in Warren, then left him to Jim. She'd waved good-bye to Jim after the meeting Roberta had called about Jillian, and had never seen him again. The Fellowship was the only family she had now, and it was a pragmatic, busy family. Did she want to ask Jillian about items in her file? Of course. Was she curious about the details the file didn't contain? Yes. But she knew better. Training with Jillian, working with her . . . she'd worry when Jillian finally went off on her own, and Sam didn't like that. She didn't need it. She didn't want it.

But she'd try to smooth Jillian's ruffled feathers. They were still working together. "I play early in the mornings—except for the services, but you don't attend those, otherwise you'd know."

Jillian's face darkened. "Give me a break. All those times I've said something about my guitar, you didn't once think to say, 'Oh, by the way, I play the piano and the organ?'"

"No, I guess I didn't," Sam said tersely. She clasped her hands behind her back. "Do you think you can get Linda to introduce you to the financial advisor on Sunday? We need to start moving things along."

Jillian gave her long look. "Assuming they're both there, yes. Linda's offered, and she knows we've signed a lease here, so it shouldn't be a problem." She glanced at the desk. "I'll be glad to have a bit more room."

"Only ten more days until we're in the condo. Anyway, I'll let you get back to it. See you tomorrow."

"Yeah. See you tomorrow."

As Sam walked to the door, she could feel Jillian's eyes on her back. Ten more days, and then how many more weeks and months until she could work on her own again?

While Jillian listened to Linda chatter on about her adult children, she kept an eye on Leanne, the financial advisor, and hoped for a natural break in the conversation. Good, Leanne was still talking to Richard—and Linda had stopped speaking. What had she just said? Something about . . . "Does Ellen work during the summers when she's home?"

Linda nodded. "She's worked at the same store for a few years now. This will be her last summer, though. She'll graduate next year. My baby, graduating," she wailed. "Where did the time go?"

When Linda paused to reflect, Jillian seized the opportunity. "Talking about time, we'll be moving into our condo next weekend, and since I sold my house, I have some money to invest. Some of it will go into the business, but I'll still have a good chunk of change left over. I was wondering, can you introduce me to Leanne? You use her for your investing, right?"

Linda's eyes lit up. "Yes, and she's wonderful. Of course I'll introduce you. Don't go to the banks. They nickel and dime you and make it difficult to get your hands on your own money."

"Is it easy to withdraw from your investments with Leanne?"

"Oh god, yes. All you have to do is call her. It's not instantaneous, but it doesn't take long."

What was Leanne doing from the time of the call to issuing the cheque or initiating the transfer? Withdrawing it from a legitimate investment, or figuring out how to cover the withdrawal using someone else's money? To do the latter, she'd need a constant stream of new cash. "The funny thing is, I'm good at math, but when it comes to anything related to finances, my brain just doesn't work. It's my kryptonite."

Linda's brows drew together.

"Superman," Jillian said, then decided to drop it when Linda's expression remained confused. "Anyway, I'd really appreciate an introduction."

"Let's do it right now," Linda said after glancing over her shoulder. "Come on."

"Do me a favour and head off Jean," Jillian said to Sam when she saw Linda's mother bearing down on them. *"I'm about to meet Leanne and I'd rather do it without her commentary."*

"*I'll talk to her about the Bible study.*" Fortunately, Sam managed to grab Jean's attention in time.

"Sorry to interrupt, Leanne, but I'm about to throw some business your way," Linda said.

When Leanne and Richard gazed at them with strained smiles, Jillian wondered if they'd intruded on an intimate conversation. "I'll talk to you later," Richard murmured, moving away.

Leanne waited until he was out of earshot, then gripped Linda's arm. "Thank you. I don't know why he's not getting the message." She shook her head. "I wish I hadn't given him my phone number. I thought he had money to invest."

"He'll move on." Linda grimaced. "He's not been the same since Mila left. Just be firm."

"I don't know how much firmer I can be, but let's not bore . . . Jillian, right?"

"Yes." Jillian extended her hand. "We've shaken hands a few times during the service."

Leanne pumped Jillian's hand. "I should have introduced myself earlier, but I'm a bit shy."

Linda chuckled. "Don't listen to her. Now that you've been introduced, she'll talk your ear off."

Irritation flashed across Leanne's face. "You said you have business to throw my way?" she said, her tone light.

Jillian jumped in. "I was telling Linda that I've sold my house and have some money to invest. She'd mentioned that you're her financial advisor."

"For a couple of years now." Linda quirked a brow. "She's also my mother's. Trust me, anyone who can satisfy my mother is gold."

Jillian smiled. "I'd definitely be interested in consulting with you, if you're taking new clients."

"I'm always willing to squeeze in someone from the congregation," Leanne said.

I'll bet you are. "Great. Can we set up a time? I have to warn you, I'm a slow student when it comes to financial matters. All I know is that it's bad to keep lots of money in your bank account, so I'd like to shift what's there sooner, rather than later."

"Let me check my book." Leanne flipped open the purse slung over her shoulder and pulled out a pocket calendar.

"Have you considered keeping your calendar online?" Jillian asked, recalling the notes she'd made about websites and online business tools.

Linda elbowed Leanne. "She's a website designer. She's in business with her sister."

"Ah, the quiet one," Leanne said, leafing through her calendar. "Not you, your sister. I've noticed she prefers to hang out with herself during coffee hour. I've thought of saying hi, but why force someone into conversation?"

"She's not a people person," Jillian said. "That's why she works behind the scenes. I'm the public face of the business."

"Makes sense." Leanne focused on her calendar and pursed her lips. "How about this Thursday at 7:30? Will that work?"

Jillian pretended to think about it. "Sure. Pencil me in."

"Your sister isn't interested?"

"It's my money, not the business's." She and Sam had agreed that Leanne might feel threatened if it was two against one.

"Fair enough." Leanne recorded the appointment. "I could come to you, or we could meet in a coffee shop."

"I'm in a hotel until next weekend. Why don't we meet in the restaurant there?"

"Sounds good to me." Leanne wrote down the details Jillian gave her, then turned to Linda. "Things will heat up again next week."

Linda snorted. "You mean when Patrice is back. God, I'm so tired of it. Her sermons are good. It's all the fuss outside the services I can't stand."

"She's back next week?" Jillian asked innocently.

"Tomorrow."

"Oh. Sam's going to some fundraising meeting on Tuesday and the Bible study on Wednesday."

"We'll see if she shows up for the Bible study," Linda said, exchanging a knowing glance with Leanne.

SAM LISTENED TO Sandra, the head of the fundraising committee, rattle off who'd be doing what regarding the bake sale they'd hold in a couple of weeks. Knowing that she needed to appear as if she cared, Sam reluctantly cleared her throat.

Sandra peered through glasses that were too large for her face. "Don't worry that you won't be helping out, Sam. We'd already decided most of this at our last meeting. There will be plenty for you to do at our next event."

"Actually, I was wondering if you'll post the information about the bake sale on your website." Four blank faces stared at her. "Do you have a website?" Sam drawled.

Sandra and Helen looked at each other. "We have something," Helen murmured. "I don't know who takes care of it. Barbara, probably."

"If you don't mind, I'll talk to her about it."

"Go right ahead." Sandra drew breath to say more, then looked over her shoulder when someone knocked on the room's open door.

A woman in a blue blouse and jeans strolled into the room and smiled. "Good morning. I thought I'd drop in and see how you're doing."

"Good morning," everyone echoed.

The woman's gaze settled on Sam. "I don't believe we've met. I'm Reverend Patrice." She rounded the table and stuck out her hand.

Sam shook it. Patrice's grip was strong. "I'm Sam. Pleased to meet you."

"Barbara mentioned you. You're the one who comes with your sister."

"Right."

"I'm sure everyone's already given you a warm welcome, but welcome to the church."

"Thank you."

Patrice turned back to the table. "Barbara says you're raising funds for a new fridge and stove."

Helen frowned. Lisa shifted in her chair and tucked her dress under her behind. Donna leaned back and folded her arms. The tension level in the room palpably rose. "Yes, we are," Sandra said levelly.

Patrice pointed to her left. "I made a cup of tea in the kitchen earlier, and the fridge and stove look fine to me. They can't be more than ten years old."

"We've grown over the last ten years," Sandra said. "Our needs have changed."

Patrice's brows rose. "How have they changed?"

"Reverend Dougherty agrees that we need new appliances." Helen glanced at the others and added stiffly, "That's good enough for me."

"New appliances will be more energy efficient," Donna said. "They'll save us money over the long run."

"Perhaps, but I can't help but think the money you're raising could go to more pressing needs." When nobody spoke, Patrice continued. "Did you know that more people from this neighbourhood are using the food bank than ever before? Everyone's been affected by the bad economy."

Sandra's mouth pinched. "A larger fridge and oven will allow us to make and store more meals."

"But for who?" Patrice asked. "You do a very good job of feeding yourselves. What about the people around you who don't have enough to eat?"

"That's what the food bank is for," Sandra said with exasperation.

Sam's hands clenched. She leaned forward. "I know I'm new here, but I agree with the reverend. Instead of getting new appliances, maybe we should donate the money we raise to one of the charities that works in the poorer neighbourhoods and makes sure kids going to school are getting breakfast."

Everyone, including Patrice, looked at her as if she'd grown horns. "We'll consider that for our next fundraiser," Sandra said snippily. "We've already decided that we'll get a new fridge and stove, and Reverend Dougherty agrees."

"I just wanted to give you some food for thought—no pun intended." Patrice nodded to them. "I'll let you carry on." Sam gave her points for not rising to the bait and reminding everyone that she was the minister of this church, not Reverend Dougherty.

The moment Patrice's footsteps had faded away down the corridor, the whispers began. "Who does she think she is?" Sandra shook her head. "Coming in here and telling us what we should do with the money we raise. We're the fundraising committee. Doesn't she get that? We're not asking her to give us the money from the church's budget."

"It happens every time," Helen said.

"She was just making a suggestion about priorities," Sam said, knowing she was only digging a deeper hole.

"And implying that we're all selfish," Donna said. "That we should all be out there giving our hard-earned money to people who are too damn lazy to get off their butts and find a job. They sit around, collect their welfare cheques, and spend it on cigarettes and booze. They'd just drink away any money we gave them."

"Damn right," Helen growled. "But you have to understand where she's coming from."

Good, not everyone was uncharitable.

"She deals with the, uh, disadvantaged all the time. They know how to stoke the guilt and make someone feel that they're not a good Christian if they aren't giving all their money away. Patrice is naive. She believes the sob stories."

Sam scratched her last thought, though Lisa, the quiet one at the table, wasn't contributing to the pile-on. Maybe she silently agreed, or maybe she'd learned to keep her peace during conversations like this.

"Don't mind us, Sam." Sandra pushed her glasses up her nose. "Reverend Patrice is a decent woman, and I'm sure she takes her ministry seriously. She's just not a good fit for this church. Anyway, let's finish up."

Ten minutes later, Sam stepped into Barbara's cramped office and waited for her to look up from her computer. "Hi, Sam."

"Hi. I was just wondering if you—we have a website. Helen said she thought we did."

"We do, but Tracy's son put it up for us. I don't think anyone's touched it since then. Why?"

"My sister and I are in web development. I could probably persuade her to do some updates to the site." For free? Sam was tempted to charge them, but not everyone in the congregation was like those who sat on the fundraising committee. "Of course, we'll do it at no charge."

Barbara smiled. "That would be kind of you. Let me talk to Reverend Patrice about it."

"The bake sale is coming up soon. I want to add information about it to the site."

"I'll call Tracy, put her in touch with you. Can I give her your phone number?"

Sam pulled a card from her pocket and handed it to Barbara. "It'll be Jillian you talk to." She glanced at the half-closed door beyond Barbara's desk. "Can I have a word with Reverend Patrice?"

"I don't see why not. Just knock."

Sam tapped on the door and pushed it open at Patrice's invitation to enter. "I hope I'm not intruding."

Patrice lifted her head from the book she was reading. "No, not at all. Come in." She slipped a bookmark into the book and closed it.

Sam eyed the title of a theology book she'd read a few years ago. "You mentioned the food bank. I was just wondering if you're involved with it."

Patrice stiffened. "Yes, I am. Why?"

"I was wondering if you need another couple of volunteers."

"You want to volunteer?" Patrice said, surprise raising her voice. Her shoulders relaxed. "That's not what I was expecting to hear. Are you sure you're in the right church?" She tutted and shook her head. "Sorry. You caught me at a bad moment. I don't know whether my time here is meant to test me, or everyone else. Perhaps both. Yes, we can always use more people. Do you have a car?"

Sam nodded.

"Then I can put you to work."

After they'd discussed when Sam, and potentially Jillian, would be available and she'd received directions to the food bank, Sam said, "Thanks. I won't keep you any longer." She paused at the door. "I'll be at the Bible study tomorrow."

"Good." Patrice's mouth twitched. "We might be the only two there."

Sam wouldn't mind that at all.

Chapter Five

JILLIAN SLAMMED THE laptop closed, then winced and opened it again. Fortunately, she hadn't cracked the display. She needed to calm down; throwing a temper tantrum wouldn't help. All it did was make her feel silly. With Jeremy's approval, she'd dug a little deeper into Leanne's background, put her agency skills to work, and discovered a big fat nothing. On top of that, Linda and Jean did have investment accounts at reputable banks and financial companies that listed Leanne as the financial advisor. Jillian didn't know if all the money they'd invested was there, but most shady advisors didn't invest any money at all. They spent it on themselves.

Leanne could have identities Jillian hadn't uncovered yet, and maybe she honestly invested a handful of her clients' money so she'd appear legit to anyone who looked. Or maybe she was clean. Jillian stood and gazed out the hotel room window. If it turned out that Leanne wasn't bilking people out of their life savings, she should be pleased, not upset. Maybe she didn't want to find out they were wasting their time here. Maybe she didn't want to go back on the road again and visit the few remaining churches on their list. Or maybe she was looking forward to staying in a condo with Sam for a while. Pathetic.

She whirled when someone knocked on the door, then opened it when she telepathically heard Sam's voice.

Sam strode into the room. "I met Reverend Patrice. I've volunteered us to work at the food bank. We're going down there on Friday morning."

Jillian gaped. "We're supposed to be running a business. You're already on the fundraising committee. When exactly are you supposed to be working?"

Sam shrugged. "We have flexible work hours. Maybe I prefer to work in the evenings."

"Except on Wednesdays when you go to Bible study." Jillian slowly exhaled. "What's she like?"

"Patrice? One of the good ones."

"And you know this how?" Jillian asked petulantly. "You've only known her for five minutes."

"She dropped into the fundraising meeting and didn't seem too impressed that they want to treat themselves to new appliances." Sam chuckled. "They don't like her very much."

"We already knew that. What does she have to do with the food bank?"

"I don't know the details. I just know she's involved with it and they need volunteers."

It wasn't like Sam to jump at something without a reason. "Are you sure we should help her out? We want to fit in at the church, which means not aligning ourselves with her."

Sam's face tightened. "I'm helping them buy appliances they don't need. She's doing something useful."

Yes, and she was apparently a devout little Christian who fed orphans at Christmas. Just Sam's type. "What happened to, 'We have to appear to believe and do things we might not personally agree with?' Sure, I'd rather spend my time at a food bank than fundraising for selfish people who already have too much, but it's not about what we want to do."

"I know that. I'm wondering if we're in the wrong place."

"What do you mean?" Jillian said, not wanting to make it easy for Sam by admitting that she was having similar thoughts.

"Let's say Leanne is emptying bank accounts. How many people are affected? Ten? Fifteen?"

"She works as a financial advisor. She has more clients than those in the congregation."

Sam nodded, but said, "Still, it's too small. Two Deiforms spending so much time? I know you don't believe Roberta's guided by God, but I do. Something doesn't make sense."

"God wouldn't care if only ten of his flock were being fleeced?"

"Yes, but He'd probably work through someone else to handle it, not His Deiforms."

Out of respect for their unspoken agreement, Jillian bit back a retort that she wasn't anyone's Deiform. "My gut says something is here."

"The funny thing is, so does mine." Sam chewed her lip. "We've assumed that whatever we're looking for is confined to the church. What if the church was only a clue, like everything else Roberta saw?"

"You mean, the church was meant to help point us to a town? That whatever's wrong isn't connected to the church, per se?"

"Yeah."

Time to quash her petty jealousy and behave like an adult. Her stupid crush would pass. "You could be right. I can't find anything on Leanne. She could be very good at hiding what she's up to, or she could be clean. I want to check her out by investing money, but I'm starting to have doubts, too."

"Even if she turns out to be dirty, we'd just report her to the appropriate authority. It's too small."

"Then why are we getting more involved with church-related activities like the food bank?"

"Because Patrice could help us find what we're supposed to find. She's more aware of what's going on around town than we are, and if we're wrong and something *is* going on at the church, she might have information about that, too."

"You're right." *And I'm an ass.* "But only you go to the food bank," Jillian said, despite dying of curiosity to meet Patrice. "We shouldn't both cozy up to Patrice, because it'll put us at odds with the group that hates her. I'll keep my distance. You work with her."

"Okay," Sam said, a little too quickly for Jillian's liking.

JILLIAN WATCHED LEANNE fill in the financial advisor's section of the application form. "You'd think it would all be electronic these days."

Leanne looked up and shook her head when the hotel restaurant's waiter offered to refill her coffee cup. She didn't speak until he'd moved to another table. "Some firms accept electronic applications. It also depends on the type of account you're opening."

Jillian's two accounts apparently required paper. Was that so Leanne could shred the applications when she got home? She could fake an electronic application, but why go through the trouble when she didn't have to?

Leanne slid the application in front of Jillian and handed her a pen. "I need your signature here, and your initials here," she said, tapping the form in the relevant spots.

Jillian took the pen, added the initials *JW*, and signed *Jillian Westwood*. "I'm glad Linda mentioned you. I didn't want my money sitting in my account doing nothing, but I also had no clue what to do with it."

"If everyone knew what to do, I'd be out of a job," Leanne said with a grin. "It's not unusual to be confused when it comes to investing. I have to do a lot of work to keep up. New account types, changing markets, changing regulations . . . you don't have to worry about that anymore. I do that for you."

Would she spend Jillian's—or, rather, the Fellowship's—money, too? Jillian knew Leanne lived in a several-million-dollar home in an affluent neighbourhood, but the Fellowship's file on her explained why. Was Jillian wasting her time here? Would Dad always make her associate church and money with criminal activity?

Leanne ripped the yellow copies from both applications she'd completed and handed them to Jillian. "These are yours."

"Thanks," Jillian said, folding them in half and shoving them into the side pocket of the satchel at her feet. She'd send the account numbers to Jeremy. "How long will it take for the money to transfer?"

"It can take a few days for new accounts to make their way into the system." Leanne cocked her head. "By the end of next week? You'll get something in the mail. You'll be in your condo by then, right?"

"We're moving in on Saturday." Jillian lifted her teacup and tried to come up with a way to ask her about Patrice without it sounding as if she cared.

Leanne solved the problem for her. "Will you be at church on Sunday?"

"I should be," Jillian said.

"It'll be your first service with Patrice."

"Yeah." She put her cup down. "Nobody seems to like her." Except Sam.

Leanne swallowed a mouthful of coffee. "The old-timers certainly don't like her, and let's face it, that's about eighty percent of the church. I get where she's coming from, but she goes about it the wrong way. Hasn't she learned that you attract bees with honey? Poking at the hive with a stick just gets them worked up."

"Sam, my sister, has already met Patrice. She's on the fundraising committee. Apparently Patrice dropped in on them."

Leanne leaned back in her chair. Her eyes narrowed. "Your sister's a keener, isn't she?"

"Well—"

"I heard she goes to the Bible study, too."

News travelled fast. "I'll admit, she's into the whole church thing a lot more than I am. I hadn't gone to church for years until we started checking out possible places to settle. When she asked me to go with her, I decided to make the effort for her."

"So they won't be seeing you after-hours, then?" Leanne said, her tone light.

"No. How about you?"

Leanne patted her copies of the application forms. "I see this as doing my bit. To be honest, I started going because my ex-husband went. Now I mainly go for social reasons. I'm not looking to meet anyone," she quickly added, "but it gets me out of the house on Sundays and keeps me in touch with some of the neighbours. And to be honest, when my marriage broke up, going to church every Sunday helped me keep my sanity."

Jillian already knew the basics concerning Leanne's divorce, but there was nothing like getting it from the horse's mouth. "You were married?"

"Oh, yes. It's how I got the house. I couldn't have afforded it on my own." Leanne's face froze. "Don't get me wrong. I'm not a gold-digger. I loved Kenny. *I* wanted our marriage to survive. Guilt is a wonderful thing when you're hammering out who gets what."

"Did he have an affair?"

Leanne wagged her finger at Jillian. "You know, to this day, I'm still not sure. He left me for another woman, but he's always claimed that nothing happened until he separated from me. They've been married for ten years now. I was the greatest wife, the love of his life, until he suddenly didn't need me anymore. Apparently," Leanne put on a vacuous look, bobbed her head from side to side, and grinned widely, "the cute little receptionist at his investing firm had caught his eye. I wasn't needed anymore. Not that I'm bitter or anything."

Jillian didn't have to feign sympathy. "I'm sorry."

"Don't be. It was hell at the time, but I actually like being on my own, and Kenny takes good care of me. He's never missed an alimony payment, never griped, still calls to see how I am. I get all the good things from a marriage without having to pick up dirty socks and underwear. Well, most of the good things," Leanne added, her eyes bright. "He even helped me when I said I wouldn't mind going to school. As I said, guilt is a wonderful thing—when it's someone else's."

"He must be doing well," Jillian said, knowing damn-well that Kenny's wealthy parents had made a healthy donation to his bank account when he'd turned twenty-one—more than most people would make in a lifetime.

"His parents are loaded. They must have been horrified when he married the girl who served him drinks at the country club. But Kenny knew what he wanted. Or thought he knew what he wanted." Leanne was silent for a moment. "I don't know why I agreed to go on a date with him. I'd sworn to myself that I wouldn't get mixed up with anyone at the club. I never imagined I'd go for one of the snooty rich boys. But you can't help who you fall for."

Nope, you certainly couldn't. "You said that going to church helped you. Did you start going after he left you, or had you been going together?"

"Kenny had belonged to our church since he was in diapers. All part of the image. Of course, after you've dumped the devoted wife for someone who looks thirteen, the halo slips a bit. He stopped going, and then he moved away—after they got married. I don't know if he attends Sunday school with the new wife. Did I say I'm not bitter?"

Jillian chuckled.

"How about you? What's your story? Have you ever been married?"

"No," Jillian said, suddenly uncomfortable. "I've always been focused on work. Sam says I'm a workaholic. Maybe I am. Why not spend my time doing what I enjoy? I'll never say never, but I've never felt the need to hook my life to someone else's."

"Well, congratulations. You took the direct route." Leanne raised her mug to Jillian, then sipped her coffee. "I took the scenic one."

"At least your ex-husband isn't a complete asshole."

Leanne smiled slyly. "It helps that I know some things about him that he probably wouldn't want everyone to know."

Ah, so she could be ruthless.

"But it also helps that he isn't an asshole. I could have done a lot worse." Leanne's eyes grew distant.

Did she still love him? Jillian didn't want to feel sorry for her. She had to remain detached, view Leanne with an objective eye. That wouldn't stop her from feeling like a jerk, though. Leanne was pouring her heart out to a smiling stranger who was here under false pretenses. The familiar pangs of guilt stirred, the ones Jillian had felt as she'd sat at bars and restaurants, listening to her co-workers diss the boss and gossip about who was sleeping with whom. She'd had few honest relationships in her life—maybe that was why she was drawn to Sam. Her feelings weren't real. They'd pass. She glanced at her watch. "I should go. I have a call with a client tomorrow morning."

"Sorry, I didn't mean to keep you."

"No, I wish I could stay longer, but the client is in the UK, so I have to be up early. I have to get Sam up, too. She's agreed to help Patrice at the food bank."

Leanne's brows shot up. "I think I'll start calling her Saint Sam. You don't have anything to do for the move?"

"Nope. The moving companies already did the packing for both of us. It's just a matter of watching them carry everything into the condo."

"Good for you."

They said their good-byes. As soon as Jillian entered her hotel room, she pulled out her phone and called Emma. "I'll read you the account numbers. Paper forms."

Emma noted them down. "Thanks; we'll see if they're actually created and what's in them."

"Let me know." She hung up and stared at the wall separating her from Sam, who was probably already in bed. What Jillian had told Leanne about having to get her up was bullshit. Was she also lying to herself about her feelings for a woman who wouldn't look at her twice—hell, in this case, not even once? Crushes sucked.

JUST OVER A week later, Jillian spooned the last of her cereal into her mouth and carried her bowl to the gleaming kitchen sink. The condo was only six months old; they were the first to live in it. Because everything was new, she still felt as if she were living in a hotel room, albeit one with a living room, dining area, two full bathrooms, two bedrooms, and a lovely kitchen—and this was one of the smaller, cheaper units.

Her phone rang. "Everything looks good," Jeremy said.

"All the money's there?"

"Yep. She did exactly what she told you she'd do."

"Keep an eye on it." Jillian disconnected and leaned against the kitchen counter. What the hell were they supposed to find here? Were they in the wrong place?

She looked toward the hallway when footsteps approached. "I'm off to the food bank," Sam said.

Jillian lifted her phone. "Just heard from Jeremy. Nothing."

Sam frowned and folded her arms. "We must be missing something."

"Maybe we're both wrong."

"No. Something's here. I feel it."

"We'll have to keep looking." She set her phone on the kitchen table. "Maybe you'll get something from Patrice this morning."

"I hope so. See you later." The condo door thumped shut.

Jillian sank back into the kitchen chair and drummed her fingers on the table. They were looking for a needle in a freaking haystack. She needed to get out there more, talk to people, listen, observe. She didn't want to become more involved in church activities, so she'd look for other opportunities to rub elbows with her fellow parishioners. Now that she was a permanent resident in the neighbourhood, it was time to get out there and start socializing. Linda had mentioned getting together for lunch sometime. There was no time like the present. She lifted her phone and brought up Linda's number. "Hi Linda, it's Jillian."

"Jillian, hi!"

"I was wondering if you'd like to meet for lunch today. I know it's short notice."

"No, I'm glad you called."

Five minutes later, Jillian disconnected and rose from the table, pleased with herself. She'd never been one for sitting around, so her lunch date with Linda lifted her spirits. She'd call Sam on her way to the restaurant to let her know. Between the two of them, they'd find the damn needle.

Chapter Six

JILLIAN FORCED A smile when she entered the hall in the church's basement. Another wonderful coffee hour! She searched for Linda and spotted her selecting a cupcake from the refreshments table. Over lunch with her a couple of days ago, Jillian had learned more about certain people in the congregation than she wanted to know, but that was all. Maybe her gut feeling that she and Sam were in the right place was more wishful thinking than anything. Oh well, she might as well get herself a cup of tea.

Sam was calmly doing what she usually did during coffee hour: hiding behind a devotional, a Bible, that morning's program, or whatever else she could get her hands on. She occasionally exchanged a few words with a parishioner, but most had learned to leave her be. Sam wasn't the only loner. Jillian suspected that Rhonda fussed around the coffee and hot water dispensers and constantly tidied the refreshment table because she didn't want to talk to anyone.

Tea in hand, Jillian joined Linda. "Where's your mother this morning?"

"She's spending a couple of weeks with my brother. A vacation for both of us," Linda said, making Jillian smile.

"I received my first statement from Leanne. Thanks for introducing us."

"So you're happy with Leanne, then?" Linda said, looking pleased.

"It's early days, but she seems to know what she's doing." Leanne hadn't touched the money. What were they doing here? Being stubborn?

Maria joined them. Jillian had hardly exchanged two words with her, but Maria was familiar because she showed up for church every Sunday. She gave Maria a small smile and said, "Hello."

Maria nodded to her and gripped Linda's arm. "Did Ellen ever have trouble in school?" she asked tersely. "Me and Max don't know what to do."

Linda's brow furrowed. "What sort of trouble? Is Dylan skipping school?"

Maria recoiled and vigorously shook her head. "No, nothing like that. It's math. He might fail. His teacher warned us at our last meeting that he was struggling, and now she's asked to see us again. What are we going to do? He's not a bad kid. He does his homework. But I can't help him, and neither can Max. We don't remember," Maria waved her hand around, "arithmetic, or whatever it's called. I barely passed myself, but it didn't matter for me. It doesn't matter as much for women."

Jillian quickly swallowed some tea.

"Dylan can't fail math. What are we going to do?" Maria wailed.

Linda shrugged. "If he's doing his homework—"

"He says his teacher is bad."

Jillian inwardly snorted as Linda said, "They always say that."

"Do you know her? It's Mrs. Wallace."

"No, I don't. I teach in the public system."

"Oh," Maria sniffed.

"What about a tutor?" Linda asked.

Maria's eyes widened. "We've tried that. He had one for a couple of weeks, then he said he didn't like him and didn't want to go again."

"Try another one," Linda snapped.

"I can tutor him," Jillian heard herself say.

Both women stared at her.

She was as surprised as they were. "As I said to Leanne, I'm terrible when it comes to financial subjects, but not because I'm lousy at math. I won several math prizes at school." She wanted to add, "Even though I'm a woman."

"Let her tutor him at home," Linda said to Maria. "He'll be more comfortable there."

Maria frowned. "I don't know."

"It's worth a try," Jillian said, wondering why she was pushing. She'd rather not tutor a spoiled brat who didn't want to apply himself and would inherit Daddy's company anyway.

"Why don't I set up a meeting with his teacher and see what she thinks?" Maria suggested. "Dylan goes to private school."

Of course he did. "Sure. I'd want to speak to his teacher anyway, to see what she's teaching and where Dylan needs the most help."

Maria brightened. "That makes sense. It sounds like you've done this before."

"A few times." In an alternate reality, maybe. But now that she'd offered her services, it would seem strange if she backed out.

They exchanged phone numbers, then made small talk until everyone started to drift home.

"I've volunteered to tutor someone's son in math," Jillian said to Sam as they waited at a drive-thru to pick up lunch.

Sam's incredulous expression said it all. "Why?"

"I don't know."

"Didn't you say you wouldn't have much patience as a teacher?"

"Yeah, I did. I don't know why I offered. It just came out."

"When that happens to me, it's usually the Lord giving me a push in the right direction."

Jillian took a moment to temper her response. Half of her wanted to speak her mind. After all, she didn't have any credibility to lose on the subject. Her other half, the pathetic part that wanted to demonstrate to Sam that she could discuss the subject without judging, won out. "With me, it's usually opening my mouth before my brain engages."

Sam's mouth twitched. "On the off chance that your instinct is nudging you in the right direction, keep your eyes and ears open."

"I don't know if I'll be doing it yet. I have to meet the teacher, pass her muster." But as she said the words, somehow Jillian knew Dylan's teacher would approve.

JILLIAN DROVE UP the circular driveway and pulled into one of the guest spots. She zipped up her jacket and grabbed her satchel, stepped out of the car, and peered through her sunglasses. Jesus. Could she say loaded? Maria's family home could double as a hotel. Okay, it wasn't *that* large, but guest spots? What looked like a ten-car garage? A mansion that had probably been featured on *Lifestyles of the Rich and Famous*? If there weren't tennis courts and a swimming pool out back, she was Mary freaking Poppins.

She steeled herself and strolled up the brick path. After ringing the doorbell, she wasn't surprised when the door swung open and a maid smiled at her. "May I help you?" she asked.

Jillian felt like pulling out a business card and presenting it to her. Would she be led to a drawing room to wait for the lady of the house? "I'm Jillian Westwood. I'm here to tutor Dylan."

"Of course. We're expecting you. Please, come in." The maid stepped aside. She spoke with an accent—Spanish, Jillian guessed. She walked into an airy entranceway that was larger than most people's living rooms. The maid motioned to her right. "Dylan is waiting for you in the study."

As she led Jillian down a carpeted hallway, Jillian's stomach churned, and she only half-paid attention to the furniture and decor. Stressing about meeting a ten-year-old boy was silly, but she'd always felt uncomfortable around kids. They were too unpredictable. Why had she offered to tutor the boy again? The maid stopped outside an open door and motioned for Jillian to go inside.

Jillian hoped her smile appeared natural as she walked into the room. Good, Maria was here, sitting at a round table with Dylan. Jillian instantly warmed to him when he met her eyes, then quickly ducked his head. She wasn't the only nervous one, and she wouldn't have to deal with a sullen child who resented the tutor his mother had forced upon him.

"Dylan, say hello to Miss Westwood," Maria said.

Dylan lifted his head. "Hello, Miss Westwood."

Jillian dropped her satchel to the carpet and sat down across from him. "Just Jillian," she murmured, and extended her hand.

Dylan solemnly shook it.

Maria patted his arm. "We're glad you're here, aren't we, Dylan?"

"I don't think you'll be able to help me," he said, making Maria's smile droop.

Jillian raised her brows. "Oh? Why is that?"

"The other one didn't help."

"Well, I'm not the other one. Let's give it a try and see how it goes." Jillian pulled a folder from her satchel and opened it. "I met with your teacher," she started, then she turned to Maria. "I think we can work on our own from here." If she were Dylan, she wouldn't want her mother hanging around.

Maria's brow puckered. "Oh! Of course. I'll leave you two to your math." She rose and ruffled Dylan's hair. "Listen to Jillian. Don't talk back."

"I won't!" Dylan rolled his eyes. "Jeez, Mom."

"Jeez, Mom," Maria repeated mockingly with a wink at Jillian. Reluctant to leave, she hovered for a few seconds, then said, "Have fun," and strode from the room.

Jillian and Dylan stared at each other. "Let's get started," Jillian said, pulling a sheet from the folder.

Just over an hour later, she slid the folder back into her satchel, pleased with how the tutoring session had gone. Dylan wasn't stupid, but he wasn't a natural at math. She was certain she could tutor him to a passing grade, though. "Make sure you do the exercises, okay? We'll go over them next time."

He gave her a small smile. "Okay."

"I'll see you next week."

When she stepped into the carpeted hallway, she was relieved to see the maid waiting for her. Too busy fretting, she'd only vaguely registered the route to the study. She could have found her way to the front door, but having the maid lead her there would be better than taking a wrong turn and getting lost in another wing of the huge house.

"Mrs. Olmos would like to speak with you before you leave," the maid said.

"Sure."

Jillian followed the maid through a formal dining room and into another hallway. They rounded a corner. A woman carrying a stack of folded towels walked toward them. "What are you doing?" the maid snapped.

The woman froze and stared at them, wide-eyed. "Sorry, sorry," she whimpered.

"Go," the maid barked, with an angry fling of her arm. The woman scurried down the hallway. "I'm sorry. She isn't supposed to be in this part of the house."

"Don't worry about it. No harm done." Somehow she'd survive running into the hired help.

Maria was lounging on a loveseat in a cozy sitting room. She looked up from a fashion magazine. "How did it go?"

"He was very good. He can pass math," Jillian said. "I don't know what he thought about me."

"I'm sure he loved you." She set the magazine on the coffee table. "Now that you've met Dylan, I won't be there next time. You did the right thing, shooing me out. I'm too protective of him."

Jillian wondered if Maria had sat in on Dylan's other tutoring sessions. Maybe that was why they hadn't gone so well.

Maria stood. "We haven't discussed your fee and how you'd like to be paid."

Shit. Jillian hadn't thought about it, and noted with interest that Maria hadn't asked before the first session. *It must be nice, knowing you can afford whatever you need.* Jillian threw out the first number that came to mind. "Fifty dollars an hour."

"Will a cheque do?"

"That will be fine."

"My purse is in the living room." Jillian followed her from the sitting room.

Ten minutes later, she drove through the estate's gate and headed for home. She hated to admit it, but she'd enjoyed tutoring Dylan. It helped that he wanted to learn. All he needed was extra time that his teacher probably didn't have, despite the smaller class size at his private school. Well, while Sam was out earning her brownie points for God, Jillian would help Dylan get a C. No, a B. Why settle?

THREE WEEKS LATER, Jillian read over Dylan's exercise solutions and smiled at him. "You only missed one."

His face lit up. "Really?"

"Really. And the one you missed was difficult." She set the open workbook in front of him and picked up her pencil. "You were on the right track," she said, pointing at the first line of his solution. "But when you—"

"No!"

They both jumped at the shout.

"We don't need anyone else."

Jillian recognized Maria's voice, and also that she was speaking Spanish. Thanks to the gifts, Jillian could understand what Maria had said, even though she hadn't spoken a word of Spanish in her life.

"Why do you keep bringing this up? I've already said no."

"I'm only thinking of you." A male voice. "Another cleaner would help."

"Don't take me for a fool. She's too old. You want to replace her with someone younger."

"That's not—"

"Even if I agreed—and I don't—we can't risk it. You know we can't risk it."

Dylan stiffened and met Jillian's eyes.

"I don't understand Spanish," she said, hoping to convey that she hadn't a clue what they were arguing about. Whatever it was, it wasn't her business and it was disturbing Dylan, but her interest was piqued. Can't risk it? Maybe she was eager to grasp at anything that sounded remotely suspicious, but—

"I am so tired of this!" the man shouted.

Dylan clapped his hands over his ears. Jillian wanted to keep eavesdropping, but she rose and quietly shut the door. When she lifted the pencil again and explained where Dylan had gone wrong in his solution, she could tell he wasn't listening. The closed door couldn't keep out the muffled shouts. "Is that your dad?" she asked gently.

Dylan nodded. "They don't argue like this all the time. Just . . ." He shifted in the chair. To Jillian's dismay, his eyes welled up. She wasn't good with kids! "I think my dad wants to get rid of Isabel." He looked down at his lap.

"Who's Isabel?"

"She works here."

"I see. Why does your dad want to get rid of her?"

Dylan shrugged. "He says he wants to get someone to help her, but we don't need anyone else. If he gets someone new, I think he'll get rid of her."

"And you don't want him to?"

"I like her." Jillian had to lean in to hear him. "She gives me candy and stuff. She took care of me when I was a baby."

"She was your nanny?"

He nodded. "And she takes care of me now, too."

"So you've known her all your life."

With his head still down, he nodded.

From what Jillian had overheard, she gathered that Max felt Isabel was too old to be useful. "Are they talking about this a lot lately?"

Having mastered himself, Dylan lifted his head and nodded again.

What could she say? It would be cruel to offer him false hope by saying that even if Isabel left, he could still see her. "Have you spoken to your mom and dad about how you feel?"

"They won't care."

"They might. Your mom cares about you. That's why I'm here." Time to steer them back to a more comfortable subject. "She wants you to do well at school, so let's try to focus on your exercise, okay?" It would help if Maria and her husband shut up.

"Okay," Dylan said.

Although the arguing stopped five minutes later, the remainder of the hour was a struggle. Jillian gave Dylan an encouraging pat on the shoulder. "You're doing well. I'll see you next week." Thankfully she didn't need to see Maria on her way out. After Jillian had received Dylan's seal of approval, Maria had paid her a month in advance. Jillian wouldn't accept any more unless she knew for sure that she'd be around to tutor Dylan. If she and Sam didn't stumble across anything soon, they'd have to consider moving on to the remaining churches on their list. Could the argument between Maria and Max be significant? From now on, Jillian would keep her eyes and ears open when she was around Maria and in the Olmos home.

Chapter Seven

Two weeks and tutoring sessions later, Jillian was feeling discouraged again. It wasn't that she wanted Maria and her husband to argue, or to discover terrible skeletons in the Olmos's closet, but her gut told her they were in the right town and at the right church. How long should they stick around before they gave up?

After breakfast, she asked Sam the same question. "I don't know," Sam said, shrugging. "We have a few churches left on the list. Maybe we should go check them out."

"As long as I'm here on Mondays to tutor Dylan."

Sam frowned. "Don't get too entrenched."

"Where did you say you're going now?" Jillian asked lightly.

"The food bank," Sam mumbled.

She tried not to look smug. "I don't know why, but I feel it's here."

"Me, too. We'll have to be patient."

Too bad patience wasn't her strong suit. After Sam had left, Jillian watched the news channel for a bit. Maybe she should have lunch with Linda again? Sitting around watching TV wouldn't find the needle they were searching for. She called Linda, and was pleased when Linda agreed to meet for lunch. Jillian hung up with a sigh. At least Linda wasn't boring.

Time to take a shower—or, no, a bath. Normally she wasn't one for baths, but she wouldn't mind a long soak in the brand new Jacuzzi tub next to the shower stall in the main bathroom. Just this once, she'd indulge herself. Her best ideas usually came to her when she was relaxed and not consciously working on a problem, so maybe something brilliant would hit her that would make finding the needle easier.

She ran herself a hotter bath than most people would find comfortable. Mom always used to say she'd burn herself, but Jillian tolerated the heat well, and the water quickly cooled, anyway. She turned on the motor, adjusted the speed and air flow, and lowered herself into the tub with a contented sigh. Should she feel guilty because she was pampering herself while Sam was at the food bank? No. She wasn't with Sam because she wanted to treat Patrice the same way Linda and company did, though after listening to Patrice preach last Sunday, it would be difficult to remain aloof with her. Patrice came across as sincere. Jillian wouldn't like snubbing her, but one of them had to fit in with the church's status quo. Sam certainly didn't. *Stop thinking.* Jillian rested her head against the wall and closed her eyes.

Twenty minutes later, she was towelling herself dry in the bathroom when her phone rang. Maybe they'd been wrong about Leanne and she was finally making a move. Jillian wrapped the towel around herself, headed into the kitchen, and picked up her phone. *K. T. Patrice.* Huh? Why would Patrice call here when Sam was at the food bank? "Hello."

"Jillian?"

"Yes?"

"This is Karen Patrice. I'm sorry to have to tell you this, but Sam's been taken to the hospital."

"What? What happened?"

"She passed out. We tried to revive her, but we couldn't, so we called 911."

Jillian's heart felt as if it was leaping from her chest. "Do you know which hospital they've taken her to?"

"Mount Sinai."

Shit, Sam was out there alone and vulnerable. What the hell was going on? "How long ago did it happen?"

"The ambulance left about five minutes ago. It took some time for me to get your number. I had to call Barbara—"

"Th—thanks. I have to go. I'm sorry. Bye." She disconnected and ran into her bedroom. Jesus! The Beguilers would love to get their hands on Samantha. She swore as she fumbled with the zipper on her jeans. *Rushing won't help.*

With her phone in her hand, she raced from the condo and pushed open the door to the stairwell. On her way down, she called Roberta. "I don't know," she said, when Roberta asked about the circumstances around Sam's collapse. "I figured I'd get to the hospital, then ask questions. She's alone, damn it!"

"All right, all right," Roberta said soothingly. "I'll see if Jeremy can pull the 911 call. You get there, and when you're sure she's safe, call me."

"All a Beguiler would need is a lab coat and a smile."

"They haven't made a play for Sam for years, and you haven't spotted them since the cemetery."

"We've been here for a while. They must know where we are."

"But you're clearly not looking for a Fledgling. They're also terrified of Sam, and you've bested them twice. They're not focused on you two right now. They have easier games to play."

"I hope you're right," Jillian said, sprinting through the parking garage to the car that had arrived the same day they'd moved in—thank god. "I'll call you."

Five minutes later she silently fumed as she sat at a red light. Who was the moron who programmed these things? She'd just wasted time at the last light. *Hello? Is it that difficult to time the green lights on the same street so that traffic will keep flowing? Stop, start, stop, start. Morons!* When the light turned green, she resisted the urge to floor it. Getting pulled over for speeding was the last thing she wanted.

At the hospital, she rushed into the crowded emergency room waiting area and searched for someone who could direct her to Sam. A sign on the wall instructed people to take a number, but she wasn't willing to wait. When a spot opened up at the station that triaged walk-ins, Jillian darted to the counter. "I'm looking for my sister. She collapsed and was rushed here."

"Name?" the woman asked.

"Samantha Westwood."

The woman tapped away on her keyboard. "I'll ask a nurse to come out and see you." She reached for her phone.

"I want to see my sister. Where is she?"

"Let me call a nurse," the woman repeated. "What's your name?"

"Jillian Westwood." Jillian shoved her hands into her pockets, then managed a smile when the woman pointed and said, "If you wait outside that corridor with the blue curtains, someone will be out to see you."

"Thank you." She wanted to project and find Sam, but doing so in this crowded waiting room would be risky. Instead, she rocked on her heels and waited.

A nurse finally emerged from behind the curtains. "Jillian Westwood?" she called.

"Right here. How's my sister? Can I see her?"

"She's still with the doctor."

"Do you know what's wrong with her?"

"We're examining her now." The nurse's brow crinkled. "Do you have a family history of fainting or any other condition that would cause loss of consciousness?"

"No. Can I sit with her?"

"When the doctor is finished."

Jillian groaned. The doctor could be a freaking Beguiler.

"Dr. Wong is very good," the nurse said.

Or maybe not, but he could work for the Beguilers. "I'd really like to see her now."

The nurse's smile was strained. "I understand that you're upset, but the best thing you can do is let Dr. Wong examine her."

"I need to call my mother."

The nurse nodded. "I promise that as soon as Dr. Wong is finished, I'll come get you, okay?"

"Yes. Thank you."

The nurse gave Jillian's arm a reassuring pat and stepped through the curtains. Jillian found a relatively quiet spot where she could still see the curtained Promised Land. She desperately wanted to project, but there was too much chaos in the waiting area and the nurse could return at any time. Fortunately, the chances were slim that the Beguilers had heard about Sam *and* made it to the hospital before she had. Keeping her eye on the blue curtain, she called Roberta. "I think she's okay. The nurse knows the doctor." And she wasn't a Beguiler. Jillian's heart wasn't pounding because the nurse had set it off. "They haven't figured out what's wrong with her yet. Did Jeremy find the 911 call?"

"Yes."

"What did it say?"

"We'll discuss that later. Right now, I want you to tell me why you saw Peter."

Jillian snorted. "I'm sure you know."

"No, I don't know," Roberta snapped. "I could have asked him, and he would have told me, but I decided to respect your privacy. I can't do that anymore. Why did you see him? Don't tell me you had a sore throat."

Jillian switched the phone to her other ear. "You think it might be related to what's happened to Sam," she stated, even though she couldn't see a connection. She'd never passed out, but as Peter had suggested, the source behind her and Sam's episodes could be "Deiformic in nature."

"It might be, yes."

For Sam, then. "I had a couple of weird turns." Jillian told Roberta everything she'd disclosed to Peter. "I never fainted, though."

Silence, then, "What were you doing this morning, while Sam was at the food bank?"

"Relaxing."

"What exactly were you doing?" Roberta said evenly.

"I called church Linda to arrange lunch." Shit, she hadn't called to cancel. "I tried out the Jacuzzi tub in the condo, soaked for twenty minutes or so. I'd just gotten out when Patrice called to tell me about Sam."

"Was the water hot?"

Jillian barked a laugh. "Yes, it was."

"I want both of you to come back to the island."

"Why?"

"We need to have a chat. Take care of Sam's problem, then get her out of there as soon as you can without causing a fuss. Tell whoever cares that she needs to relax over the weekend so you won't be at church."

"Okay, but—" The nurse emerged from the curtains and glanced around. "I have to go. Sam's nurse is looking for me." She disconnected and strode over to the nurse.

The nurse beckoned to her. "There you are. I'll take you to your sister now."

"Thank you." She followed the nurse through the curtains and into a bustling emergency ward. Drawn blue curtains lined each side of the corridor. The nurse stopped outside a set and drew them back. Jillian stepped into the makeshift room. A lump rose in her throat. "She's still out," she whispered, her eyes on Sam's pale face.

The doctor near the gurney turned around. "You're Samantha's sister?"

"Yes."

"I'm Doctor Wong. Would you mind stepping outside with me for a minute?"

Jillian joined him in the corridor. "We're running tests, but we don't know yet what's wrong with her. I can't explain why she's still unconscious."

Deiformic in nature.

"Our next step will be to do a CAT scan."

"You think it might be neurological?"

"At this point, we have to consider everything," Wong said, in that annoyingly bland tone doctors used when they didn't want to upset anyone. "Has anything like this ever happened before to a member of your family?"

Christ, maybe, but the cause of Sam's collapse would be outside Dr. Wong's expertise, and that went for every medical professional in this hospital. "Not that I'm aware of."

"We'll take her for the CAT scan in about fifteen minutes."

"Can I sit with her until then?"

"Of course."

"Thank you." Jillian gave him a worried smile, then went over to Sam's bedside. "Hey, Sam," she said, for the benefit of anyone lingering outside. *"You there?"* Silence. Shit. Jillian sat next to Sam and reached for her hand. *Sorry.* She closed her eyes and probed, imagined a ray of light travelling from her inner being into Sam, illuminating—

Jillian dropped Sam's hand and shot up from the chair. She'd found it, the dissonance in Sam's system that prevented her from waking. Was there a medical term for it? It didn't matter. Jillian drew the curtain shut, sat down, and held Sam's hand again. This time, she bathed Sam in warmth, and energy . . . and love. The dissonance morphed into harmony.

Trembling and light-headed, Jillian drew back and rubbed her free hand across her forehead. *You'd better wake up, damn it.* Sam's fingers grabbed Jillian's. "Sam?" she breathed.

Sam's eyelids fluttered. "Mom," she murmured.

"No! Jillian."

"I should have known better," Sam whispered.

"It's Jillian." She pried Sam's fingers from around her own and gently shook Sam's shoulder. "Come back."

Sam's eyes flew open. She gave Jillian a startled look, then pushed herself up on her elbows. "What's going on?"

"You're in the hospital," Jillian said. "You collapsed at the food bank."

"What?"

"I just took care of the problem. We need to get you out of here. We're going back to the island."

Sam's expression grew more confused.

"Lie down," Jillian said, amazed at the colour returning to Sam's face, even though she was behind it. At times like this, she was in awe of the gifts. She didn't have to believe; they were remarkable and mysterious, and science would eventually explain them. Too bad. "Lie down," she said again, pressing on Sam's shoulder. "I'll find someone to release you." *"You up to taking on a Beguiler if one shows up?"*

Sam lay back. *"I think so. Yeah."*

"I'll be back in a minute."

Jillian slowly stood; the room didn't spin. She went into the corridor and glanced around, but didn't spot Wong or the nurse. No luck in the waiting area, either. She was about to go back to Sam when the name "Westwood" caught her ear. She scanned those at the triage counter, ready to escort a Beguiler outside, then relaxed when Patrice turned away from the triage nurse. She wasn't wearing her collar, but Jillian had stared at her for an hour on Sundays and briefly chatted with her during coffee hours. She waved.

"I thought I'd drop in on my way to the office," Patrice said when she reached Jillian. "How is she?"

"She's doing all right," Jillian said. "I'm just looking for someone to release her."

"Do they know why she collapsed?"

"They're not sure. It could be stress. We've just moved, she's working hard at her new business . . ."

"And doing a lot for the church." Patrice grimaced. "I shouldn't say this, but she should drop the fundraising committee. We need new appliances as much as we need a hole in the roof. I'm being selfish here, but I need her at the food bank." She lifted her hands and dropped them. "Of course, given what happened this morning, I'll understand if she doesn't want to go back."

"Sam's made of stronger stuff than that."

Patrice frowned. "Are you all right? You look a little pale."

She could use a chair. Healing Sam hadn't knocked Jillian out, but she'd doze on the plane. "I guess now that I know she's okay, I'm feeling the shock. I should get back to her."

"I won't keep you. Please let her know that I'm glad to hear she's all right and that I'll pray for her—for both of you."

"I'll let her know," Jillian said, hoping her smile appeared genuine. Jesus, she was reacting like a teenager again. Nothing would ever happen between her and Sam. She had a stupid crush that would burn itself out. Patrice was more Sam's type—not that Sam would get involved with her. Right? "Thanks for stopping by. I appreciate it. Oh, we won't be in church on Sunday. Sam needs to take it easy over the next few days. I don't want to leave her alone."

"I'll call her, see how she's doing," Patrice said.

"You have her cell number?" *See, I can be an adult.*

Patrice nodded. "Take care."

"You, too." She watched Patrice walk toward the exit, then whirled and headed back into the emergency ward, feeling like an idiot. Patrice's file didn't cover her relationships, but the odds were that she was as straight as a freaking arrow. She didn't ding Jillian's gaydar, and given Patrice's position, it was natural for her to show concern. And honestly, did Jillian believe that Sam would get involved with anyone? It couldn't last, not with an outsider, and Sam wasn't the type for a fling. Nope, with Sam it would have to be an "until death us do part" sort of thing. Did Sam's file contain any information about her relationship history? When Jillian's adolescent feelings had passed and she didn't care so much about Sam opening up to her, she'd read the damn thing.

The nurse emerged from Sam's enclosure and beamed at her. "She's awake."

Jillian gaped. "Really? Oh my god, that's great!"

"I'll find Doctor Wong." She strode away.

Sam was perched on the edge of the gurney. "Let's go."

Jillian held up her hand. "Let the doctor release you." She sank into the guest chair.

"You all right?"

"Just tired."

"Thanks for getting me on my feet," Sam said.

"I don't think we're quite even yet." "Patrice dropped by. I told her we won't be in church this week. She said she'd call you . . . and that she'd pray for you."

"When I was coming out of it, I remember talking to . . . someone. Was it you?"

"No. You didn't say a word. You must have been dreaming." Jillian scratched her nose.

Someone pulled the curtain farther back. The nurse gestured toward Sam. "See?"

Wong's brows shot up. "How do you feel, Samantha?"

"Sam. I feel fine."

He held up his fingers and ran through a few basic tests to verify that Sam wasn't addled and could see. "Have you ever fainted before?"

"No."

"We should still do the CAT scan."

"No. I'm fine. Save the machine for people who really need it."

"But—"

Sam sprang off the gurney. "I'm leaving now."

Wong's lips pressed into a thin line. "I can't stop you, but I strongly recommend that you see your family doctor for a follow-up."

"I'll do that. Thank you."

Jillian murmured her thanks and followed Sam into the corridor. "I'm parked outside," she said, taking the lead.

They didn't speak again until they were on the road. "So what happened?" she asked Sam.

Sam's brow furrowed. "I don't know. I suddenly felt really hot. The next thing I know, I'm waking up in the hospital."

Hot . . . *Was the water hot?* "Do you know why Roberta would want to see us?"

"You spoke to her. What did she say?"

"She asked me about why I saw Peter. After I told her, she said to come see her."

"Why did you see Peter? The real reason."

It was her own freaking fault that she had to tell the same story over and over again. If she'd been honest . . . "I had a couple of weird turns," she began, and told Sam what she'd told Roberta. When they stopped at a light, Jillian turned to her. Sam's arms were folded. She looked pissed off. "Roberta asked me what I was doing when you collapsed. I was in the tub. I like the water hot."

Sam grunted. Dismayed, Jillian refocused on the road. She'd expected sympathy, not anger. The temperature in the car had definitely dropped, and if Sam was any tenser, she'd pull a muscle. For once, Jillian wouldn't prod her with a stick to see what happened. They were on their way to Roberta, who'd damn-well better have some answers that weren't riddles.

Chapter Eight

Sam strode into the library and glared at Roberta. "You think we're experiencing empathysense."

Roberta looked up at her. "Yes, I do. I know it's not what you wanted."

"You're damn right it's not what I wanted. I don't want somebody knowing what I'm doing." Half of her wanted to rage; the other half wanted to weep.

"You know that's not how empathysense works, and don't deny it, because I know you've researched the joint gifts since our conversation about them. So have I." Roberta's voice lost its edge. "She doesn't know exactly what you're doing. You can only receive physical hints, and right now, those hints are distorted. They're too intense. That's why you collapsed."

Sam dropped into a chair. "Apparently that's normal when empathysense first stirs." Her surroundings blurred. She successfully held back the tide, but her sense of defeat, the darkness infringing on the light . . . Deep down, she'd expected this since her conversation with Roberta about what had happened at the soul healer's cabin, but expected deaths were still a shock. Life still changed—forever.

"Remember, they're gifts." Roberta paused. "He wouldn't bestow them without good reason."

She wasn't seeing the good reason right now.

"It's not her fault," Roberta said softly.

Sam slowly exhaled and stared down at her hands. Sulking wouldn't help. She'd do what she always did: accept His will. Believe that whatever happened was in her best interest, either in this life or the next. "I meant it when I said I'd tell her if I suspected we had the joint gifts. She lied to me about why she wanted to see Peter."

"And you didn't push." Roberta didn't have to say they both knew why.

"I should have. I know how scary it can be to involuntarily experience a gift. I'll go tell her."

"No, let's talk about it together."

When Roberta extended her hand, Sam swallowed and took it. She tightened her fingers around Roberta's.

"You have to accept this, Sam. I know it's a hard pill to swallow, but it's what the Lord wants."

"I know. His will be done." *Your will be done. In time, I'll understand. I'll see the silver lining that must be there.* The one she wasn't seeing right now.

With her free hand, Roberta lifted her phone from the round table. "Jillian? You can come up now." Still holding Sam's hand, she disconnected and bowed her head.

Sam bowed her head too, but she couldn't still her mind, and her determination to be positive stalled on the runway.

Why?

Was she being punished? Did she not pray enough? Had her disdain for creeds angered Him? Was being tied to Jillian supposed to teach her something? If so, had there not been a way to learn it without receiving a life sentence? She'd already come to terms with one of those.

Maybe it wouldn't be so bad. Jillian seemed to understand her need for solitude. Sam could sometimes tell that Jillian wanted to spend more time with her, but she had her reasons for holding Jillian at arm's length—reasons that were moot now, but they still mattered to her.

She didn't want this. She'd won her inner battles and achieved peace and acceptance, but now she'd struggle again to not resent the life thrust upon her. *Is that why?* Had her spiritual life lacked challenge? Training Jillian and working with her had sometimes tested Sam, but knowing it was a temporary situation, or so she'd believed, had tempered the struggle. Now she'd run through the fire again, but this time she'd undergo the trial with someone who didn't even believe in Him. It didn't make sense. What had she done wrong? *I don't understand, not this time. Why her?*

JILLIAN HUNG UP on Roberta and shoved her phone into her pocket. She'd take her sweet time heading up to the library. She didn't appreciate Roberta telling her to buzz off while Sam found out what was going on. Jillian hadn't ended up in hospital, but she'd experienced two frightening episodes of disconnecting from her physical environment. *Was the water hot?* Sam had felt hot. How could her time in the Jacuzzi have had anything to do with Sam collapsing? Time to stop pouting. She wanted answers.

When she entered the library, Sam and Roberta were praying. What was going on? With the exception of saying grace, they rarely prayed in front of her. She sank into the other chair facing Roberta, reminded of the first time she'd sat in this library with these two women. She hadn't known them then. They'd wanted to train her; she'd told them it would never happen. Sam had been angry about Jim's death. What was upsetting her today? Jillian had received the silent treatment all the way back to the island. She'd bet that Sam had already known what Roberta was going to say and wasn't happy about it. *But why is she mad at me?*

Sam and Roberta let go of each other's hands and drew back. Jillian's concern over Sam grew. Sam looked different. Her slumped shoulders, downturned mouth, dull eyes . . .

Roberta gazed at Jillian. "I won't beat around the bush. I think the two experiences you told me about are due to a gift called empathysense."

Jillian tensed. "I thought I knew all the gifts."

"Sam taught you all she knew, and what most Deiforms know." Roberta leaned forward. "There are a second set of gifts. Rare gifts we call joint gifts. You have to go back to the twelfth century to find the last time a Deiform in our cell possessed them. They can't be learned. You either have them, or you don't."

"And you think I have these gifts?"

"Yes."

Was it because she viewed the gifts differently? Was she able to tap into inner resources that the others couldn't use because they were focused outside themselves? "What does empathysense do, because all it's done for me so far is made me think I'm losing it."

Roberta's expression didn't change. "They're called joint gifts because they require two Deiforms. Empathysense allows you to sense another Deiform's physical circumstances. You can also send your physical circumstances to the other Deiform. You can't learn it, but you can refine it and learn to control it. Right now, the sensations you feel are too intense and using the gift is involuntary. You—"

Jillian held up her hand. "Wait, wait. Okay, so I was sensing Sam." Who else could it be? Was that why Sam was unhappy? Would this empathysense gift enable her to determine Sam's emotional state, once she'd learned how to control it? If so, she could understand why Sam was freaking. Jillian certainly wouldn't want her emotions to be an open book. She turned to Sam. "I have no idea what you're feeling right now."

Sam curtly shook her head. "You weren't sensing what I was feeling. It doesn't work like that. You were sensing how I was moving. You'll also be able to sense other factors about my environment, like hot, cold—"

"So me relaxing in the Jacuzzi *did* make you collapse." *Oh, shit.* Sam was often in her thoughts. Right now, using empathysense was involuntary. Brooding about Sam must have caused her to feel as if she was immersed in hot water. "I didn't ask for this." But Sam would resent her anyway, and who could blame her? So would the other Deiforms Jillian would work with. "I can see how empathysense could be useful, and I assume the other joint gifts are also handy. So much for working alone." If she couldn't work with Sam, she'd prefer not to work with anyone. She wasn't as introverted as Sam, but unless she really liked someone, familiarity bred contempt. "Will I have to work with Deiforms in other cells, go where I'm needed? If these gifts are rare and useful . . . I haven't experienced anything else."

"Actually, you have," Roberta said. "Remember when you sensed Sam at Junior's cabin, when she was projecting?"

Wondering when Sam had told Roberta about that particular event, Jillian nodded.

"You weren't supposed to be able to do that, but we weren't sure whether it meant the joint gifts were stirring or it was just a fluke.

You might have subconsciously figured that Ruth and Sam would find the cabin, and you just happened to reach out at the right moment."

Jillian's jaw dropped. "Do you mean that you and Sam have known all this time? Why didn't you tell me?"

"Because we didn't *know*. We weren't sure."

"You still could have mentioned it." Jillian pressed her hand against her chest. "I had no idea what was going on. I was on my hands and knees in a *freaking restaurant*."

"In hindsight, we should have included you in our conversation," Roberta said.

Sam remained silent. Maybe she was resentful because the atheist Deiform had tapped into these rare joint gifts. Jillian wasn't entirely pleased herself. "If I'm honest, I don't like the idea of bopping around to where I'm needed." Her voice rose along with her dismay. "I like the island. I want to feel as if I have a home." And that she was part of a "family," a need that was too personal and new for her to voice aloud. Right now, she also wanted to be near Sam, but she hoped—no, expected—that her crush would eventually disappear. "I don't want to be 'that Deiform' everyone calls on when the joint gifts will help, but nobody really knows her because she's only ever around for five minutes, and then she's on to the next place she's needed."

Sam's shoulders hunched. She clasped her hands on her lap.

"The joint gifts don't work that way," Roberta said.

"I thought you said they took two Deiforms."

"They do." Roberta moistened her lips. "The same two Deiforms."

Oh. *Oh*. She gave Sam a sidelong glance. She wanted to be with her, but not like this. She'd wanted it to be a choice she'd thought they wouldn't have, because Deiforms worked alone. What would happen when her feelings ran their course? How long before familiarity bred contempt? "It doesn't mean we always have to work together."

"In the past, the Deiforms who share the joint gifts have stayed together. We've always seen it as the Lord's will."

"I don't," Jillian stated calmly. "What would happen if we didn't stay together? Would we shrivel up and die? Would we lose the gifts—all of them?"

"I've only come across one instance where the two Deiforms were separated for a time, because one was imprisoned. The other one didn't lose the gifts, or shrivel up and die—but he stayed nearby." Roberta's eyes narrowed "He found that straying too far interfered with his peace of mind."

Great, apparently they'd go crazy unless they remained in each other's back pockets. "That doesn't mean—"

"Stop questioning it," Sam snapped.

"What?"

"For once, just accept it. It's the Lord's will. I know you don't care about that, but I do."

Jillian was surprised by how frustrated Sam sounded. By trying to find out if they could work apart, she'd thought she was doing what Sam wanted. "Okay. No more questioning." In the heavy silence that followed, she thought back to her two weird turns. "So I was sensing Sam."

Roberta nodded. "The first time, Sam was driving. The second time, she was in the elevator, coming down to the hotel lobby. Because your empathysense is just stirring, what you're sensing is distorted. It's too intense. I'm not even sure which one of you involuntarily initiated the gift. At the cabin, it was definitely you, but the rest . . . were you reaching out to Sam, or was Sam reaching out to you?"

Jillian had a strong suspicion of the answer, and had the good sense to keep her mouth shut. Had she caused this? It wasn't God, so had her longing for a closer relationship with Sam somehow linked the sources of their gifts together?

"Either way, you need to get a handle on it."

"How?"

Roberta turned her attention to Sam. "Do you remember how you dealt with your time shifting?"

"Yeah," Sam said flatly.

"I'd try the same thing," Roberta suggested.

"It doesn't sound like it was empathysense at the cabin," Jillian said.

"It wasn't. It was a gift called astral telepathy. There's also astral sight. When that gift stirs, you'll be able to see what the other one is seeing when she's projecting."

Now, that would be handy. "What else is there?"

"I've left a couple of books out in the undercroft's library. You should spend some time there over the next couple of days."

"And these gifts are just going to happen to me—to us—when they first stir?"

Roberta grimaced. "Yes. I know that's unfortunate."

"It'll be unfortunate if it happens when we're in the middle of driving, or some other activity that requires us to be in full control of our faculties."

"It won't happen then," Sam said.

Jillian bit back a comment that she wished she had Sam's faith. She'd already shot to the top of Sam's shit list, assuming she hadn't been there already. "We'll need to talk about how to turn involuntary into voluntary," she said meekly.

Sam grunted.

Great. Then again, if Sam remained surly, maybe Jillian would stop hoping that Sam would see her as more than an inconvenient sidekick. It would sure make working with her unpleasant, though.

"If there's nothing else for now, I have a few things I'd like to do," Sam said.

"Go," Roberta murmured.

When Jillian rose, eager to go to the undercroft, Roberta motioned for her to sit back down. She did so, and listened to Sam stomp from the library and down the hall. "You could have told me," she said to Roberta. "Sometimes I feel you don't trust me."

"It wasn't because of you." Roberta jutted her chin toward the door. "Sam wasn't ready. She still isn't, but the Lord has a reason for bestowing the joint gifts."

"Does He?" Jillian barked a laugh. "I'm not sure what He got out of having me on my knees in a restaurant. You'd figure He would have tried it when I was in a church. And this god of yours has a weird way of treating those who bust their asses for Him. He doesn't reward Sam for her loyalty all these years. He drops a freaking anvil on her head. You should all form a union."

Roberta tutted and gave her an indulgent look. "Are you finished?"

"No, I'm not. Why would He bind two Deiforms together when we're in such short supply? You'd figure He'd choose more Deiforms, or at least make efficient use of the ones He has. But then, logic has never been one of His strong points."

To Jillian's surprise, Roberta laughed. "You've certainly made things more interesting, Jillian."

"Well, thank you," she said. "I'm always glad to be of service."

Still smiling, Roberta said, "I wanted you to stay behind so I could ask how you feel about the joint gifts." They certainly knew how Sam felt.

"Astral sight sounds useful." Jillian could think of a couple of practical uses off the top of her head for that one. She supposed astral telepathy could help when plain old telepathy wasn't possible. Empathysense? No, thank you. "Empathysense has a longer range than telepathy, but I'm not sure how helpful it will be. I can see how astral sight and astral telepathy could be useful."

"I didn't ask for an evaluation of each gift you know about. I asked you how you feel."

God, she hated touchy-feely crap, and why the hell did it matter? She shrugged. "I haven't had any time to think about it." She let that hang between them for a moment. "All I can say is that I'm not thrilled, because it's going to make things tense between me and Sam for a while. I already feel like I'm in her face too much."

Roberta frowned. "Is she being rude?"

"No, but let's face it. She makes most introverts look like extroverts." Jillian suddenly wanted to bite her nails, but brushed imaginary lint off her jeans, instead. "I'm sure she already resents me."

"And if she does, that would bother you?"

"Of course it would bother me."

"You care about how Sam feels about you."

She stiffened. Had she just heard the click of a trap? She gazed into Roberta's eyes. As usual, she couldn't read her. Damn it! Sometimes she wondered if Guides could tap into every Deiform's source and, from there, into their hearts and minds. She forced herself to relax. Her agency days had taught her that the most convincing lies were 99 percent true. "Yes, I do," she said levelly. "She brought me in. She trained me. She . . ." *She was there for the most confusing and transformational time in my life since Dad's suicide.* "She saved my life. And frankly, I like her." She kept her eyes on Roberta's face.

"I don't deny that she might close in on herself for a while." Roberta raised a finger. "But she'll come around."

Jesus, if Sam closed in any more on herself, she'd disappear. "I hope you're right."

"You have to figure out how to control the gifts that have stirred. She knows that."

"I'll give her some time before I push her." She decided to change the subject. "I'm not sure about this church we're investigating. Both our guts told us we'd found the right one, but we haven't uncovered anything sinister yet. We've gone through the trouble of getting involved with the congregation. We have a condo. What happens if we decide in two weeks that we're pulling out? Everyone will wonder."

"Yes, they'll wonder, but they'll soon forget about you. You have other family. Someone could be ill. You could leave the church without leaving the community. You wouldn't be in town, but you'd keep the condo for a while. But don't give up yet. If you both have a gut feeling, I suspect you're in the right place."

Jillian wished she shared Roberta's confidence. She was starting to suspect that her gut feeling was indigestion. "Can I go now? I'd like to go to the undercroft and find out what's in store for me and Sam."

Roberta chuckled. "You have a good attitude." She paused. "Be patient with Sam."

"I will." Whether Sam would reciprocate was another question.

AN HOUR LATER, Jillian lifted her head from one of the books Roberta had selected and touched her face—something real. Christ, if a couple of the joint gifts she'd just read about had manifested out of the blue without her knowing anything about them, she would have checked herself into a psychiatric institution, assuming the shock hadn't killed her. The good news: she'd still be a private person. No mind reading. No seeing exactly what the other Deiform—Sam—was doing. Empathysense was limited to environmental cues, like hot, cold, motion. Pain and pleasure—no, or at least the Deiform pairs she'd read about hadn't recorded experiences along those lines. Had they censored themselves? She hoped not.

She and Sam had to master the ones they'd experienced pronto. It couldn't wait until Sam stopped sulking. Maybe she believed that God would prevent a gift from stirring at the worst possible moment, but Jillian didn't have that luxury. At best, she could believe that since they themselves were the source of the gifts, they would subconsciously know when it was safe to experiment. Yeah, she was stretching.

The sooner she and Sam had a conversation about this and cleared the air, the better. They were in the middle of an investigation. They were freaking living together right now. Jillian would refrain from pointing out that "right now" would probably become "most of the time." Sam was already painfully aware of that, and Jillian wasn't sure how she felt about it herself. She closed the book and rose. *Time to face the music.*

When she couldn't find Sam at the house and a call to Ruth eliminated that possibility, Jillian set off for the place she'd go if she was troubled. She spotted the huddled figure sitting on the rock and stopped walking. A lump rose in her throat. *Just shoot me now. It'll be quicker.* With a sigh, she strolled to Sam's side and looked down at her. "I'm probably the last person you want to talk to, but we need to talk about how to get these gifts under control."

"I know it's not your fault," Sam said, gazing at the water.

"I'm sure that doesn't help a hell of a lot. Should I sit down, or do you want me to go away?"

Sam still didn't look at her. "Sit." She hugged her legs to her chest.

Pondering how to open what she expected would be a tense conversation, Jillian lowered herself down next to Sam. "I'm sorry I didn't tell you the truth about why I saw Peter," she said, deciding to be conciliatory. "I honestly thought I might be ill. I didn't want to bother you with it." Sam continued to stare at the lake. "When he didn't find anything wrong with me, I let it go. I didn't *want* anything to be wrong with me." Silence. Jesus. "We need to trust each other more," Jillian said, struggling to control her frustration. "Especially now. How did you overcome your involuntary time shifting?"

"Intentionally doing it taught me what it felt like to start moving out of time," Sam said softly. "I could recognize it. I was able to stop it."

Jillian thought back to her two episodes. "I don't remember having any warning. One second I was fine, the next I was falling or hurtling through space."

"But you knew something was happening to you."

"Yes. I suppose I could try to stop it." She'd never consciously pulled away from her centre. "I'll have to try it." She swallowed. "We'll have to try it. We'll have to try to provoke empathysense and shut it down."

"Roberta was right, though. We don't know whether we've been inadvertently reaching out, or sensing."

Jillian studied the side of Sam's head. "We'll have to intentionally try to do both. I could soak in a hot bath for a while," she said lightly.

Sam slowly turned to her. Jillian winced at Sam's frowning, taut face. "You don't seem very upset about this." Sam's fingers drummed against her legs. "I thought you were looking forward to working alone."

That was what she'd wanted Sam to believe. "Yes and no," she said, applying the 99 percent rule again. "When I was with the agency, I couldn't wait to be alone, because everything was fake. When I was undercover for a case, my job was fake, my relationships with my co-workers were fake, *I* was fake. When I was between cases, I couldn't remember what it was like to be myself." It hadn't helped that she'd never built a life for herself and neglected Mom and Danny, always using the excuse that there was no point, because she'd be away for long stretches. Well, tons of people had jobs for which they travelled or spent months overseas. They still managed to nurture relationships, maybe because someone close to them hadn't blown their world away with a bullet to his head.

"Before the Fellowship showed up, I was wasting my life away at bogus jobs or in front of the TV. I'd convinced myself that I loved being alone. And then Jim happened, and everything changed. I'm not saying I've turned into a people person, but feeling like I have a second chance . . . leaving behind my parents . . . I don't know, maybe I've realized that I want . . ." *To care? Someone to care? Both?*

"I won't mind having someone who's there most of the time." And now she'd shut up, or she'd approach 99.9 percent and regret every word that came out of her mouth.

Sam turned back to the lake. "It could get old quickly."

"Sure," Jillian swiftly agreed. "But we won't be attached at the hip. I know you prefer your own company. So do I, to some extent. We'll work it out."

"We have to, don't we," Sam snapped. Then her shoulders sagged. "I know this isn't your fault."

"But you can't help being mad at me. I get that."

Sam shook her head. "I'm not mad at you."

"Who are you mad at, then?" Jillian didn't require any gifts or super-duper spidey senses to feel Sam's anger.

She looked up in dismay when Sam jumped to her feet. "Look, I can't talk to you about this stuff."

"What stuff?"

"The important stuff. Because I know you'll judge. I know that no matter what you say, inside you'll be judging." Her hand sliced through the air in an angry, dismissive gesture. "I don't want or need the joint gifts. It doesn't matter who it would have been, so it's not about you. But I do wonder why He's linked me to an atheist. Because if I'm going to be stuck with someone, it would have been nice for it to be someone who doesn't believe I'm deluded, or a throwback to the Middle Ages." She glared at Jillian, then shook her head. "Shit," she breathed. "Look, it is what it is. Why don't we meet after dinner and see if we can't learn to control empathysense a little better."

Her throat tight, Jillian nodded. She looked back at the lake, and blinked into the mist that wasn't there a second ago.

Chapter Nine

Sam finished stocking the canned soup shelf at the food bank and added the empty cardboard box to the stack waiting to be used for more pickups. "Can you do the fruit juice next?" called Megan as she strode by.

"Sure," Sam said, certain that Megan's mind was already somewhere else. As the food bank's manager, Megan was always juggling five thoughts at once. After asking how Sam felt, Megan had quickly put her to work. Patrice had mentioned the car when she'd roped Sam into volunteering here, but Megan hadn't sent her on a pickup yet. Maybe she worried that Sam would pass out while driving. After all, she'd hardly been here five minutes last time before she'd commented about how hot it was and collapsed. Since arriving today, she'd noticed a couple of the other volunteers looking her way every few minutes, their brows creased.

It wouldn't happen today. She and Jillian had spent the week practicing empathysense and believed they had it under control. Still, Jillian was forbidden from getting into the Jacuzzi or doing anything else that could inadvertently trigger it. Hopefully Sam's driving hadn't set it off too quickly for Jillian to stifle it. If she fell and hit her head, there wasn't anyone there to help her.

Sam opened a container filled with juice boxes, then gave in to her nagging concern and pulled out her phone. "You okay?" she asked.

"I'm fine," Jillian said. "I'm being very good. I'm practicing my guitar. About the only danger you're in is that your ears might ring."

Sam chuckled.

"Jeremy called. Nothing's going on with the money. It's still there. No abnormal activity." Jillian paused. "I don't think there's anything shady going on with Leanne. Unless she starts by legitimately investing the money to see if the new victim gets cold feet, but no . . . I think she's above board. I think she's sincerely giving her fellow parishioners a break. So . . ."

What were they doing here? "Let's—" Sam broke off when she sensed someone behind her. "I have to go. I'll talk to you later." She disconnected and turned around. "Reverend Patrice."

Patrice lifted her hand. "Please, call me Karen."

"All right, Karen," Sam said, even though she felt uncomfortable addressing Patrice by her first name. She preferred to keep her contact with outsiders professional, especially when it came to members of the clergy. Patrice made that difficult, which was probably why she was starting to get on Sam's nerves. If she'd realized that Patrice would be around so much at the food bank, she would have found another way to help in the community while they were searching for whatever the Lord wanted them to find. Thank goodness Jillian worked the coffee room after services.

"Megan told me where I could find you. How are you feeling?"

"I'm fine. I fainted, that's all. I followed up with a doctor here in town, and everyone's concluded that it was stress. We'd just moved, new business, adjusting to living with someone again . . ."

Patrice nodded. "How's Jillian? She seemed very worried at the hospital."

Worried that a Beguiler would take advantage of Sam's unexpected circumstances. "She's fine." Actually, she wasn't. Jillian was too acquiescent lately—since the conversation they'd had on the island, after Roberta had told her about the joint gifts. Maybe Sam shouldn't have said that she'd rather not discuss matters of faith with Jillian, but if they were going to work together from now on, they needed to be honest. Why would Jillian care, anyway? It wasn't because she'd no longer be able to push Sam's buttons; she didn't require a religious topic of conversation to do that. Sam almost missed it. She preferred the feisty Jillian to the one who smiled and nodded. It kept her on her toes. Fortunately, the awkward period would pass. Jillian wouldn't be able to keep it up, and Sam didn't want her to.

She refocused on Patrice. "I'm sorry about the fuss I caused."

Patrice quirked a brow. "You don't have anything to be sorry about. But maybe you're doing too much. You didn't have to come today. You could have returned next week."

"No, I'm fine. I was actively involved in my last church, and worked long hours. I've just experienced too many changes at once, that's all. Being involved with the church and food bank helps. It's familiar."

Patrice patted her arm. "I'm glad. Anyway, I should continue my rounds. I just wanted to see how you were."

"Thanks." Relieved, Sam turned back to the juice boxes.

"Oh, did Jillian tell you that the fundraising committee is a waste of your time?"

Sam looked over her shoulder. "She mentioned it."

"It's just that I have something else you might be interested in," Patrice said.

Forcing a smile, Sam faced her again. "What is it?"

As THE MAID walked with her to the study, Jillian mentally reviewed what she wanted to cover during the tutoring session with Dylan. According to his teacher, he'd done better than expected on his last test. Jillian had bit back the comment that his teacher should adjust her expectations; alienating the woman would only hurt Dylan. As they approached the study, she heard the murmur of voices within.

The maid frowned, then marched ahead. "What are you doing in here?" she asked in Spanish.

Jillian stepped into the study. Dylan sat with his head down. Next to him, a woman shrank back from the maid, her eyes wide with fear. Jillian couldn't be certain, but she thought it was the same woman they'd bumped into during her first visit, the one carrying towels.

The maid's hands went to her hips. "You know you're not to be in here. Mrs. Maria will be upset."

The woman cringed. "No, no, don't tell her."

"I have to tell her."

"I won't do it again. Please, don't tell her. Please!" She covered her mouth and fled from the room.

The maid towered over Dylan. "You should know better. You're not a baby anymore."

Dylan lifted his head. "I don't understand." His voice quavered. "Why can't I talk to her?"

"Because your parents don't want you to. She works for them. She's not your friend. Your mother won't be pleased." She turned to Jillian, switched to English. "I'm sorry."

Realizing that she cared more about Dylan's feelings than not upsetting the maid, Jillian didn't want to say anything that would come across as siding against him. She dropped her satchel to the floor. "We should get started," she said.

The maid nodded. She gave Dylan one last glare, then left. Jillian sat down and focused on Dylan. Damn, his eyes were wet. Torn between wanting to ask if he was okay and not wanting to embarrass him, she chose to get down to business, but the awkward start to the session hung between them for the entire hour. Dylan's mind was clearly elsewhere.

Jillian tried not to show her frustration as she prepared to leave. It wasn't Dylan's fault. Maybe they should meet somewhere else. She pushed back her chair and gave him the widest smile she could muster. "You'll pass your test tomorrow. You're ready. I'll see you next week, okay?" She turned toward the door.

"Jillian?"

She whirled.

Dylan stared up at her and lowered his voice. "If I give you something, will you promise not to tell anyone?"

Knowing the maid was always lingering nearby, waiting to escort her to the front door, Jillian pushed the door shut. "Is it something bad?"

"No!" His hands clenched, and he rocked in his chair. "Isabel told me to give it to you."

"Isabel? Is she the woman who was here?"

He nodded. "I don't want to get you into trouble."

"Nobody will know," Jillian said, intrigued. "If you give it to me, I'll put it straight into my bag. I won't look at it here, and I'll never tell anyone, okay?" Hopefully she could keep her promise.

Dylan continued to rock while he considered her proposal.

"You've mentioned Isabel before," she said. "She's the one who gives you candy, right?"

He nodded again. "She knows you come to see me. She said it's important."

"Then you'd better give it to me."

"Promise you won't tell anyone."

"I promise."

He stopped rocking and reached into his pocket. Out came a candy and an elastic band. He dug into his pocket again, then reached his hand toward Jillian. She took the crumpled piece of paper and quickly slid it into her satchel's side pocket. "Thank you. I'd better go now," she whispered. With a wave, she pulled open the door and casually strolled along the hallway to where the maid stood dusting a vase.

Five minutes later, when she was out of sight of the house, she pulled over to the side of the road, dying of curiosity. She smoothed the crumpled piece of paper and stared at the two words scrawled across it: *Help me.*

Chapter Ten

JILLIAN BLEW ON her tea, then sipped it to test the temperature. Too hot. She quickly swallowed it and looked across the table at Sam, half-expecting to see her clawing at her throat. But Sam was fine. She was wiping her salty fingers with a napkin. "Jeremy didn't find anything too suspicious," Sam said, pushing aside her plate.

Nope. The Olmoses checked out. Married for twenty years. One son. No criminal records. No suspicious activities. But nobody with the first name Isabel had filed a tax return tied to them. "I understand they might not pay her enough, or they're paying her under the table. But something's definitely wrong."

"She could want money, or another job. You said they want to get rid of her."

Jillian straightened. "Or it could be something else. They treat her like garbage."

"That's not unusual when it comes to the help."

"We need to investigate this," she said, through clenched teeth. "This could be what we've been looking for."

Sam made a calming motion with her hand. "I just don't want to jump to conclusions. We need more information. We need to talk to her."

Jillian shook her head. "I'll never get her alone. I'm escorted to and from the front door." It hadn't seemed suspicious to her—until now. "I wonder what the maid knows."

"Probably everything, but she's loyal to the Olmoses. She won't risk her job." Sam sipped her water. "We have to come up with a way to get Isabel alone, but before we do, why don't we take a look around inside, find out if there are others who don't file returns, where she sleeps, that sort of thing?"

"The maid sticks to me like glue when I'm not in the study."

Sam gave her a withering look.

Right. "I was thinking about when I show up to tutor Dylan," she said lamely. "And I think you should do it. I know them. I'll feel funny looking around their house."

"On the other hand, you've seen Isabel. You'll recognize her. You're also familiar with one wing of the house."

True. "Okay, I'll do it." She glanced at her watch. "It'll be dark soon." Unfortunately she couldn't flick on lights when she was projecting. "I'll have to do it tomorrow."

Sam nodded. "I want an early night tonight, anyway. We'll go in the morning."

JILLIAN ROLLED OVER and fumbled around the top of the nightstand for her phone. She stared at the time: *1:42*. Great. She'd already lain awake for at least fifteen minutes, thinking about Linda, Dylan, Max, and Maria. Dylan was getting better grades on his math assignments, which pleased her more than she'd expected. That was the problem.

They'd lived here for several months. They were a part of this affluent community now. She preferred it when they were in and out, case closed. During her agency days, the protective shell she'd surrounded herself with had prevented anyone from getting through—or maybe ingratiating herself with white-collar workers hadn't offended her moral sensibilities as much as making small talk during church coffee hours. She also had to admit that getting in touch with the gifts had also put her back in touch with her humanity—compassion, empathy, honesty. Even if she wanted to, she'd no longer be capable of sitting on her ass in front of a TV all day, pretending the rest of the world didn't exist. She felt again. She was alive. She couldn't go back, and she didn't want to.

She was starting to appreciate that being a Deiform, working with the Fellowship, would hurt. She—

Was that the front door? Her heart pounding, Jillian sat up and strained to listen. The floor in the hallway creaked. *What the hell?* How had someone gotten in? They'd chosen this condo because there was twenty-four-hour security. Whoever was out there had slipped past the security guard and the doorman, and let themselves into the apartment.

Holding her breath, Jillian slowly got out of bed and slid open the nightstand drawer. Pistol in hand, she crept to her bedroom door and opened it a crack. Light was spilling into the hallway from the kitchen. *"Sam!"* she barked, hoping to wake her up.

"What?" Sam immediately replied, startling Jillian.

"Someone's in the condo. They're in the kitchen."

Silence, then, *"It's me."*

"What?"

Footsteps, then Sam appeared in the hallway and waved. "It's me."

Jillian lowered her pistol. "What the hell are you doing?" Why was Sam dressed? She was wearing her jacket! "Were you going somewhere?" She set the gun on the dresser and marched into the hallway. "You scared me. If you were going out, why didn't you tell me?"

Her irritation flared into anger when Sam beckoned to her and went back into the kitchen. Seeing Sam leaning against the counter, casually drinking a glass of water, didn't help. "What the hell is going on?"

"I wasn't going out. I've been out. Patrice—"

"Patrice!" Jillian spat, then she cursed herself. *Get a freaking grip or you'll say something you'll regret.* "What about her?" she asked, wishing her pyjama bottoms had pockets.

"She told me about a group that checks on the homeless when it's cold. It's below zero out there. I went out to drive around a couple of people who hand out hats, mittens, and coffee."

"And you didn't tell me? What if I'd woken up and realized you were gone?"

Sam shrugged. "I'm always home by around this time, and I've always left you a note in the bathroom. I figured if you got up in the night, you'd go there."

Wanting time to think, Jillian whirled and stomped to the bathroom. She snatched up the note on the toilet seat and flicked on the light. *I'm out with a group that ministers to the homeless. I'll be back by 2. Sam.* She crushed the note in her hand and let out a long, exasperated sigh. If she'd woken up while Sam was still out, she wouldn't have known Sam was gone. Sam's bedroom was the last place she'd go in the middle of the night. So okay, Sam had left a note to let her know, anyway. That wasn't the point. They were supposed to be a team. They were supposed to trust each other. And frankly, it hurt that Sam didn't share stuff like this with her. She knew her crush was a lost cause, but that didn't mean she was okay with being treated as an afterthought. It was freaking rude. She wouldn't stand for it anymore.

She strode back to the kitchen and flung the crumpled paper at Sam. "Thanks for the note!" It bounced off Sam's arm and fell to the floor. Jillian's eyes felt moist. *Damn it!* "Look, I know you hate working with me. I know it's worse now with the joint gifts. I'm sure you resent the crap out of me. But that doesn't mean you can treat me like I don't exist." She slapped herself on the chest with both hands. "We work together. How would you react if you woke up and discovered that I'd just flitted off on my own in the middle of the night?" There was a time Sam wouldn't have let Jillian out of her sight. Did she care that little now?

Sam quickly set the half-empty glass on the counter. "I'm sorry. I didn't realize it would upset you so much."

"How could you not realize? I don't get it. I don't get you. I would never do this to you." She pointed toward the hallway. "You're out there helping the homeless and feeding the hungry, while you treat the person you work with like shit. Does that make sense to you?"

Sam's face tightened. "Saying I treat you like shit is a little strong."

"You're inconsiderate. Does that work better for you?"

During the heavy silence that followed, Jillian wondered why the hell she had feelings for Sam. God, she was a sucker for silent types who stuck to their principles and didn't follow the crowd. That Sam had just returned from showing a little kindness to the homeless didn't help. It wasn't as if she'd been out getting laid. Not Sam. Jillian massaged her forehead and slowly exhaled. "Okay, maybe I'm overreacting a bit, but you drilled how vulnerable we are into me, and going off in the middle of the night without telling me is inconsiderate. I'm sorry, but it is."

Sam sank into a chair and held her head in her hands. "You're right."

Great, now Jillian felt terrible for lighting into her. But she couldn't let Sam off the hook, or it would happen again. Why hadn't Sam asked whether Jillian wanted to go with her? Sam wasn't the only one who could help those ministering to the homeless. But then, she was used to doing everything by herself. "Is this how you rebel?" Jillian asked, as she pulled out the chair opposite her. "You act as you wish things were, rather than how they are?"

Sam lifted her head and met Jillian's eyes. "I'm sorry. I should have told you."

A dull ache flared in Jillian's chest. "Am I really that bad?"

"It's not you," Sam said forcefully.

"Yeah, I know, it wouldn't matter who it is."

Sam thumped her fist on the table. "I've spent most of my life trying not to get attached to anyone, because either I leave, or they do. The homeless we helped tonight . . . they didn't see me. I didn't see them. I drive. The others hand out the coffee."

And at the food bank, Sam stocked shelves and avoided dealing with those who relied on it. What about Roberta? Ruth? Warren and Brian? *What about me?* "I'm not going anywhere."

"I know." Sam lifted her hands, then clasped them on the table. "I'm not used to having the same person with me all the time. I've never had to give an account of where I am and what I'm doing. I usually work with Supporters. It's a temporary arrangement, and I'm always the one calling the shots. You and I are equals."

"Are we?"

"Yes."

Jillian let that sink in. "You've been in the Fellowship for almost twenty years. You're close to everyone."

"I've worked with the others a few times, but not for long, and I never know when I'm saying good-bye for the last time." Sam suddenly pushed back her chair and went to the counter. "When one of us dies, you quickly grieve and keep going, because you have to," she said, her back to Jillian. Her voice dropped. "Look at Jim and Joanna."

Normally Jillian would surrender at the mention of Jim and Joanna, but this time she wouldn't let her guilt get in the way. And she'd be damned if she'd not allow herself to care about anyone because they could die at any moment. That was true of everyone.

Sure, those in the Fellowship were in harm's way more than most, but anyone crossing a street was taking their life in their hands. A beating heart could stop at any second. A blood vessel in the brain could rupture without warning while someone sunbathed on a beach. Hell, you could be sitting in front of the TV in your living room and have a plane crash into you. Death was a part of life. It would happen to everyone; it was only a matter of when and how. People still cared about each other. Jillian had already been numb for too many years to not care.

How honest should she be? "I heard you come in because I was lying awake in bed thinking about how bad I'll feel when we decide to move on. I'm starting to understand why it's best to remain detached as much as possible." Now for the tricky part. "But I can't hold *you* at arm's length. We work together." Hell, they lived together. "I have to care about what happens to you. I have to consider you. It would be unprofessional of me not to." Part of her wanted to tell the truth, the whole truth—that her feelings for Sam were often unprofessional. Maybe Sam needed to hear that someone deeply cared about her and would grieve for a long time.

Jesus. Jillian wanted to roll her eyes at herself. More than likely, she was suffering from a bad case of wishful thinking. If the unthinkable were to happen, she wouldn't be the only one whose world would tilt on its axis. Roberta, Ruth, the others . . . yes, they'd get on with it, but because they had to, not because they hadn't loved Sam and wouldn't miss her terribly.

Sam turned around and folded her arms. "It's not because I don't care about what happens to you. I do. If I wasn't confident that you can take care of yourself, I never would have left the condo without telling you."

"Why didn't you tell me, anyway?" Now that her anger had died, Jillian was genuinely curious. "It would have been the courteous thing to do."

Sam took her time answering. She shook her head. "I don't know. Maybe I am rebelling against the idea that I have to let someone into my life a little more than I'm comfortable with."

Jillian gave her a point for honesty. "I know it's not easy."

"It's not a matter of how easy it isn't." Sam chewed her lip. "You know, when I think of my parents, I have to remind myself that I'm seeing them as they were twenty years ago. I could pass them on the street, and I wouldn't know. The same goes for Alex. The last time I saw her, she was sixteen. My memories of them . . . they're a time capsule."

The same would happen for Jillian. In twenty years, she'd still see Mom and Danny as they were the last time she'd visited. Mom in front of the TV watching her silly shows, Danny poring over his coin magazines, neither having aged a day. As it was, they didn't intrude on her thoughts every hour, as they had after her "death," and it hadn't even been a year. They were dead to her. She thought of them in the past tense. Like Sam's, Jillian's past life was frozen in time, and like Sam, she'd always miss them, even though she might not think of them every day.

She had the impression that Sam's family had been a close one. It wouldn't have mattered that Sam knew what was happening. Losing both parents and her sister at nineteen must have rocked her world. Jillian was beginning to understand why forming bonds with others wasn't high on Sam's priority list. She needed time, and Jillian would have to be patient. Not one of her strong points, but she'd try. "If you ever feel like telling me more about your family, I'd love to hear about them."

"I don't see the point." Sam's hunched shoulders and strained voice told Jillian it would be too painful for her.

Shit. It took every ounce of willpower for Jillian to not go and put her arms around her. "Will you at least tell me your last name?" she said softly.

Sam quietly snorted and shook her head. "I don't have a last name. I haven't had one for almost twenty years." She looked at her watch. "I'm going to bed. You should, too. We have work to do tomorrow."

Considering that Jillian hadn't thought of herself as "Jillian Campbell" for a while, she wouldn't protest. She got up and picked up the crumpled note. "Sorry about this."

Sam waved away her apology. "I deserved it." She walked to the hallway and turned around. "You've been subdued lately—since the island. I'm glad you're back to your old self."

Warmth radiating through her chest, Jillian had to consciously prevent herself from gaping.

"Good night."

"Good night," Jillian managed to mumble. She stared after Sam, then ripped up the note and threw the pieces into the recycling bin. She'd just had what she'd hoped for—an honest conversation with Sam that went beyond discussing the weather—but it had unsettled her. She didn't have a crush on Sam. It was worse than that.

SEARCHING FOR SOMEWHERE to park that wouldn't be too conspicuous, Sam cruised past the Olmos estate and took the next right. Jillian covered her mouth and yawned, then sipped her tea. "Did we really have to come this early?" she mumbled.

Sam chuckled. "It's 7:00, Jillian."

"Exactly."

"Didn't you have to get up when you worked nine to five jobs?"

"Not this early, and we were up in the middle of the night. You were out for some of it. You should be exhausted."

When she'd agreed to drive the group last night, she hadn't known they'd finally have a potential lead. Despite going to bed earlier than usual, she was a little tired, but . . . "I'll survive."

Jillian slipped her tea into the cup holder. "Max might not be there. I heard them arguing that day around 4:30, so maybe he goes in early, comes home early."

"Or maybe he just happened to be home at that time on that day. I know they're probably not all still in bed, but we can't wait until the sun is rising earlier. You might be able to tell where Isabel sleeps, anyway."

Jillian's brows drew together. "Why does that matter?"

"It'll give us an idea of how she's treated." Sam pulled into a driveway and turned the car around. Finding an inconspicuous spot was proving difficult. Nobody parked on the street in this neighbourhood. "Do you know if there's a park nearby, or a store?"

"There's a spa not far away from here, on King. Maria was telling me about it."

Figured. "Will you be okay travelling to the house?"

Jillian tensed, but nodded. "Drive to the stop sign and turn left."

Sam did as directed. When they reached the spa, she pulled into the parking lot, but drove around to the back of the complex and parked there.

Jillian pointed to a sign. "You might have to move, or they'll ticket you."

"Then I'll move." Sam smiled at Jillian's wide eyes. "Don't worry. You're attached to your body. You'll make it back."

"How will I know where to go?"

"You'll know. Do you remember telling me about how you slammed back into your body at Junior's place?"

"It was Jackson's, and yes, I do remember."

"You didn't have to think about where you were."

"So if you're not here when I come back, I just have to panic?" Jillian quirked a brow. "I think I can manage that. But don't move unless you have to, okay?"

"I won't." Sam twisted and reached for the knapsack on the back seat. She plopped it on her lap. "I'll have a pad and paper ready when you get back."

Jillian unfastened her seatbelt. "Maybe you should try astral sight," she said as she adjusted her seat and leaned back. "If I see anything interesting, you can write it down."

"I wouldn't know how to do it. We have to wait for it to happen."

"Maybe today will be the day." She gave Sam a sidelong glance. "You can always ask the boss to make it happen."

"Time to get going," Sam growled.

Jillian cleared her throat and closed her eyes. "I'm off."

Sam watched her visibly relax. Jillian's body looked as if it were deflating. She grew paler. Her breathing slowed. How long would it take her to cover the distance to the house? She could be gone for a while. Sam undid her seatbelt, carefully lifted her tea from next to Jillian's, and gulped some down. She wasn't sure what to make of the note Jillian had brought back from the Olmoses. She wouldn't wish distress and pain on anyone, but she hoped they were finally on their way to discovering their purpose for being here. It would be disappointing if Isabel's cry for help turned out to be a request for money.

When she'd finished her tea, she unzipped the knapsack. Jillian should be in the house by now. Sam wanted to be ready when she returned. She wasn't experiencing astral sight, so Jillian would have to write down any important details she didn't want to forget. As Sam pulled out what Jillian would need, she fumbled the pen; it fell right next to Jillian's foot. Shit. She slowly leaned over and reached out with her fingers. They brushed Jillian's leg.

Whoa!

She was moving down a hallway. No, she was in the car, behind the spa, but she could see a hallway. This must be astral sight. It was similar to daydreaming. Sam knew exactly where she was. In fact, she could see Jillian's foot, but in her mind, she was seeing what Jillian was seeing. Just as when daydreaming, or thinking intensely—you always knew where you were, but the mind was elsewhere. Did she have to touch Jillian to make it happen? The other Deiforms hadn't mentioned that, but Sam had only read about those in her cell, and they might not have written down every detail about the joint gifts. She pulled her fingers away, then slowly straightened as she moved into a kitchen. Apparently touch wasn't required to maintain the connection.

"Jillian," she pushed out, wondering if the connection would support telepathy. Jillian—they—stopped moving.

"Sam?"

"I can see what you're seeing, and I guess telepathy works, too."

Movement again. *"That'll come in handy, especially since it has a longer range this way."* They passed from the kitchen into a bathroom. *"Women use this,"* Jillian said, lingering near the toiletries lined up on the counter next to the sink. *"Let's hope Isabel's bedroom is nearby."*

"Have you seen her yet?"

"No." Through another doorway . . . *"This could be it."*

The cramped room contained a single bed, a bureau, and a round area rug. Atop the bureau were two unlit candles. *"Pretty bare."*

"At least she's not sleeping on the floor," Sam said, thinking of other cases in which those she'd rescued had lived in deplorable conditions. *"Check the other rooms."*

"Here she is," Jillian said when she entered a laundry room. The woman inside was ironing a shirt.

"She doesn't look very old," Sam observed.

"No, she's about our age," Jillian said.

"You said they were thinking of getting rid of her because she's old."

"That's what I heard."

"When they were arguing, did they say her name?"

Silence, then, *"No. Dylan told me they argue about her."*

Maybe Dylan had it wrong, but Sam would wait until Jillian was back to continue the discussion. *"Keep looking around."* So far, they hadn't seen anything that told them why Isabel had reached out to Jillian.

Fifteen minutes later, the colour returned to Jillian's face. She opened her eyes and turned to Sam. "That was a complete waste of time."

"No, it wasn't. We know her living conditions are okay. The room is small, but comfortable. We need to talk to her."

Jillian frowned. "How? I can't get her alone. I'm escorted to and from the front door."

"I've been thinking about that."

"Can you think while you're experiencing astral sight? Because that's what just happened, right?"

Sam nodded.

Jillian's eyes glinted. "You took my advice, then."

"No, I dropped the pen near your foot." Sam shoved the pad and pen into the knapsack and tossed it onto the back seat. "When I bent over to get it, I touched your leg, and bam."

"Don't tell me you were bent over the entire time."

"I pulled away to see if the connection would break. When it didn't, I decided to try telepathy."

Jillian's brows shot up. "Glad to see you're being adventurous."

Sam humoured her with a smile. "I don't know if we'll always have to initiate it that way, or if touching you caused the gift to stir, and now we won't need to."

"I guess we'll find out. So, how are we going to talk to Isabel?"

"The way I see it, we have a couple of options."

Jillian adjusted her seat until she was comfortable, then looked at Sam. "I'm all ears."

AFTER SLIDING HER notes into her satchel, Jillian clasped her hands on the table and smiled at Dylan. She'd hoped she wouldn't have to involve him, but her subtle attempts to get Maria to tell her what she needed to know during Sunday's coffee hour had failed, so now she had to trust a ten-year-old boy to be discreet. Fortunately he was fond of Isabel, and he'd kept the note a secret, so . . . "Do you remember the note from Isabel?" she said softly, even though she'd closed the door halfway through the session.

He vigorously nodded. "I wanted to ask you about it, but I didn't want to get into trouble," he whispered.

"I need to talk to her, to—"

"Is she in trouble?" he asked.

Jillian hesitated. "I don't know. I need to talk to her—alone. Do you know if she ever goes anywhere? By herself?"

Her heart sank when Dylan shook his head. "She always goes with a driver," he said.

"Where?" Jillian asked, her hopes rising again.

"She picks up food Mom and Dad like. Dad says it's the only place that makes the real thing, not imitation shit." He froze. "Sorry."

"Doesn't matter," Jillian murmured. "Do you know where?"

"No."

"Is there a particular day she usually goes?"

His faced scrunched up. "I think Wednesday mornings."

"Does she go out any other time?"

He shook his head.

"Thank you." She met his eyes. "You can't tell anyone about this, okay?"

He straightened. "I won't! I don't want to get her into trouble. They already hate her."

"Are you sure? Hate is a strong word."

"Why do they argue about her?" His voice conveyed his bewilderment. "She hasn't done anything."

"I don't know." But she'd find out. "You can't tell her about this, either, okay? If she doesn't know, she can't get into trouble for it."

"Okay."

"She's lucky to have a friend like you." Jillian smiled at him. "I'll see you next week."

As soon as she got back to the condo, she relayed the conversation to Sam. "Our best bet is to stake out the house Wednesday morning."

"You should be able to talk to her inside the store. The driver won't go in. He'll probably have a smoke or talk on the phone."

"What if it's a small boutique store?"

Sam lifted a glass of juice from the end table next to the sofa. "Then you'll let me know and I'll distract the driver."

"I could always offer to give her a lift home. I could tell the driver that I tutor Dylan and I know Isabel."

"No. The Olmoses wouldn't like it. Heck, the maid, or whoever rules the hired help, wouldn't like it. We don't want to tip them off that we're looking into anything, especially when it comes to you. We don't want to lose your access to the house." Sam frowned. "If I thought Isabel would trust someone else, I'd talk to her and leave you here. But she'll be skittish. The last thing she'll want is for you to involve the driver."

Jillian narrowed her eyes. "You seem to know a lot about how the upper crust and their servants behave."

Sam took a long sip of her juice. "We'll need a translator."

"Isabel might speak English."

Sam shook her head. "You would have gotten a longer note."

"A translator could spook her."

"We'll have to take that chance. Let me call for a translator. Then we'll work out the best questions to ask." She rose and strode from the living room.

Jillian wished tomorrow was Wednesday, instead of Tuesday. After months of searching, she was eager to speak to Isabel. Hopefully the translator wouldn't intimidate her. Why couldn't the gift have allowed Jillian to speak every language, too? Sam believed the gifts were pale imitations of God's abilities. Since Jillian believed the gifts came from within, she figured being able to speak *and* understand every language would be logical, but logic didn't play a huge role when it came to the gifts. Frustrating.

She gazed toward the hallway. Where was Sam? Why couldn't she have fetched her phone and called the translator in the living room? Jillian would be the one working with him or her—in fact, maybe she should have called, rather than Sam. But Sam was used to doing everything herself. Jillian imagined Sam in her bedroom, probably sitting on her bed, the phone pressed to her ear, explaining—*what the hell?*

Sam leaped up from her bed and gaped at Jillian. "Whoa!"

Dazed, Jillian looked up at her, then oriented herself. Her knuckles were touching the hard floor. So was her bum. She was no longer sitting on the living room couch. She was in Sam's bedroom.

"I'll call you back." Sam ended the call and stared at Jillian, then reached down and nudged her shoulder. "You're definitely here. Translocation?" she suggested, at the same time Jillian thought it. "It has to be. The joint gifts are coming fast and furious now."

Jillian glanced at Sam's closed bedroom door, then pushed herself to her feet. "When I read that it works through walls and other physical barriers, I didn't quite believe it."

"How did it happen? What did you feel?"

"Nothing. I mean, one minute I was on the sofa, the next I was here."

"But something must have initiated it." Sam's brows knit together. "When you . . . arrived, I was talking about you. You were in my mind."

"I was thinking that you were speaking to the translator," Jillian said. "According to the records, it only takes one of us to initiate it."

"Yeah, but it's easier if we're both focused on the same arrival point, or at least both thinking about the other one." Sam sank onto her bed. "You didn't feel anything?"

Jillian shook her head. "Nothing."

"It didn't feel like shifting?"

"No. It happened as quickly as someone snapping their fingers, but I wasn't outside of time. One minute I was in the living room, the next I was here. No warning. No weird turn. Nothing."

"Now that the gift has stirred, we need to practice. We can't do this every time we both happen to think of each other at the same time."

Jillian smiled. "You might get some unexpected help at the food bank."

"Yeah." Sam grinned. "Though I don't think translocation has that range."

"It might have a longer range than telepathy."

"Even if it does, I bet it'll be most useful when we're in telepathic range. We'll need to coordinate our thoughts. I suppose we could go by time, but that won't help when we need to use it to get one of us out of a sticky situation." Sam dropped her phone onto the bed. "Go back into the living room. Let's try it again."

An hour later, they'd each successfully translocated several times from one end of the condo to the other, and while carrying objects, an experiment Jillian had suggested based on what previous Deiforms had reported. Sam had pointed out that their clothes were translocating with them, but Jillian had wanted to confirm that carrying an item would work. She didn't want to translocate and find herself without her pistol and identification at the other end. As for translocating fully clothed, if she'd arrived at her destination naked, she would have filed the gift under "use only if it will save my life"; she was sure Sam would have done the same.

Chapter Eleven

Jillian watched Isabel enter the store that specialized in Mexican food, then turned to Sam. "I guess I'm on." She shivered and blew on her hands. "I should have worn my gloves."

Sam leaned over and flipped open the glove compartment. "Here," she said, pulling out a pair of wool mittens.

Jillian slipped them on, figuring they must be left over from one of Sam's late-night excursions. She stared at the mitts, admiring their rich brown colour and appreciating the sensation of the soft wool against her fingers. "Can I keep them?"

"Sure."

"Thanks." She twisted toward the translator sitting in the backseat. "You ready?"

Julie nodded.

"Don't let Isabel know that you understand her," Sam cautioned. "Let Julie translate for you."

With a nod, Jillian got out of the sedan. Julie gave Jillian a tight smile. "I'll follow your lead."

"Why don't you walk on my left?" Jillian said, hoping to stay out of sight of the driver as much as possible. Not that he'd care. As Sam had predicted, he was already outside the car with a cigarette dangling from his lips, despite the chilly temperature.

When they entered the store, she was grateful for the warmth. Damn, the interior wasn't that large, and apart from themselves and Isabel, there was only one other shopper. She raised her brows at Julie, then eyed the prepared dishes as she moved closer to Isabel, not wanting to make a beeline for her.

All right, here we go. Big smile. "Isabel!" she said. "Hello."

Isabel whirled toward Jillian. Her eyes widened.

"This is my friend, Julie," Jillian said slowly.

"Pleased to meet you," Julie said in Spanish.

Frozen in place, Isabel stared at them.

"Tell her I got her note from Dylan and I'm here to help," Jillian said.

"Jillian got your note. Dylan gave it to her. She wants to help."

Isabel swallowed and looked out the window. Jillian did the same. The driver was leaning against the car with his back to them. "I want to leave," Isabel whispered, after checking to see what the other shopper was doing.

Jillian opened her mouth and turned to Julie, then clamped it shut. *Wait.* "She wants to leave," Julie said.

"The Olmoses? She doesn't want to work for them anymore?"

Julie repeated Jillian's question in Spanish.

Isabel nodded. "I want to get out, but I can't. I don't want to end up like the others."

Jillian waited for Julie's translation, then said, "What others? And if she wants to leave, why can't she hand in her resignation?"

Julie turned to Isabel. "Who else are you talking about? And Jillian wants to know why you can't just leave. You can tell the Olmoses—"

Isabel gasped. Words tumbled out. "I can't leave. I have nowhere to go. I have no papers. They took them. And those who try to leave, they disappear. Nobody sees them again. Even if that wasn't true, I can't leave. I can't go, but I can't stay like it is now. My life is wasting away."

Jillian's mind raced as Julie duly translated. "I don't understand. Tell her we can get her papers." Hell, if the Fellowship couldn't track them down, it could create another identity for her.

Julie conveyed the information to Isabel. "No, no," she cried, shaking her head. "I can't just go." Her voice rose. "I can't just go, don't you understand?"

"Ask her—"

"I don't know what you're doing," a deep, accented voice said, "but if you don't want to make her life more difficult than it already is, I suggest you leave her alone."

Jillian turned around. A man wearing an apron and hair net glowered at her. "I'm trying to help her. She asked for my help," she said.

He looked at Isabel. "She says you asked for her help. Is that true?"

"I have to get out. But I can't." Isabel's eyes glistened. "I don't know why I thought she could help me. It was stupid. But I don't know what to do."

The man's eyes flicked to Julie, then settled on Jillian. "Can you help her?"

"Yes, I can."

He studied Jillian, then gazed past her, out the window. "Come with me." He beckoned to Isabel. "Come." They followed him to the counter. He pulled a set of keys from underneath it and unlocked a nearby door. "Be quick, otherwise he'll come looking for her."

The three women crowded into the cramped storage room. When the door closed behind them, Jillian felt claustrophobic. She sucked down some air. "Ask her why she can't leave if we get her papers and sneak her out," Jillian said to Julie.

Julie translated the question for Isabel. "Can you get the others out, too?" Isabel asked.

Jillian's frustration rose. "What others?" she hissed, after waiting for Julie's translation.

"I'm not the only one. They bring others. They take their papers, too," Isabel said to Julie. "They say we'll get them back when we've paid off our debt, but how long does it take? I heard Mr. Max and Mrs. Maria talking about getting someone else. What will they do with me? I don't know what will happen if they don't want me."

Julie translated Isabel's concerns for Jillian. "If she wants to leave, wouldn't it be good for them to get rid of her?" Jillian asked, wishing she didn't have to pretend that she didn't understand. Waiting for Julie to translate was wasting time.

When Julie translated the question, Isabel vigorously shook her head. "No. Nobody ever leaves. Nobody. They disappear. Nobody ever sees them again. They say they went to another job, but that's not true."

Knowing they didn't have much time, Jillian focused on Isabel. She'd worry about the others later. "But we can get you out and keep you safe." Julie conveyed as much to Isabel.

"I can't just leave," Isabel repeated.

Jillian's hands clenched. "Why can't—"

They all jumped when someone banged on the door. It swung open. "You have to get out," the man in the apron said. To Isabel: "He's wondering where you are."

With a cry, Isabel pushed past Jillian and into the store. Jillian and Julie hurried after her.

"It's okay, he's talking to someone," the man said, "but you'd better hurry up."

"Tell her I can help her," Jillian whispered to Julie. She didn't understand the reason for Isabel's fear, but she knew it was real. "If she wants to leave the Olmoses, I can get her out safely. Nobody will be able to hurt her. She'll be safe."

Julie did so, but Isabel ignored them. She quickly told the man what dishes she wanted. As he silently packed her order, Julie murmured, "Maybe we should go."

"No. Let's move away, though." She walked to the window. Sam was talking to the driver and probably hating every minute of it, especially when he took a drag of his cigarette and exhaled. Footsteps rang on the tile floor. Jillian heard the whoosh as the store's glass door opened. She watched Isabel walk across the parking lot to the car, then went to the counter.

"You know why Isabel needs help," she stated to the man. "I'd like to help her, but I need to know more."

He made a show of tidying up the stack of glossy brochures next to the cash.

"Please."

"She's gone. She doesn't want your help," he said without looking at her.

"She's scared."

He didn't respond.

"You want to help. You let us—"

"I didn't think," he snapped. "She doesn't want your help. Please leave. And don't come back." He pushed open a swinging door and disappeared behind it.

Jillian waited for a moment, then conceded and left the store, with Julie on her heels. The Olmoses' car was gone. Sam was back behind the wheel of their car.

"I have more questions than answers," Jillian said as she slid into the passenger seat. *"I'll tell you about it when Julie's gone."*

She waited until they were back at the condo. "I don't know what to think. She's scared, the guy at the counter is scared, but nobody wants to talk."

"What did Isabel say?" Sam asked.

"She kept saying she wants to get out, but she also said that those who leave disappear. Oh, and she said someone took away her papers, so she can't leave. They have to pay off a debt, and she's not the only one in this situation."

After a moment, Sam said, "It sounds like human trafficking."

Jillian snorted. "What? The Olmoses? Come on."

"You'd be surprised. They might not even know, though they probably do."

"I read a couple of Fellowship cases about trafficking rings involved in the sex trade," Jillian said. "Isabel's a cleaner, or cook, or something. She's not turning tricks."

"Forcing people into domestic labour isn't unusual at all."

"But why?" Jillian said, bewildered. "Why would people like the Olmoses . . . You're suggesting they're holding her captive, that—"

"She's a slave?" Sam nodded. "Yeah, that's what I'm suggesting. We've run into this before. There are more slaves today than there's ever been in history, and lots of those slaves are in the western world. They're not out in cotton fields, though some of them are farm labourers. Most of them are hidden behind closed doors, just like Isabel. Now, maybe the Olmoses don't know, but I'm betting they do."

"I'm sorry, but I just can't believe they'd knowingly keep a slave."

"They probably don't look at it that way." Sam's eyes widened. "This could be big. It sounds like the Olmoses aren't the only family using forced labour. We could be dealing with a trafficking ring."

"Isabel can leave at any time. There's nothing stopping her from going to that store and slipping out the back door."

"And then what?" Sam asked softly. "I'm willing to bet that she has no money, no ID, no one to call, and she's probably been told that she can't trust anybody, that it's a dangerous world out here, that the authorities will beat her, maybe even kill her. You said yourself, she's terrified, especially since those who've tried to flee are never heard from or seen again."

"How would she know that, if she's isolated?" Jillian wondered, still unable to accept that Maria, so polite at coffee hour, was a slave owner.

"Gossip has a way of finding ears. She overhears conversations between the Olmoses, visitors, tradesmen, the guy at the store . . . Assuming she's from another country, it's possible that she didn't arrive alone. But not all slaves are foreigners. Some are native Canadians, Americans, Brits . . ."

Jesus. "Okay, let's assume for a minute that she's there against her will—"

Sam held up her hand. "She might not have started there against her will. She said that she has a debt to pay off. That suggests to me that she paid someone to get her into the country, probably someone who promised her a decent job and citizenship. However it happened, she knows she's trapped now. I wonder how long she's been there."

"Dylan said she took care of him when he was a baby."

"That's at least ten years. We need to get Jeremy and Emma on this."

"For sure. So let's say you're right. What do we do? I can't go back to that store. We can't kidnap Isabel . . . or maybe we can. Why don't we just go in and grab her?"

"If she was the only one, I'd say yes, let's do that. But it sounds like she isn't, and swooping in without having the whole picture could hurt others." Sam pulled out her phone. "Hey," she said when the person at the other end answered. "We think we might have found the problem." As Sam recounted her suspicion that they could be dealing with a human trafficking situation, Jillian gathered that she was speaking to Roberta.

Sam hung up. "Okay, Jeremy's on it. We need to know more before we do anything, both from him and Isabel."

"How? Like I said, forget the store."

"We'll have to get her alone some other way, away from the house."

"According to Dylan, she only goes out on Wednesday mornings," Jillian said.

"Then we'll have to get her out another time. Maybe someone Maria trusts can suggest that she needs Isabel and the other servants to help her with her good work."

"And who—" Jillian broke off. "Patrice." Reverend freaking Patrice.

Chapter Twelve

SAM WAITED WHILE Barbara conferred with Patrice about the unexpected arrival who wanted to speak to her right away. Barbara stepped from the office, a tight smile on her lips. "You can go in."

"Thank you." Sam went into the office and closed the door.

Patrice's eyes searched Sam's face. "I was going to say hello to you at the food bank tomorrow." She paused. "How are you feeling?"

"Fine."

"Please, sit down. Is there something wrong?"

"As a matter of fact, there is." Sam reached into her back pocket and pulled out a business card, but she held onto it as she sank into one of the guest chairs. "It's a delicate matter. I need to know that this conversation won't go any further than you and me."

Patrice's brows drew together. "That goes without saying. What is it?"

Sam hesitated. She hated lying to clergy. Lying to anyone bothered her—when they were big lies, not the little lies everyone told to spare feelings and get along. But lying to clergy sometimes felt like lying to Him, even though she knew that wasn't possible. Well, one could try, but He always knew the truth. "I haven't been honest with you."

Patrice's expression didn't change. "How haven't you been honest?"

"I'm not a technical person. I don't run a web business." Sam leaned forward and offered Patrice the business card. "I'm a private investigator."

Patrice reached for the card and took a minute to read it over. She set the card on her desk. "And what about Jillian? Who's she?"

"She's also an investigator."

"I see." Patrice's shoulders hunched. "I have to admit, I'm disappointed. I honestly thought you were a Christian."

"I am. I only lied about my job."

Patrice gave her a long look. Her voice hardened. "Are you investigating me? The church?"

"No. We came here because we were asked to look into a possible human trafficking ring. The information we had led us to your church, and since then we've identified a possible victim of the ring." Sam moistened her lips. "We need your help to find out exactly what we're dealing with."

"Who sent you?"

"Our client information is confidential." *But you know Him.*

"I don't understand how this church can be connected to a human trafficking ring. I'm certainly not involved. The same goes for Barbara."

"It's not the staff."

Patrice jerked forward and splayed her hands on her desk. "You think someone in the congregation is involved?" she said, her voice shrill.

"That's what we need to confirm."

Patrice slowly exhaled. "Who is it, or am I not allowed to know?"

"It can't leave this room."

"You have my word."

Sam met Patrice's eyes. "We think that one of Maria Olmos's workers might be there against her will."

Patrice gaped. "Maria?" She shook her head. "No, I can't see it."

"Excuse me for saying this, but most slaveholders don't look like slaveholders."

"Slaveholder?" Patrice breathed. She fell silent.

"We've managed to speak to the servant once, but she's frightened and she only leaves the house once a week, always in the company of a driver. We need to talk to her alone. We were hoping you could help us with this." Sam sat quietly while Patrice digested information that had obviously shocked her to her core.

"Jillian is tutoring Dylan," Patrice murmured.

Sam nodded.

"I thought that was rather nice of her. Now I understand why she offered."

"No," Sam said, knowing that Patrice would return to Maria when she was ready. "When Jillian offered to tutor him, we had no idea that the Olmoses might be involved." At the time, they'd still been in the dark about why they were here. "As I said, we had information that led us to your church, but we didn't know who was involved."

Patrice's brow furrowed. "I don't understand. Why would you be led here with no idea of who to investigate? That doesn't make any sense."

Sam shrugged. "I can't tell you any more than that." When Patrice didn't protest or demand to know more, Sam continued. "We need to speak to the servant alone."

"Yes, you said." Patrice swallowed. "I don't know how I can help you with that."

"You do a lot of work that needs volunteers. If there was something coming up that required more hands on deck . . ."

"I'm not sure what you mean."

"You could ask Maria to lend you some of her employees."

"I don't know if she'll go for that," Patrice said with a frown. "Maria comes every Sunday, and that's it. Max and Dylan used to come, but Dylan decided he was too old for Sunday school and Dad quickly agreed that Sundays would be father-son bonding time. He's so busy during the week." She grimaced. "I disagreed, but God rarely wins these days, as we see out there." She pointed at the wall. "But I'll speak to her. The church bazaar is coming up. There's always a lot to do."

"That sounds promising," Sam said, pleased that Patrice would help. "It'll be busy, which means it'll be easier to speak to the servant alone for a few minutes without raising alarm bells."

Patrice's expression turned pained. "I'm of two minds about this. I don't like going behind people's backs."

"Even when it could mean saving others from a terrible situation?"

"Perhaps if we spoke to Maria," Patrice began. "We—"

"No," Sam said firmly. "Regardless of whether or not she knows what's going on," and if she didn't, Max certainly would—it had to be one of the Olmoses, "telling her could lead to disastrous consequences." She paused. "We've heard rumours about some servants disappearing."

"Surely not. We would have heard."

"No, we wouldn't have. When it comes to bringing in slaves from other countries, nobody in the new country knows the person exists, except those who have the key to the shackles."

Patrice stared at Sam, then slowly shook her head. "In my position, I hear a lot. I don't mind saying this conversation is particularly chilling. I'll do what I can." She raised a finger. "No promises. Maria could say no."

"All we want is for you to try."

"I'll certainly do that."

Sam felt her shoulders sag as tension drained from her. "Jillian and a translator will speak to her—Isabel."

"She's the one you think might be there against her will?"

"Yes."

"What language does she speak? Spanish?"

Sam nodded.

"I can speak Spanish. I'm not perfect, but I can stumble along."

"Does Maria know that?"

"I don't think so."

"Even better. And don't worry. Nobody will protest if you ask Jillian and Isabel to help you with something," Sam said.

"You're sure this is the only way?"

No, there was a Plan B, but it was risky. Definitely last resort material. "If we thought there was another way, we wouldn't involve you." Sam leaned forward. "I know it feels underhanded, but if this woman *is* being held against her will, we need to help her. She reached out to Jillian, but now she's terrified. And there may be others."

Patrice recoiled. "At Maria's?"

"We don't know. But it's possible that we could break up a ring and rescue a lot of people."

"Rescue . . ." Patrice picked up Sam's business card and peered at it. "I expect you want me to keep your and Jillian's secret?" She dangled the card between her thumb and forefinger. "Didn't you do something on the church's website? Don mentioned you'd worked for him, too."

"We're here as a web development company."

"You're living a lie, in other words." When Sam drew breath, Patrice beat her to it. "The ends justify the means? When I was younger, I would have railed against that, but the years in this chair have turned my black and white glasses to gray. That doesn't mean it always feels right, though."

Sam was more familiar with that sentiment than she'd ever wanted to be. She stood. "Thank you for hearing me out. I won't take up any more of your time. You'll let me know how it goes with Maria?"

"I'll speak to her on Sunday."

"Thank you." Unfortunately, Patrice would have time to think about it and could change her mind, but at least they would have tried for Plan A before moving to B.

Her phone rang as she was walking to the car. "Hey," she said to Jeremy.

"I got your message, and the answer is yes, three people on record as working for the Olmoses. Two men, one woman."

"Professions?"

"Chauffeur, maid, gardener. Oh, and it was the cook, in the study, with the candlestick."

"You win," Sam said dryly. When Jillian had projected, they hadn't seen anyone other than the Olmoses, Isabel, and the maid. Sam would be surprised if the Olmoses had more hired help beyond the chauffeur and gardener. Their estate wasn't *that* large, and there were only three family members.

"I need a last name for Isabel," Jeremy said. "I can't find out anything without her full name."

"We're working on it. Thanks." Sam hung up. Okay, so Isabel was the only one unaccounted for at the Olmos household. If Isabel was wrong about there being others, they might not be dealing with a trafficking ring after all, but that didn't matter. One person in bondage was one too many.

JILLIAN PULLED ON a sweatshirt and stared at herself in the full-length mirror mounted on the bedroom door, something she could have done without. Today was her one-year anniversary with the Fellowship—and one year since she'd "died." When she'd turned thirty-seven in the weeks following the showdown with Junior, she'd missed the customary phone call from Mom. Had Mom picked up the receiver and then remembered? How many times had irritation flicked across her face when Mom had called on her birthday? Why had she kept looking at her watch, tapped her foot, rushed Mom off the phone? Would fifteen minutes have killed her?

Would Mom and Danny think about her today? Would they visit her grave? Not wanting to see herself any longer, Jillian swung the door open. *Don't be maudlin today, Mom. I don't deserve it, and I'm fine.*

And thankfully, she'd be busy. When she'd heard that the church bazaar would fall on her first anniversary, she'd been grateful that she wouldn't be sitting around, twiddling her thumbs. She had a job to do.

When she strolled into the kitchen, Sam looked up from her cereal and said, "Good morning."

"Morning," Jillian said, wondering if Sam would acknowledge her milestone. When she'd turned thirty-seven, Sam hadn't wished her a happy birthday. Now that Jillian had been with the Fellowship for a year, she knew she'd definitely missed Sam's birthday. She'd considered asking Sam about it, but she'd figured she'd get the same old grunted, "It doesn't matter," answer, and Jillian had gathered that the Fellowship didn't mark birthdays. They weren't religious holidays, and some of its members were technically dead. She glanced at the kitchen clock. "You should have woken me up. We have to be at the church in half an hour."

"It only takes us five minutes to get there," Sam said, shrugging.

Forty-five minutes later, they huddled with Patrice in the corner of the busy main hall. "Don't pounce on her as soon as they arrive," Sam said. "You're sure she's bringing Isabel?"

"She didn't seem too pleased when I pressed her to bring her entire household, but I told her I was desperate and that I don't badger her to bring everyone to church every Sunday, so maybe she could do me this one favour." Patrice scowled. "I don't like guilt-tripping people."

"Helping out here will make them all feel good," Sam said. *"If Maria does bring everyone, I might slip out and pay her house a visit."*

"I'll call you if they leave before you're back." Jillian smiled at Patrice. "Why don't you tell me what I can do, and I'll find you when I think it's a good time to speak to Isabel."

"There's quite a lineup outside," Sam said.

Patrice beamed. "With three halls packed with bargains, you can't go wrong." She lowered her voice. "Maria just arrived."

Jillian looked toward the hall's entrance and spotted Isabel. "She's here. She's the one in the brown coat."

"I'll go take care of them. Why don't you two busy yourselves in the kitchen? I think they need help carrying everything to the baked goods area."

"Is everyone here?" Sam murmured when Patrice had left.

Jillian took another surreptitious look. "I don't see the chauffeur, and we've never seen the gardener."

"He's seasonal. Okay, when things really get going and Patrice can believe I'm lost in the crowd, I'll take off."

"What about the chauffeur?"

"He must be outside. If not, I can avoid him at the house."

"Don't be long."

Jillian spent the next while carefully moving all sorts of goodies between the kitchen and baked goods tables, a task that became ten times tougher when the doors opened and bargain hunters streamed into the hall. She felt as if she were at a Boxing Day sale. Patrice had assigned Isabel to a table packed with used toys and conveniently located near an exit. Jillian would give it fifteen minutes, then find Patrice. She didn't want to risk the Olmoses cutting out early.

As she threaded her way through the mob for the tenth time, her phone vibrated. Expecting it to be Sam, she pressed her finger against one ear and the phone against the other. "Hello," she shouted. She could make out a woman's voice, but not the words. "Just a minute." She elbowed her way back to the kitchen, where it was noisy, but not overwhelming. "Sorry about that."

"It's all right," Roberta said. "I just wanted to congratulate you on your first year with us. I'm glad you came to us."

"Oh. Thank you." Jillian paused. "I wasn't sure the Fellowship acknowledged the dates we joined."

"We certainly do acknowledge them."

"I haven't seen anyone do it."

"You haven't been here when it's one of our turns."

"What about birthdays?" She'd been on the road with Sam when hers had passed. It was possible that Sam hadn't said anything because she was being her usual quiet self, but Roberta hadn't called her, either.

"We usually don't, because we consider today to be your birthday. Joining us is a rebirth of sorts."

Jillian wouldn't quibble.

"That doesn't mean you shouldn't wish someone a happy birthday on their old birthday, though. It's up to you." Roberta was silent for a moment. "I gather you haven't read about us."

"No."

"Why not? Don't you want to know who you're living and working with?"

A baking tray fell to the floor with a loud *clang*. Jillian caught the eye of the woman in charge of the kitchen and pointed toward the kitchen door. "Hold on. I'm going somewhere quieter," she said to Roberta. She ducked out a side door and stood shivering in the near-zero temperature. It had been warmer this time last year, a time she'd never forget. "I feel it's an invasion of privacy. I'd rather hear it from you all. Most of you don't have a problem telling me a little about your pasts." Well, Roberta hadn't said much, but Jillian hadn't asked. Now that she felt comfortable with her, she'd give it a try next time they were in the same room together and see how Roberta reacted. "I should have asked about your anniversaries." Why hadn't Sam freaking told her?

"It's not the most important thing to know about someone."

"What about Sam's, um, Fellowship birthday? Did I miss it?"

"It passed when you were living undercover as a soul healer."

Okay, she had an excuse for that one. "What about her old birthday? You said we don't celebrate them, but . . ."

"It was two months ago."

Shit. "Please tell me it wasn't her fortieth. I would have said something for her fortieth."

"No. Her thirty-ninth." Silence, then, "I can perhaps understand why you'd prefer to get to know us through conversation, except in Sam's case. She brought you in. She trained you, and now you're linked to her. I would have expected you to get to know her."

"I'd like to. I've asked her about her past, but she's private."

"That's why I would have expected you to read her file," Roberta said.

"I'd like to hear it from her." Jillian shifted her weight and shoved her free hand into her pocket. She was chilly, and she didn't want to discuss Sam with Roberta. The woman had an uncanny way of figuring out, or just knowing, what someone was thinking or feeling. Jillian didn't want that right now. "I should go. We're at a church bazaar. We're hoping to speak to Isabel."

"I won't keep you, then. Enjoy your day."

"Thank you. I appreciate that you called," Jillian said, meaning it. She hung up and hurried back into the warmth.

To appease the kitchen matron, she carried another load of goodies to the baked goods area. Man, these people were snapping up the treats faster than Jillian and the others could restock the tables. Fortunately there were more cookies, cupcakes, and brownies in the kitchen, but Jillian predicted that the baked goods area would close before the bazaar did.

She glanced at her watch. It was still early, but she didn't want to take any chances. She found Patrice in the smaller hall, near the tables stacked with used books. "I think we should try to speak to Isabel now," Jillian murmured. "You should go to get her alone. I might spook her."

Patrice nodded. "I'll bring her to my office."

Jillian headed there, and only had to wait a few minutes until Patrice ushered in a nervous Isabel. As soon as Isabel spotted Jillian, her eyes widened and she turned to leave.

"No, don't go," Jillian barked.

"We only want to talk to you," Patrice said in passable Spanish.

"Mr. Max and Mrs. Maria . . . they won't like it."

"They won't know. You told Jillian that you want to leave the Olmoses, but you can't. Is that true?" Patrice asked, without any prompting from Jillian.

"I have to leave, but I can't."

"Why can't you leave?"

"I told her!" Isabel said, pointing at Jillian, who was content to let Patrice handle the conversation for now. "They took away my papers."

"Who?"

"Mr. Max and Mrs. Maria."

Patrice's face tightened.

"And where would I go? I have nowhere. No money. Nobody," Isabel added.

"What's she saying?" Jillian asked, wanting to jump in, and frustrated that she couldn't let on that she understood every word.

"So far, she's confirmed what you told me. She wants to leave, but she doesn't have papers or anywhere to go."

"Ask her what her last name is," Jillian said.

"Torres," Isabel said, in response to the question.

Jillian mentally filed away the information. "Tell her we can get her papers."

Patrice did so. Isabel vehemently shook her head. "No, if I leave, they'll kill me. The others . . . they never come back. They're never seen again."

"Who'll kill you?" Patrice asked.

"I don't know. I just know it will happen."

"Who are these others?"

"Others like me. They work in houses, with no papers. We came here for a better life, but they tell us we have to pay off a debt. But for how long?"

Patrice turned to Jillian. "She's afraid. She says they'll kill her if she leaves. Not the Olmoses. She doesn't know who. And apparently she's not the only one. There are others in the same situation."

"Tell her we can protect her, and if she leaves and helps us, we'll help the others."

Patrice's forehead puckered. "Can you do that? Protect her?"

"Yes."

"You'd better mean it." Patrice grasped Isabel's shoulders, and relayed, "We can protect you, and if you help us, we'll protect the others, too. Let us get you out. You can leave right now. You don't have to go back into the bazaar."

"No, no, I can't do that," Isabel cried, stepping away from Patrice.

Jillian was against it, too. They wanted to get Isabel out in a way that wouldn't endanger everyone else and tip off whoever was running the trafficking ring, assuming there was one. "Is she still afraid?

Tell her that if she wants to leave, we'll come up with a plan that will ensure she's safe. It will take us some time."

"Oh, sorry, I just told her she could leave now."

"No, that might prevent us from finding the others, and the people responsible." If the buck didn't stop at the Olmoses . . .

"I'm not used to dealing with this sort of thing," Patrice said, sounding irritated. She looked back to Isabel. "Jillian says it would be better that you not leave today, but we'll get you out as soon as we can."

"I can't leave," Isabel said. "I want to, but I can't. I shouldn't have asked for help, but that day, I had hope. I thought she could help me. I don't know why. If I stay, they'll kill me because the Olmoses don't want me anymore. If I go, even if you protect me, I'll never see him again. I'd rather die than not see him again."

"Not see who again?" Patrice asked.

Tears filled Isabel's eyes. She shook her head.

"Is it someone at the Olmoses'?"

Isabel hesitated, then nodded. Jillian looked on in confusion. As far as she knew, the only men at the Olmoses' were Max, the chauffeur, and the gardener. Could she be in love with one of them? "What's the problem?" she asked Patrice.

"She doesn't want to leave because it means she won't see someone again, someone at the Olmoses'. A man."

"Is it a lover?"

"Is it someone you're involved with, your lover?" Patrice asked Isabel.

"No!"

"Is it a relative?" Jillian asked. She didn't have to understand Spanish to know that Isabel had said no.

Patrice relayed the question to Isabel, who hesitated again. She swallowed, then whispered, "Yes."

A brother? A cousin? Wait. Another male lived under the Olmoses' roof. A snatch of conversation with Dylan ran through her mind. *"She gives me candy and stuff. She took care of me when I was a baby,"* he'd said. Maria's voice rang out in Jillian's head. *"She's too old. You want to replace her with someone younger."* Oh my god. "Ask if Dylan is her son."

Patrice's jaw dropped. "What?"

"Ask her if Dylan is her son," Jillian snapped.

"Is Dylan your son?" Patrice asked quietly.

Isabel shrank in on herself. Tears spilled down her cheeks. "Yes."

The blood drained from Patrice's face. Jillian went to Isabel and gave her shoulder a reassuring squeeze. "Ask her if Max is the father."

"I doubt—"

"Ask her."

Patrice's shoulders slumped. "Who is Dylan's father? Is it Max?" she asked Isabel.

Isabel slowly nodded.

"I don't want to start throwing false accusations around, especially when it could hurt a child," Patrice said. "She could be lying about Max and Dylan. We'll have to talk to Max."

"No. There's another way to find out. Ask her if we can take a couple of her hairs."

"What?"

"For DNA testing."

"Oh." Patrice relayed the question to Isabel. With her consent, Jillian plucked two hairs from her head and murmured a thank you. She'd find a baggie or plastic wrap in the kitchen. She'd also try to get a sample from Max by taking him a coffee and whisking away his empty cup. Checking his coat for hairs was another possibility, if she could figure out which one was his. "Tell her you'll take her back to the bazaar and that we'll figure something out. Tell her we won't do anything to jeopardize her position with the Olmoses."

A subdued Patrice relayed the information to Isabel, adding that she'd take her to the ladies' room first. "I'd like to speak to you and Sam about this," Patrice said. "Where is Sam? I haven't seen her since you arrived."

Jillian shrugged. "Helping out somewhere, I guess. We'll find you at some point." She looked toward the door. "I'll wait here for a few minutes to give you a head start. Please thank her, and tell her she's brave."

"I will." Patrice patted Isabel's arm and spoke quietly to her as they left the office.

When she was sure they were out of earshot, Jillian pulled out her phone and called Sam. If she was still prowling around the Olmoses', her phone would be on vibrate.

Sam picked up. "Hey."

"Are you at the Olmoses'?"

"Yeah, and nobody's here. Have you spoken to Isabel?"

"Yes, we did. Things just got a whole lot more complicated."

Chapter Thirteen

JILLIAN HAD TO hustle to keep up with Sam as they walked through the condo's parking garage to the elevator. To her surprise, Sam had put off meeting with Patrice after the bazaar; instead, they'd meet with her before church tomorrow. When they'd stopped at a UPS Store on the way home to send off the hair and the coffee cup Jillian had grabbed from Max, Sam had been impatient with the clerk—meaning she'd said "please" and "thank you" tersely, rather than politely. "What's the rush?" Jillian asked.

"No rush." Sam stepped into the elevator and mashed the *Close Doors* button.

Maybe she needed to go to the bathroom.

When Jillian entered the condo, the aroma of cooking meat stopped her in her tracks. *Huh?* Ruth stepped into the hallway, a mug in her hand. "You're back. Good. Dinner won't be ready for another couple of hours." She raised her mug. "Tea?"

Jillian shook herself. "What are you doing here?" she said, feeling a grin spread across her face.

"Sam twisted my arm." Ruth smiled. "She didn't have to twist it too hard. Happy birthday." She handed her mug to Sam. Jillian didn't protest when Ruth embraced her. God, she was turning into a sappy, sentimental pile of mush. "It's good to see you."

"And you." Ruth threw her arm around Sam and carefully squeezed her, not wanting her to spill any tea. "You two are certainly living in luxury."

"We have to keep up appearances," Sam said. "Everyone at the church is loaded."

"They're all old money, or entrepreneurs with successful companies." Jillian sniffed the air. "It smells good. When did you get here?"

"A couple of hours ago." Ruth lifted her arm from Sam's shoulders and took back her tea. "Come into the kitchen and tell me all about this case you're working on."

Jillian wanted to thank Sam for the nice surprise, but she'd have to do it later. "Where do you want us to start?"

"At the beginning. We have time." Ruth flicked on the electric kettle. "I'm staying here tonight. I'll go back to the island tomorrow." She turned to them. "So, I know about Roberta's vision and that you've stumbled onto something here. Fill me in."

Jillian glanced at Sam, then said, "It was luck." She couldn't help but smile when Sam and Ruth raised their brows at each other. "I offered to tutor this boy . . ."

By the time she finished telling the tale, they'd moved to the living room.

Ruth's brow furrowed. "So Isabel claims that Dylan is her son."

"Jeremy's trying to find out how and when Isabel entered the country," Sam said.

Ruth raised her second cup of tea to her lips and took a sip. "I wonder if her information about the others is true. She's probably getting snatches here and there."

"If we can ever talk to her for more than five minutes, we might be able to get other names," Sam said.

"The guy at the food store knows something, but he refuses to help." Jillian thought back to her brief conversation with him. "He's afraid, just like Isabel."

"That suggests a trafficking ring, perhaps with connections to organized crime," Ruth said. "We've run into this before." She looked at Sam. "Warren broke up that sex trafficking ring, remember?"

Sam nodded. "Assuming we're dealing with a ring, we need to find out if they're still operating."

"They must be," Jillian said. "Otherwise why would Isabel be afraid to leave?"

"She's been around since before Dylan was born. A ring might have brought her in, but are they still involved?"

"The Olmoses might not be aware that they were dealing with a ring," Ruth added. "Maybe they went to an agency—a front, of course—to hire help. Maybe they never had her papers, or the agency asked for them and never gave them back. Maybe they were told that Isabel owed the agency fees for immigration services, and the Olmoses paid them off years ago."

"Then she'd leave," Sam pointed out. "Okay, maybe the people who brought her in threatened and brainwashed her. They probably told her the Olmoses are bad people who would hurt her, or deport her, if she said boo. But if the Olmoses weren't in on it and treated her right, you'd figure any threats would have lost their teeth by now." She paused. "Then there's Dylan—if Isabel is telling the truth."

"Mr. Olmos may or may not have taken advantage," Ruth said, "assuming he's the father. If he is, the man of the house sleeping with the servant doesn't mean she was put into his service against her will and has been trapped there ever since."

"You're saying that she may have had a consensual affair with him?" Jillian said.

"Yes. Even if it wasn't consensual, it doesn't mean they got her through a trafficking ring."

Blood pounded in Jillian's ears. "No, but it means the woman's probably lived through hell," she snapped. If she was correctly interpreting the argument she'd heard between Maria and Max, he wanted to throw Isabel away like a piece of trash because she was too old for him.

Ruth motioned for her to calm down. "I know," she said quietly. "We're just discussing all the angles, not making any judgements or trivializing anything."

Aware of her chest rapidly rising and falling, Jillian went to fold her arms, then decided it would make her look defensive. It would help if she could talk about illicit affairs without thinking of Dad. Maybe she should have heeded Sam's warning and not read the Fellowship's file on him, but it was too late now. She'd have to hope that she'd eventually stop hyperventilating whenever she heard about a man sleeping with someone who saw him as an authority figure.

The timer in the kitchen dinged. Ruth straightened, then rose. "Dinnertime. Come along, you two. I can use your help."

"Sure," Jillian said, grateful for the break in the conversation. One thing was for sure—this new Fellowship birthday was an improvement over how she used to celebrate her real birthday: spending the day with temporary fake friends or sitting alone in her apartment, dreading Mom's call. She swallowed. Funny, how today she'd love to pick up the phone and hear Mom's voice at the other end.

JILLIAN SWUNG THE dishwasher door shut, but since they were getting ready to go to bed and Sam would sleep in the living room, she didn't start a wash. The dishes had sat on the counter all evening while she, Sam, and Ruth chatted. They could wait until morning. She listened to the conversation going on in the hallway.

"You don't have to give up your bed," Ruth was saying. "I can sleep on the sofa."

"It's only one night," Sam said.

"Exactly. I'll survive."

"Don't be stubborn."

"I'm not the one being stubborn," Ruth countered.

Deciding to cast a vote, Jillian joined them. "Let Sam sleep on the sofa. You're our guest. I'd have volunteered my bed, if Sam hadn't beat me to it."

"You're the birthday girl. I would have turned you down." Ruth held up her hands in a gesture of surrender. "But I see I'm outnumbered, so I'll sleep in your bedroom, Sam. Thank you, and good night. I'll see you both in the morning."

"Do we have a spare pillow and blanket?" Jillian murmured when the door to Sam's bedroom closed.

"Yeah, I picked them up a few days ago."

Jillian watched Sam pull them from a hall closet they didn't use, then trailed after her into the living room. "Thanks for inviting Ruth over." *And for listening to me and Ruth gab all night.* Though Sam had thrown in the odd word. "I'm sorry I missed your birthday. Both of them."

Sam dropped the pillow onto the sofa and turned to Jillian. "You finally read my file."

"No."

Sam's brows drew together. "Why not?"

Here we go again. "I want to hear it from you." She kept her voice low, hoping Ruth couldn't hear her.

Sam's frown deepened. "Have you read anyone else's?"

Jillian shoved her hands into her pockets. "I've peeked at a few, but nobody I see a lot."

"You're usually curious."

"I want to hear it from them."

Sam gazed at her, then shrugged and unfolded the blanket. "I won't like you reading my file, but you have my permission to do it. Just don't badger me with questions."

That hardly sounded like permission. "I'm not going to read it."

"Why not?" Sam asked, an edge to her voice.

"Because you don't want me to. I'll wait."

Sam shook her head. "What will me telling you about myself prove?"

"I don't know. That you trust me," she said, providing half the answer.

"I do trust you."

"But not enough to tell me anything beyond the trivial. Okay, you've shared a little about what was going on in your life when the Fellowship found you, but that's it."

Sam blew out an exasperated sigh. "It's not that I don't trust you."

"What is it, then?"

"My former life, before the Fellowship, is a distant memory. It's so far removed now. I don't want to talk about it."

"Was it terrible?" When Sam didn't answer, Jillian figured this conversation was going to end the way it always did when she tried to glean a shred of information about Sam's past.

But then Sam sat on the blanket she'd just spread and looked up at Jillian. "No, it wasn't terrible," she said flatly. "But sometimes I wish I could know what type of person I would have been, what my life would have looked like, if I wasn't a Deiform." She stared at her hands. "I envy you. You had time to find out."

Shock momentarily rendered Jillian speechless. She kicked herself into gear, not wanting to squander this opportunity or give Sam the impression that she didn't care. Nothing could be further from the truth. She moved to sit down in a chair, then changed her mind. "You envy me?" she said, sinking onto the sofa next to Sam. "There's nothing to envy. Trust me, my life wasn't much until the Fellowship rudely snapped me out of my zombie state. Maybe it looked great from the outside. Confident woman, successful career, financially comfortable. Sounds wonderful. But I had nothing. No meaningful relationships, no dreams, no life. I was wasting my freaking time, waiting for the grim reaper to show up."

"Maybe I would have been the same. I don't know. I never had the chance to find out."

"No. You wouldn't have been the same."

Sam turned to her. "Why not? Because my father didn't—I didn't have the same background as you?"

"No, that's not it." Jillian took a moment to put into words what she instinctively knew. "I don't know many details about your past, but I do know you," she said, with a flash of comprehension. "I've spent more time with you than I have with anyone since I moved away from home. Sure, I was friends with some of my work colleagues when I was working a case. But they weren't true friendships. They were based on a lie. This." She swung her fingers between them. "This is authentic." And it was why she'd prefer not to learn about everyone by reading their files. She'd done that when she worked for the agency—learned about vices, weaknesses, what mattered to a person. She'd judged words on a screen, slotted people into little boxes. This time, she wanted to listen.

"You care about stuff. Your whole life has been about that, or at least it has since you entered the Fellowship." Sam was introverted and didn't wear her emotions on her sleeve, but she cared. She reached out in ways that made sense for her. When she came across as detached and indifferent, it was because she cared too much and was protecting herself, not because she was numb, as Jillian had been.

"You can't get emotionally involved," Jillian continued. "Or at least you have to try to keep your distance. Like you warned me, I'm learning the hard way that I have to strive to do the same. But you feel it." She recalled her first real conversation with Ruth, when they'd discussed Sam's love of reading. "You're the opposite of what I was. You never would have been what I was. If you weren't doing this, you'd be doing something else to make things better. Being a

Deiform, belonging to the Fellowship . . . you're doing exactly what you should be doing."

"Don't get me wrong, I'm humbled that the Lord has chosen to work through me," Sam said. "I'm just saying that when I was younger, after I first came in, I couldn't help but wonder. But I came to terms with it a long time ago." She met Jillian's eyes. "That's why I don't want to rehash it again. So when you do get around to reading my file, don't ask me a ton of questions. It's not my life."

Jillian sensed the same pain she'd picked up on when they'd spoken in the kitchen in the middle of the night. Maybe she was lucky that she'd only discovered the gifts when she was thirty-six, right when she was starting to question her life. "Let me ask you one question. You said you were at university, in religious studies."

Sam nodded.

"What were you planning to do? Become a minister?"

Sam chuckled. "Can you see me as a minister? I don't have the patience. I'd do the same thing you said you'd do if you were a teacher."

Jillian chuckled along with her. "Was the religious studies degree going to lead into something else, then?"

"I don't know," Sam said, slowly shaking her head. "I knew I wanted to serve the Lord, but I didn't know how. My parents wanted me to go to university, so I went into religious studies and hoped for guidance, I guess."

"It looks to me like you got it," Jillian said, "though I wouldn't put it that way. I'd say the gifts stir at the right moment, when we're at a crossroads, truly questioning or seeking."

Sam gave her an indulgent look. "And the Fellowship just happens to come along at the same time?"

"You and I now share some gifts. It's possible that we're all connected in some way, so we can sense when someone is ready—or rather, Guides have a gift that allows them to do it."

Sam's expression grew more skeptical. "You once accused me of doing mental gymnastics. From where I'm sitting, you're pretty good at swinging around those uneven bars yourself."

Jillian couldn't help but smile. "I suppose we all do it at times."

"Can I get that in writing?"

"No." Jillian knew that Sam's dancing eyes mirrored her own. They sat in comfortable silence for a minute, both lost in their thoughts. Jillian felt like she could say anything to Sam, which was dangerous, given some of the thoughts running through her mind. Best to bring the conversation back to where it had started. "I can imagine that if I'd come in as early as you, I might wonder about what I would have done with my life. All I can say is that you're doing exactly what you wanted to do, in a way that works for you." She shook her head. "No, it's stronger than that. You're doing exactly what you were meant to do. If you weren't a Deiform, you might never have found a way to serve God that was comfortable for you. Your life might have sucked."

"Gee, thanks," Sam said.

"You know what I mean."

"Yeah, I do. I appreciate your perspective." Jillian's throat tightened when Sam added a soft, "Thank you."

Shit, time to go, before she did something stupid. "Anyway, I don't want to keep you up." She stood. "Thanks again for the nice surprise. It was great to see Ruth."

"It could be a while before we're back on the island."

"For sure." Jillian lingered, reluctant to leave. Maybe she should have kept the conversation rolling. *No.* The last thing she wanted to do was get on Sam's nerves. Short, heartfelt conversations were better than drawn-out, shallow ones. "I'll see you tomorrow." She forced herself to move, then spun around. "I know you think it's weird, but I'm not going to read your file. I'd still like to hear it from you, even if you don't want to tell me anything beyond the facts."

"Have it your way." Sam's eyes narrowed. "You could be waiting a while."

That was fine with her. She wasn't going anywhere.

SAM CHEWED THE last of her toast as she read her devotional for the day. She'd managed to sneak into her bedroom and get the book without waking Ruth, and it would be at least an hour before Jillian got up. Sam relished the peace and quiet and always loved how mornings felt, how they demonstrated renewal and enticed optimism. Normally she wouldn't feel so tired; she was the "spring out of bed and greet the day" type. But she'd lain awake long after Jillian had gone to bed last night, not because the sofa was uncomfortable, but because the surprising conversation with Jillian had got her thinking.

Before her life had begun to spiral out of control because of her involuntary shifting, her future had troubled her. She'd never forget Dad's face when she'd told her parents that she'd decided to apply for the religious studies program. He'd struggled, and failed, to mask his disappointment. In the absence of the son he'd wanted, he'd assumed that she'd be the one to accept the torch from him, and she'd tried to convince herself that it would be the right thing to do, that she must honour her mother and father, that duty was a Christian virtue. But her desire to dedicate her life to Jesus had proven too strong to overcome.

It hadn't helped that she'd despised what Dad stood for, and had despised herself for benefitting from it. She'd wanted to break out and distance herself from her family, despite loving them very much. She'd felt torn, trapped; every possible path had led to ruin. Forced to choose one, she'd put herself first, for once, even though she'd had no idea what she'd do with her degree. She'd felt selfish. Every conversation with Dad about her future had condemned her, even though, to his credit, he'd accepted her decision and never outright stated his dismay. But he'd often asked the questions that plagued her. "What will you do when you graduate, Sam? If you don't want to be a minister or work overseas, what will you do?"

Mom had assumed that her daughter would travel the academic's path, but Sam had wanted to work in the world, not in an ivory tower. When she'd said as much, Mom had said, "Don't worry, something will turn up." She'd never know that she'd been right. No, as far as Mom knew, her prayers had been futile, or worse—they'd led to a devastating resolution that would have evoked the warning, "Be careful what you ask for." When Sam had asked Jeremy to find out if Alex had become a vet, she'd also asked whether her parents still attended church, and was relieved to find out they did. She couldn't have borne the knowledge that she'd turned her parents against God, and she'd realized that worrying about it had shown a lack of trust in Him. He would never have called her to His service if her parents' faith wouldn't have survived her death.

When the shifting had started, Sam had wondered if her guilt over not honouring her parents, and her worry over what she'd do with her life, had ripped her mind apart. She'd refused to believe the psychiatrist's diagnosis. At the same time, something had obviously been wrong with her. Every day she'd lived in dread, not knowing when she'd enter the weird alternate reality that terrified her. Then Brian had arrived, manna from heaven. He'd explained everything. He'd given her the answer. She'd eagerly grasped it and leaped without hesitation.

When reality had set in, when naivety had given way to maturity, she'd wondered whether the Lord had rescued her from the unproductive life she would have led because she couldn't figure things out on her own. She was a Deiform not because of her devotion and faith, but because she'd let Him down. She'd never considered that perhaps she was always meant to serve the Lord as a Deiform, that He hadn't rescued her. Maybe her life had proceeded exactly as He'd always expected it to proceed, and that was why, that one time, she'd found the strength to disappoint her parents. Maybe that was what He'd wanted to see from her. Calling her to be a Deiform hadn't been a lifeline thrown with disappointment. It had been an invitation.

She couldn't know for sure. But the possibility had lightened her spirit. She'd made her peace with the course her life had taken, but that didn't mean she never thought about it, especially recently, with the stirring of the joint gifts. From now on, she'd choose to believe that she was doing exactly what she'd been meant to do from the moment the Lord had given her life. She'd also stop wondering why she'd been linked to Jillian, of all people. She'd rather not be linked to anyone, but given that she didn't have any choice in the matter, Jillian wasn't the worst person to be with. She was smart, reliable, and often came at things from a different angle than most in the Fellowship. Ruth had said that Jillian worked for God, whether she realized it or not. Sam would add that God worked through Jillian, too—whether she realized it or not.

She had to get over her fear that Jillian would be killed. It would be easier if she'd managed to stay aloof. She'd tried, but how could she not care about her when they were together all the time? It was strange, working with someone she was starting to consider a friend. It had been so long. She was close to those on the island, but Roberta was almost like a mother to her, and Ruth was her mentor; Jeremy and the others were friends, but the sort you saw a few times a year to catch up. Jillian was a constant presence.

Her phone rang. She picked it up from the table. "Yeah."

"Good morning," Jeremy said cheerfully.

"You're calling early. It's not even seven yet."

"I figured you'd be up. I have lots to tell you."

"What did you find out?"

"Isabel Torres entered the country from the US fourteen years ago and then disappeared. No taxes, no medical records, no credit, nothing. Five others entered with her."

"How do you know?"

"Same date and time, same paperwork, same authorizing signatures, and that's the last of them in the system, too. I have no idea where they are. I'm sending the names and all the info I found to you . . . now."

"What about Dylan?"

Jeremy coughed. "Sorry. Yeah, Dylan. Well, he has a birth certificate that names Max and Maria Olmos as the father and mother. He was born at home, using a midwife."

So far, it sounded like he was Max and Maria's child.

"A couple of red flags, though," Jeremy continued. "He didn't see a doctor until he was six months old, and the Olmoses spent a year in Vancouver."

"Let me guess, they left when Maria wouldn't have been showing, and returned with a baby."

"Ding-ding-ding! I also found out that Maria and Max had tried in-vitro fertilization a few times. No luck. That doesn't mean she couldn't have gotten pregnant naturally, though."

Sam turned the information over in her mind. Nothing was conclusive. The Olmoses could have been desperate for a child, tried all the medical avenues in vain, and then lightning had struck. Or, Isabel had become pregnant, probably by Max, but not necessarily, and they'd decided to "adopt" the baby. "Did they ever look into adoption?"

"They applied and wanted an infant, but the waiting list . . ."

Yeah. "You said Isabel came in from the US. Was that her country of origin?"

"No, Mexico."

"How long have the Olmoses been married again?"

"Twenty years."

"Have they always lived here, in this city?"

"Yes."

"Are they originally from here?"

"Yes. But Max has relatives in Mexico."

"I want you to look into the midwife and anyone who had a hand in bringing Isabel into the country. Send me the information as soon as you can."

"Will do," Jeremy said.

"Is Roberta up?" Sam asked, knowing the answer.

"I'll transfer you."

She waited, then spoke as soon as she heard Roberta's voice. "Has Jeremy told you everything?"

"Not yet," Roberta said,

Sam filled her in. "Jillian and I will follow the leads we can up here. We need someone in Mexico to find out anything they can about Isabel, and to check into Max's relatives."

"I'll call Anita and have Jeremy forward them everything."

"Thanks." Sam hung up and rubbed her eyes. Right now, she had more questions than answers, but that was better than having neither.

Chapter Fourteen

JILLIAN WATCHED RUTH pass through the security check, then smiled and waved when Ruth looked over her shoulder. Anyone observing them in the bustling airport terminal would think two daughters were seeing their mother off. She fell into step with Sam as they strolled to the parking garage entrance.

They could be back here soon, to board a flight to Vancouver. As Jillian and Ruth had eaten breakfast, Sam had brought them up to speed. Rather than being daunted by the numerous leads they needed to investigate, Jillian felt energized. She waited until they were in the car before bringing up the investigation. "We'll have to work Vancouver around my next tutoring session. I don't want to give Maria any reason to think about me more than she has to."

"Cancelling one session won't be the end of the world," Sam said.

"Okay, maybe I just don't want to let Dylan down," she admitted, and she'd better change the subject before Sam changed her mind about both of them taking the trip. Not surprisingly, Sam had initially wanted to go by herself, but Jillian had protested. She didn't want to sit around twiddling her thumbs. Plus, two heads were always better than one, and maybe the joint gifts would come in handy. Sam had reluctantly agreed. "What are you thinking about Dylan's parentage?" There hadn't been time to discuss theories before church, and the conversation on the way to the airport from there had been about the service and those at coffee hour.

"I'm leaning toward Isabel having told the truth." Sam inserted the parking stub into the machine and drove out of the garage when the gate lifted. "Given their fertility problems, the Olmoses would have been paranoid about the baby's health. They definitely wouldn't have waited six months before taking Dylan in for a check-up. I'm guessing they saw a doctor off the record, until they felt that they'd gotten away with claiming the child as Maria's."

"You could be right." Jillian felt as if her head would explode. For the longest time they'd had nothing; now they were swimming in avenues to explore. "I need to get DNA from Dylan. And what are we going to do about the immigration lawyer?" One of the names Jeremy had sent was the lawyer who'd arranged for Isabel and the others to enter the country.

"That's where we're going right now. He won't be open, so we'll see what the situation is. Maybe we can get in, maybe we'll have to wait."

Jillian's stomach knotted, as it always did when they were about to do something illegal. It didn't matter that their motives were good. It didn't matter that they wouldn't be breaking in to steal. It didn't matter that the Fellowship had its own set of rules. She still felt as if she were doing something wrong. "I hate breaking into places."

Sam glanced at her. "Sometimes it's the only way."

True, but she'd never entirely agreed with "the end justifies the means." Jillian knew what Sam would say if she voiced her reservations: "God's law isn't man's law. We follow God's law." If breaking into this lawyer's office would contribute to freeing people in bondage, who was she to argue? How would she explain to Isabel and the rest that they'd remain imprisoned because it was more important to Jillian that she not get her hands dirty, that she follow the letter of the law, even when it meant letting innocent people languish? Wouldn't she essentially be saying that she cared more about the rights of the guilty than she did about saving the innocent? It would be a different story if she were in law enforcement, where—

Sam's phone rang, breaking into Jillian's thoughts. She pulled over and reached into her jacket pocket. "Yeah." She listened. "Okay, so this is ongoing, then. We're on the way to the lawyer's office now. We might need you . . . Okay." She hung up and turned to Jillian. "Jeremy found more people who've entered the country through this lawyer and then dropped off the radar, some as recent as six months ago. We knew someone was at least keeping tabs on those that came in with Isabel, but we weren't sure whether they were still actively bringing people in. Now we know."

Ten minutes later, they sat in the car outside a high-rise office building, on a street with heavy foot traffic, even on a Sunday. "I'll try the door." Sam climbed out of the car.

Jillian watched her wait for a break in traffic. Sam sprinted across the street and pulled on the glass door. Nope, they weren't getting in that way, and it was too busy to let themselves in. Sam disappeared down the alley that ran between the office building and a coffee shop. A couple of minutes later, she sank back into the driver's seat and shook her head. "There are a couple of back entrances, but there's a security system. Too bad there isn't a parking garage." She raised her brows. "Do you want to go in and check out the system from the inside, or should I? Visiting the lawyer's office to get the layout would come in handy, too."

"It's on the fifteenth floor." Jillian peered out the passenger side window and counted the floors until her eyes settled on the fifteenth one. The prospect of projecting up to it made her feel queasy.

"Why don't I go, and you can try astral sight? Instead of me having to write down the details, you can do it while you're actually seeing everything."

Jillian quickly agreed, wondering if Sam had sensed her reluctance. "Remember as much as you can, in case I can't do it. If it's not working for me, I won't be able to tell you."

"If I don't hear from you, I'll know."

Sam fired up the engine and drove onto a quieter street a block away. "You might need to touch me to get it to work."

Jillian nodded. "I'll get what I need from the trunk."

By the time she returned with the paper and pen, Sam was already projecting. Jillian waited a couple of minutes, then rested the pad on her lap and touched Sam's arm.

Jesus! Seeing through Sam's eyes as she projected was freaky—and effortless. She pushed out, *"I'm with you."*

"Good. I haven't seen any security guards." Jillian involuntarily flinched when Sam approached a door marked *Security* and passed through it. *"Nobody."* Just a couple of empty chairs in front of three monitors. *"The door is locked."*

"I wonder what time they show up and leave."

Sam didn't reply. *"Here's the security system panel."*

As Sam recited any numbers she could see and remained focused on the panel, Jillian furiously scribbled away. Her stomach lurched when Sam shot through the ceiling, emerged in the middle of a typical open-space office, and headed for the next ceiling. Jillian had never been one to ride the roller coaster, and shutting her eyes wouldn't help. She gritted her teeth and kept her fingers on Sam's arm.

"Here we are," Sam said, floating into immigration lawyer Benjamin Seaman's office. *"Great, he has his own alarm system."*

"Good to know." They would have assumed that disarming the building's security would be enough. Jillian wrote down the model number and repeated it to Sam, then sketched the layout of Seaman's office as Sam explored it. Typical—a separate waiting room with a receptionist's desk, and a spacious office with a degree hanging on the wall and a computer, phone, and datebook on the desk. Wait, there was another door near Seaman's coat rack. Sam passed through it. Ah. Filing cabinets.

"There are files from the late nineties here," Sam said. *"Looks like they might have switched over to electronic records around 2006."* She went back into the office. *"I'll just have a quick look at the rest of this floor."*

Ten minutes later, Sam groaned and stretched her arms and legs. "Give me the pad," she murmured, then pulled out her phone. "Here's what we've got for you." She relayed Jillian's scribbled notes to Jeremy. "Call me when you have something." She disconnected.

"I'm hungry, and there's a Kelsey's on the corner," Jillian said. "Want to go there for lunch?"

Sam shrugged. "Sure."

Jillian was finishing off her chicken when Jeremy called Sam. "What did he say?" she asked, when Sam hung up.

"Not much." *"The building alarm will be easy. Seaman's alarm will be tough. We pretty much have to be inside the office to disarm it."*

"Great."

"I have a plan. I'll tell you at home."

"Okay," Jillian said, finding Sam's use of the word "home" endearing and sad.

Jillian watched the elevator's floor number change and consciously slowed her breathing. It was 9:10 a.m., the Monday after Sam had projected into Seaman's office. "His date book was open, and I noticed that he has a 9:00 a.m. tomorrow, and then nothing until 10:00," Sam had said when outlining her plan. "Except for the receptionist, the waiting room should be empty."

They hoped. What if a delivery guy showed up? What if the 9:00 a.m. had brought a friend or family member for support and left them in the waiting room? *"I hope this works."*

"If we can't do it today, we'll figure out another way."

The elevator door opened on the fifteenth floor. Jillian followed Sam into the corridor, then took the lead. When they reached Seaman's office, she pasted a smile on her face and swung the door open. Empty chairs. So far, so good. Conscious of Sam behind her, Jillian planted herself in front of the receptionist.

The woman peered over her monitor and beamed. "Can I help you?"

"Yes, I was wondering if Mr. Seaman handles real estate transactions," she said, knowing he didn't. "A friend of mine used him for a family matter and highly recommended him. I was hoping—" She stopped when Sam elbowed her in the side.

"I'll meet you next door," Sam muttered.

"Sure. Grab me a tea, okay?"

Sam nodded.

Jillian turned back to the receptionist and met her eyes. *Keep looking at me, lady.* "Sorry. What was I saying? Oh, yeah." When the office door clicked shut behind her and the receptionist didn't gasp or leap to her feet, Jillian breathed a sigh of relief. Her part was done, for now. "I was wondering whether Mr. Seaman handles real estate."

The receptionist grimaced. "I'm sorry, he doesn't."

"Oh, that's too bad. Can you recommend someone?"

"There's an attorney down on the eleventh floor that we've used before. I think I have her card." The receptionist pulled open a drawer and rummaged through it. "Yes, here you are." She handed the card to Jillian. "Let her know that we sent you, okay?"

"I will, thanks. Have a great day." Jillian left the office and strolled back to the car. The whole day stretched ahead of her. Apart from an hour tutoring Dylan, she'd watch a little TV, play some guitar, read, and be back here bright and early tomorrow morning.

SAM THOUGHT SHE'D counted eight people entering then leaving Seaman's waiting area, though she could never be sure when observing from outside time. The receptionist had been gone long enough that Sam was certain she'd left for the day. Seaman was gone, too. It was dark. Nothing was happening. Sam stepped back into time. Colours burst into life. Ambient sounds surrounded her. The world felt three-dimensional again.

She gave her eyes a minute to adjust to the darkness, then shrugged the knapsack off her back and pulled out a flashlight and a pair of latex gloves. After snapping the gloves onto her hands, she flicked on the flashlight and tried Seaman's door. It opened. He hadn't locked the door to the archived files, either. Sam started with the year Isabel had entered the country. There wasn't a file labelled Torres or Olmos, which wasn't surprising, because Seaman wouldn't have been working for either of them. Hoping something would jump out at her, she flipped through the files in the drawer until she came to one marked *7445-G22*. Not only was it the only file she'd come across that wasn't identified by a name, it was thicker than the others.

She pulled it out, rested it on top of the files in the open drawer, and flipped it open. Bingo. The top sheet listed Isabel and the others Jeremy had identified as arriving at the same time. Underneath was the full paperwork filed for each individual. She was particularly interested in who had sponsored them. The electronic records Jeremy had hacked into yesterday held everyone's location and date of entry, nothing more. *Zachary Diaz.* She scribbled the name on the pad she slid from the knapsack, just in case it didn't come out clearly in the photos she'd take.

Sam methodically photographed every sheet in the file with her phone's camera. Once she'd placed the file back into the drawer, she thumbed through the rest for that year, and stopped at one labelled *7445-G23*. More names with the same sponsor. She photographed those, as well.

When she'd finished searching the last drawer a couple of hours later, she'd located more files with labels that started with *7445*. As of 2006, they were up to *G35* and she'd switched to a backup camera with more memory.

Sam was itching to call Jeremy, but she didn't want anything to place her in this office. She left the file archives room as she'd found it and sat at Seaman's desk. His computer was on. She woke it up.

Darn, it was password protected. Two alarm systems weren't enough for this guy—but then, he had things to hide. She had software she could use to crack the password, but it would mean restarting the machine. Seaman might notice. If they decided they needed a look at his hard drive, they'd find a way to hack in later.

She effortlessly unlocked his desk but didn't find anything noteworthy in its drawers. Jeremy would appreciate the business card with Seaman's cell number on it, though. Seaman's calendar was more informative; adrenaline shot through her when she found two entries for lunch with 7445. One appointment had taken place three weeks ago, the other was scheduled for next week. Were they bringing a new group in? Both were lunch appointments at a restaurant. Sam noted everything down, then bugged his phone and office. She'd do the same to the receptionist's phone before leaving.

Someone jiggled the outer door's handle. Sam snapped off the flashlight and prepared to shift. A security guard must be doing his check of this floor. Silence, then the faint sound of receding footsteps. She let out her pent breath and turned the flashlight back on.

Her remaining exploration of Seaman's office didn't turn up anything, and the receptionist's desk and computer yielded no secrets. Sam eyed the alarm system's control panel. She could try to disarm it using the instructions Jeremy had given her, but she'd also have to disarm the main building's security and avoid the guards. There was an easier way. She positioned herself as close as she could to the outer door without tripping the alarm's motion sensor, and stepped back into the quiet ethereal world.

What felt like five minutes later, she watched the receptionist dump her bag and coat on her chair, then leave the office again. Sam stepped back into time and checked her watch—*8:50*. After opening the door a crack to ensure the coast was clear, she headed for the elevator.

At 8:57, she sank into the passenger seat next to Jillian, who pointed at the cup in the holder. "Tea. I guess you don't need anything to eat."

"No, I only ate breakfast a couple of hours ago."

Jillian chuckled.

Sam picked up the tea and sipped it. "Thanks."

"Find anything?"

"The sponsor's name. Paperwork for everyone. Only up to 2006, though, except for a lunch appointment next week with someone who might be a ring member. Did you book the tickets?"

"For tomorrow afternoon."

Sam gulped down more tea. "They're still operating."

Jillian nodded grimly. "Let's shut them down."

Chapter Fifteen

JILLIAN STOOD IN line with Sam at the birthing centre where the midwife listed on Dylan's paperwork was now employed. She rarely saw so many pregnant women in one place and wondered what those in the waiting room thought of her and Sam. A lesbian couple here to check the place out, maybe? She kept the thought to herself; Sam might not appreciate the humour.

"Next, please."

They approached the counter. When Sam smiled broadly at the receptionist, Jillian swallowed. Sam should smile more often; it lit up her face, and the crinkles at the corners of her eyes were strangely attractive. Jillian shoved her hands into her pockets. *Focus, for god's sake.*

"Good morning. We were wondering if we could have a private word with Janet Fields," Sam said, using the midwife's married name. She'd been Janet Eckers back when Dylan was born. "We're investigating the disappearance of one of her former clients." She handed the woman a business card.

After peering at it, the receptionist picked up her phone and paged Fields. "She'll be out soon. You can take a seat and wait for her."

"Thank you."

They'd hardly sat down when a woman strode into the waiting area and spoke to the receptionist, who pointed at them. Jillian recognized Fields from a photo Jeremy had sent. "Ms. Fields?" Sam said, rising.

"Yes."

"Can we speak somewhere privately?"

"Uh, yeah, come with me." She led them into an office and shut the door. "What is this about?"

"We're investigating the disappearance of Maria Olmos," Sam said. "You delivered her son around ten years ago."

Fields' brow furrowed, then her eyes lit up. "Ah, Maria. I remember her. She's missing? What happened?"

"We don't know," Jillian said. "Her family reported her missing. We're combing through her background, trying to find anyone she might have contacted, or might be staying with."

"I haven't seen Maria for years."

"Since you delivered her baby?"

"That's right."

Sam pulled out her phone and swiped past several photos until she reached the one she wanted—a photo of a younger Maria. "This is Maria?"

Fields looked at the photo. "No, that's Isabel."

"Oh, I'm sorry," Sam said sheepishly. "I showed you the wrong photo." She swiped again. "This is Maria."

Fields nodded at the older photo of Isabel. "Yes."

"And you delivered her son?"

"Yes," Fields said, her brow furrowing again.

So Isabel was telling the truth. Shit. Now they just needed the DNA results to confirm the father. She'd managed to get one of Dylan's hairs on Monday. She'd smiled and picked it off his collar. Doing so had reminded her of all the times she and Mom had watched some poor couple receive paternity results on an afternoon talk show.

"Were Isabel and Maria close friends?" Sam asked.

"I got that impression. I always saw both of them, and Isabel was present when Maria gave birth, along with Maria's husband, of course."

"Max?"

Fields nodded again. "Have you checked with Isabel?"

"She hasn't seen Maria and doesn't know where she is."

"Oh."

Sam turned the phone toward Fields again. "This is Max?"

Field nodded.

"How did Maria find you?" Jillian asked. "When she was looking for a midwife, I mean. Did a doctor refer them?"

"Why?" Fields blurted, suddenly cagey. "What does that have to do with anything?"

"He or she might know something."

Fields stared at them, her face tight.

"Her family's going nuts," Sam said. "We have no leads. We need to look at everything. Sometimes it's a detail that nobody thinks is important that breaks a case."

"Look, I don't want to get into trouble."

"Then I assume you won't want us mentioning your past activities to this clinic's management."

Fields took a step back and put her hands on her hips. "It was ten years ago. I was younger. I don't do that anymore."

"Do what?" Jillian asked levelly.

Fields scratched her cheek and rocked on her heels.

"We're private investigators. We're not the police. All we care about is finding Maria." *"I wish we could read minds,"* she said to Sam in frustration.

"No, you don't," Sam shot back. "Please, Ms. Fields. Whatever you're holding back could help us find Maria."

Fields' shoulders sagged. She raised a finger. "This goes no further. I could be fired, even though I got out of that game a while ago. I do everything by the book now."

"We won't tell anyone," Sam assured her.

"All right, then. I used to deal with clients outside the system, those who weren't legal and couldn't afford to pay. An immigration lawyer would send them my way."

"So Maria Olmos came to you because she was in the country illegally and too poor to show up at a clinic and pay?" Sam said.

"Well, that, and they didn't want to draw attention to themselves."

"The lawyer told you this?" Jillian asked.

Fields nodded again. "Why?"

"We just want to make sure we're understanding you correctly," Jillian said. "Did you ever check into the women you helped, to verify their circumstances?"

"Why would I? The lawyer had already done that. He was trying to help them get papers, but babies don't wait on bureaucracy," Fields said with a small smile.

"Was he also helping Isabel to get papers?"

"I don't know. Only Max spoke English, so he translated. We stuck to Maria's pregnancy. I didn't ask a lot of questions."

"What was the lawyer's name?" Sam asked. "He would have kept in touch with Maria for longer than you did. She eventually got papers, so . . ."

Fields hesitated, then said, "Adam Rodale."

"Was he the only one who sent women your way?"

"His partner sometimes did, too. Jean Horowitz."

"Thank you," Jillian said. "You said you don't do it anymore?"

"No. When I was younger I was a bit more militant, shall we say. Then you get married, you have kids, you have a mortgage . . . well, you know how it goes. I knew I could get into trouble for what I was doing, and I wanted steady work, at a respectable clinic."

Sam shifted her weight. "Where did you work before? What would happen if there were problems with the delivery?"

"A doctor at a walk-in clinic in one of the poorer neighbourhoods helped out." Fields' mouth pressed into a thin line. "I'm not telling you who he is. He's helped lots of women, not just illegals. I'm not ratting him out. He wasn't that involved with Maria, anyway. He just signed the paperwork."

"Can you tell us anything else about Maria that might help us to find her?"

Fields pursed her lips, then slowly shook her head. "No. I didn't get too involved in these women's lives, you know. I didn't want to know too much. I just wanted to make sure they safely delivered their babies."

"If you think of anything else, please call us." Sam handed her a business card. "Thanks."

"Thank you," Jillian echoed.

In the corridor, Fields pointed the way to the waiting room and went in the opposite direction, probably glad to be rid of them. Outside the clinic, Sam called Jeremy. Jillian walked next to her, not paying attention to what Sam was saying to him. Her mind was too busy turning over what they'd learned from Fields.

So, Dylan was Isabel and Max's son. Another man taking advantage of immigrants. Too bad Max and Dad had never met; they would have had a lot in common. Jillian covered her mouth. *Oh my god, do I have any half-brothers or -sisters running around? Could Dad have been that stupid?*

Too lost in her thoughts, she didn't notice when Sam finished her conversation with Jeremy. When they reached the car, Sam said, "Ready for lunch?"

"Sure."

Unable to get Dad out of her mind, Jillian picked at her fettuccini and mustered a one or two word response to whatever Sam said. Even her after-lunch tea didn't cheer her up. Sam paid the bill and suggested that they stroll through a nearby park. It didn't occur to Jillian how uncharacteristic that was of Sam until they were walking past a pond and Sam said, "You're thinking about your father."

"No. Well, maybe." Jillian blew out a sigh. "It's hard not to. At least Max only took advantage of one woman—that we know of."

"Slow down. We're not absolutely sure Max is the father."

"Who the hell else would it be? He's an authority figure to Isabel. Just like my father was to all those women." She kicked a discarded coffee cup into a bush.

Sam gingerly picked up the cup and dropped it into a nearby recycling container. "Maybe you shouldn't have read his file."

"Well, I read it, okay?" She took a deep breath. "I wanted to know. It cleared up stuff I'd wondered about." And filled in the gaps she hadn't wondered about, until she'd thought back with the benefit of hindsight.

"What are you mainly angry at him for? The stealing, the cheating, or the suicide?"

Jillian barked a laugh. "All of the above." She shook her head. "He wasn't all bad. He was always busy. Came with the job. But when he was around, he was great—until the last couple of years. I don't know what happened. I don't know why he started to dip his fingers into the offering plate and . . . everything else." She glanced at Sam. "Okay, his file said that he wanted the money for the women, but . . ." Why? Why had he suddenly lost his mind? Why had he done that to Mom, to her? Why had he pressed the gun against his head and pulled the trigger? "He betrayed everything he'd stood for, and us. Me and my mother. He didn't even have the decency to stick around and say he was sorry."

On the other hand . . . "You'll probably think I'm awful for saying this, but part of me has always hoped he did it for us." A hope she'd unsuccessfully tried to stifle, and one that had deepened since she'd read his Fellowship file and learned the extent of his betrayal. "If he hadn't killed himself, it would all have become public. As it was, people were supportive, for the most part." Mom had found out who her friends were. "It would have been worse if they'd known Pastor Campbell was spending so much time in motel rooms—with freaking children."

"They were all adults."

"Barely." Jillian's nails dug into her palms. "Don't stand up for him. He doesn't deserve it."

"I'm not. I'm just stating a fact." Sam paused. "You told me that he shot himself in your bedroom."

"Yeah, he did. I don't know why." Had he not wanted to be alone? Had he come to say good-bye and decided to stay and do it right there? No, that wasn't possible. "I slept through it." She turned to Sam and saw the incredulity she'd expected.

"The shot didn't wake you up?"

"He'd added a little something extra to the milk he'd insisted I drink. They tested it when they had trouble waking me up." Her face and throat were so tight she was finding it difficult to get her words out. She swallowed and tried to slow her breathing. "I don't know if he did it because he wanted to be with me but didn't want me to see it, or to get at Mom. She came home to find her husband with his brains blown out and her daughter lying deathly still in her bed." *Bastard! Goddamned bastard!* Did she really believe that he'd shot himself to spare her and Mom from a trial and public humiliation? She wanted to, she really did, but she'd never know. He could have left a note, explained himself, but no. He'd left them to wonder. Maybe it *had* been all about him. "Mom's a survivor, or at least that's what I used to think. I mean, yes, she survived, but the world was never the same." For either of them. "I'm glad Danny came along."

The path in front of her suddenly blurred. Jesus, she didn't want to lose it. "Your turn. Tell me something about yourself, please! I need to take my mind off this." She could hear the desperation in her voice.

Sam must have heard it, too. "Okay." She chewed her lip. "I like to knit."

Jillian stopped short. "Knit?" Her spirits instantly lifted. "You knit? I've never seen you knit." She wiped a tear from the corner of her eye and stared at Sam's red cheeks.

"Some of the others tease me about it," Sam said sheepishly. "I wasn't sure what you'd think of it, so I've kept it to myself, but this case is dragging on so long . . . I'm usually alone. I can do it whenever I want."

"You can do it whenever you want now." Jillian bit her lip. "I wouldn't let the Beguilers know, though. It wouldn't exactly jibe with your reputation, though I suppose you could fend them off with a knitting needle." She made jabbing motions with her hand.

Sam threw up her hands. "See?" She walked again.

Grinning, Jillian fell into step with her. "That's it, I promise. I've got my teasing out of the way." She'd also stopped thinking about Dad and wanted to keep it that way. "So, how long have you been knitting?"

Sam gave her a sidelong glance. "Since high school. The church wanted volunteers to knit for some group that I forget now. I decided to give it a try, even though it wasn't cool."

"You usually don't care about that—being cool."

"I did when I was fourteen. Not enough to bow to peer pressure, but at that age, you can't help it. I mainly did it to please the minister."

Jillian bit her tongue. Most fourteen-year-olds cared about what their friends thought. Not Sam!

"I didn't think I'd like it, but I did. It's relaxing, and useful, and there's something almost hypnotic about it."

Come to think of it, there were quite a few knitted items lying around the house on the island, and Ruth was often wearing a wool sweater when Jillian visited. "Feel free to knit at the condo. I won't say anything."

"I've been knitting when you're not there."

Wait. "The mittens . . ." The rich brown ones she'd worn all the time. "Did you knit them?"

Sam hesitated a beat. "Yeah."

"Thanks for letting me have them. I mean it. So you're knitting some of the mittens you pass out to the homeless."

Sam nodded.

Jillian wouldn't mind going with Sam on those excursions, but she had to give her room, not impose on everything she did. "I'll try not to stare the first time I see you knit," she said, only half-joking. She wanted to add, "Now, was that hard, telling me something personal about yourself?" but she didn't want to be an ass. "I'm feeling better. Thanks for helping to take my mind off things. What did Jeremy say?"

"Our people in Mexico have reported back. Isabel left her village along with several others, for a better life."

Of course.

"Apparently the same people come by every year or so and dangle the same carrot. New life. Money you can send back to your families. It doesn't matter that everyone who's gone before is never heard from again."

"They're desperate."

"Well, that, and everyone is afraid of them." Sam turned to Jillian. "The people who dangle the carrots," she clarified. "Those who've publicly opposed them are no longer with us. I'm guessing that some of the women still take the bait out of hope. Others are coerced."

"Breaking up this ring won't stop it," Jillian said, a sense of futility souring her mood again.

"No, but they'll have to find another way to get people in." Sam was silent for a moment. "Our Mexican cell will do what they can. We have to focus on what's going on up here and try not to think about the rest."

Easier said than done.

"Jeremy also dug deeper into Seaman's background. He's clean as a whistle and well-connected, and the information in the files I photographed didn't lead anywhere. We won't be able to go to the authorities with this one, not directly. Roberta has a plan to draw out those involved in the ring. She'll fill us in when we're finished here."

"What about Isabel's claim that some people have disappeared up here? Has Jeremy checked John and Jane Does in the morgues to see if any match the photos on the immigration papers?"

Sam cocked her head. "I don't know. Why don't you ask him? If he hasn't, ask him to do it."

Jillian pulled out her phone.

THE LAW FIRM that had referred women to Fields had closed a couple of years earlier. One partner now practised in Alberta; the other had left the legal profession and opened a health food store.

"Adam Rodale?" Sam said to the man standing behind the store's counter.

He smiled. "That's me. What can I do for you?"

Jillian had a hard time imagining the bearded man with salt and pepper hair as a lawyer, but then again, digging into Rodale's background had revealed a man who'd handled many of his family law cases pro bono and had often shown up at the office in flip-flops and Hawaiian shirts. At first glance, he was a good guy. How the hell had he gotten mixed up with human traffickers?

"I'm investigating the disappearance of a woman you dealt with around ten years ago," Sam said, handing over her reliable PI business card.

Rodale took the card but didn't look at it. "Who?"

"Maria Olmos. You referred her to a midwife. Janet Eckers," Sam said, using the midwife's maiden name.

Rodale lowered his head, suddenly interested in the card he held.

"We're at a dead end, so we're combing through her background and talking to everyone who had any contact with her."

"Do you have a PI licence?" Rodale asked.

Sam pulled a leather folder from her other pocket, flipped it open, and held it up. "We're from Ontario," she said, as Rodale studied the licence. "That's where Maria currently resides."

"Well, I don't know anything," he said.

Sam slid the folder into her pocket. "Do you remember her?"

"I remember Maria. Vaguely. It was a long time ago."

"Eckers said you often referred women to her."

He dropped the business card on the counter. "What are pregnant women supposed to do while they're waiting for the immigration system to get its ass into gear? Hey, I know, they didn't follow the process, so why should we help them when they get knocked up?" He pressed both his hands on the counter and leaned over it. "A lot of these women are running away from abusive situations or trying to make better lives for themselves. They're not seen as good prospects, you know what I'm saying?"

"We're not here to judge what you did. We don't care. We just want to find Maria."

"Who are you?" Rodale snapped at Jillian.

"I'm also an investigator." Jillian pulled out her own fake PI licence, but Rodale wasn't interested. He was stalling.

"How did you find out about Maria?" Sam asked. "Anything you tell us will stay with us. We want to give Maria's family some closure. They're frantic."

Rodale stared at Sam, then pushed away from the counter. "A friend of mine—well, someone I knew in high school—contacted me about Maria. He said she was in Vancouver and needed help. He'd heard I might know someone. We talked about it. I took down her details, contacted her, and sent her Janet's way. That's it. I didn't have any involvement beyond that."

"What was the friend's name?"

"Ben Seaman. We went through high school together. Then I came out west. I'd heard he was a lawyer and saw him a couple of times when I was home visiting the folks. We were more acquaintances than friends."

"Did Ben ask for your help other times?" Jillian asked.

Rodale shifted his attention to her. "No, why would he?"

"How did he know about Maria?" Sam asked.

"He had a friend in Vancouver who knew her. And no, I don't know who."

"Janet said you referred other women to her. Are you sure Seaman didn't—"

"Look, I helped Ben once. That's it." Rodale ran a hand through his hair. "I helped out a couple of shelters. That's how I was involved."

"What about your law partner?"

"Jean? The same." The store's glass door swooshed open behind them. "Sorry I don't have what you're looking for," Rodale said loudly. "You could try the Internet. One of the online stores might have it."

"He doesn't know anything," Sam said. *"Let's go."* "Thank you."

"Thanks," Jillian murmured. She left the store with Sam.

"He wasn't involved in trafficking. He wasn't the sort to ask questions, either." Sam glanced at her watch. "Let's head to the airport. We won't find out anything else here."

"Maria must know that Isabel is under the thumb of a trafficker," Jillian said. "She seems like a perfectly nice person, but she has a slave and stole Isabel's son. I guess she figured whatever belongs to Max also belongs to her."

"Hold your horses. We don't have the paternity results yet."

"Still. She lied about Isabel. She falsified papers."

"But we don't know why. Maybe someone else got Isabel pregnant and the Olmoses were helping her. Even if it *was* Max, she could have willingly allowed them to adopt Dylan, and now she's having second thoughts."

"That doesn't change the fact that Max was sleeping with—"

"We don't know the circumstances around that, either," Sam reminded Jillian. "Maybe he took advantage. Maybe Isabel was in love with him."

Yeah, not everyone was her freaking father, but if Max turned out to be a knight in shining armour, she was Mary freaking Poppins.

Chapter Sixteen

Disappointed but not surprised, Jillian stared at Sam's phone on the kitchen table. The DNA results were in. Dylan was Max and Isabel's son. Jeremy had also located one of the women who'd entered the country with Isabel. He'd matched her immigration photo with her autopsy photo. Her unidentified body had been buried three years ago in an unmarked grave. That upscale, squeaky-clean house Jillian visited every Monday had more skeletons in its closets than a biology lab. Maria must know. You couldn't trust anyone. Life sucked.

"We have to draw out the ring," Roberta said, on speakerphone. "We can't confront the Olmoses. We don't know how they'll react, or whether they're still in contact with anyone in the ring. We don't know if Isabel's debt is real and the Olmoses are still paying someone, or if that's just a story they tell her. Either way, they know exactly what they're doing."

Yep. Poor Dylan.

"You said you had a plan," Sam said.

"We need someone like Isabel, don't we, or at least a couple of Supporters will." Roberta paused. "Jillian, tell Maria that you have friends who are looking for live-in help. Ask her what agency she used to hire hers. See what she says. In the meantime, we'll put a couple of people into place."

"What if she gives us the name of a reputable agency?" Jillian asked. "She has other help that aren't in the situation Isabel is in."

"Then we'll find another way, but let's try Plan A first."

"What are we going to do about Dylan and Isabel?"

"One step at a time. I'll leave it up to you whether to ask Maria on Sunday, or when you're at her house on Monday."

"She's not always around when I see Dylan. If I can, I'll ask on Sunday."

"I'll call you tomorrow and let you know the names of your friends, just in case she asks. We'll have laid enough of a paper trail by then."

"Seaman's meeting with someone next week," Sam said. "We might be able to get to the ring through his contact."

"Yes, but we might not. Either way, I'd like to see how these people operate. What do they ask for? How do you collect your purchase?"

Jillian's stomach knotted.

"Who really owns the slave? You, or the ring?" Roberta continued. "Seaman's contact might be involved with getting the slaves into the country, and that's it. He or she might not deal directly with the individual buyers."

"Having two roads into the ring is better than one." Sam clasped her hands on the table. "Anything I can do?"

"When we're ready to take on the ring, you'll take the lead. For now, support everyone else, and be there when Seaman and his contact meet. I don't want them seeing Jillian. We need the Olmoses to continue trusting her."

"Anything else?"

"Not right now."

After saying their good-byes and disconnecting, Jillian slumped in her chair and folded her arms. "Think of all those people who left their families expecting a better life, but instead, they end up imprisoned. How many are out there that we don't know about? How many live out their lives without ever tasting freedom?"

Sam rose and opened the fridge. "Too many."

"I'm not trying to pick a fight, here, but I don't understand how you can believe in a loving God when you're faced with situations like this." She watched as Sam poured herself a glass of juice, figuring that Sam had decided to ignore her.

"Do you want some?" Sam asked.

"No."

Sam put the juice jug back into the fridge and closed the door. "Here's the difference between you and me. You see suffering in the world and conclude there isn't a God. I see suffering in the world and conclude there must be a God." She lifted her glass from the counter and took a long drink.

"That makes absolutely no sense."

Sam frowned. "Why? Because if a loving God exists, suffering wouldn't?" She shook her head. "That's a little simplistic."

"Simplistic?" Jillian sputtered. "I'd say it's logical."

"Logical?" Sam snorted. "Don't talk to me about logic."

"No, I suppose you wouldn't like that, because then you'll have to admit that you don't have a leg to stand on."

"Quite the contrary," Sam said calmly, perturbing Jillian further. "From where I'm standing, you're the illogical one." She touched her chin with her finger and looked upward, clearly mocking Jillian. "You don't believe in God, but you believe life has meaning, that's why you're upset about Isabel and the rest. News flash. Without God, all meaning is an illusion, or maybe that's delusion. I'm never quite sure."

"Bullshit. Just because there's no God doesn't mean everything is meaningless."

"Sure it does. Think about the merchant who lived in twelfth century London and had ten kids."

"What about him?"

"You tell me. Tell me how meaningful his life was."

"He lived."

"So what? He doesn't anymore. For all intents and purposes, he never existed. According to you, it would make sense to live in a world where everyone who attends university is killed the moment they graduate. Everything they'd learned would be wasted, but that would make complete sense to you."

"No, it wouldn't make sense. Have you ever thought about why you believe? Maybe it's so you can make sense of life. Maybe you can't accept that life doesn't make sense."

"But it has meaning?" Sam gave her a withering look. "You'll have to do better than that. Assuming life itself has meaning, which you haven't proven in any way, shape, or form, tell me why it matters that our hypothetical merchant grew as a person, assuming he did.

Tell me why his life meant something. Tell me what meaning his life will have had when the universe as we know it dies." Sam sipped her juice and looked so damned relaxed that Jillian wanted to punch her. "The guy is dead, Jillian. He's been dead for centuries. Nobody knows who he was, and nobody cares. Any growth, suffering, epiphanies, sacrifices, were snuffed out when his heart stopped and his brain died. It was all for nothing. In your world. Not in mine."

"I'll admit there's no eternal meaning, but his life meant something."

"What did it mean? Why grow as a person just to die? Yes, growth is good and we see meaning in it. But if we die in the end, then I say that meaning is delusional. There is no real meaning. Whatever you did, whatever you overcame, ultimately it was for nothing."

"I already said there's no eternal meaning. And I can see your point." She'd wrestled with the questions Sam was asking. "So what do you want me to say? That you're right? That I'm delusional and should just shoot myself right now because my life has no meaning, and neither does anyone else's? Or maybe I should just let my hair down and live life hedonistically, because it doesn't matter what I do. Who cares if I hurt anyone?" She jabbed her finger on the table. "We're still sentient beings with brains. We have to live together on this planet."

"I agree. Just don't tell me how meaningful it all is, because I won't believe you." Sam downed the rest of her juice. She placed her empty glass in the sink, picked up her phone, and strolled toward the hallway.

Jillian slowly clapped. "Very good."

Sam turned. "What?"

"You did a great job of avoiding why a loving God allows so much suffering. You know, my original point."

"I don't know, but I believe He has his reasons."

"What reasons?"

"If I knew, I wouldn't say, 'I don't know,'" Sam said. "I'd tell you."

"And not knowing doesn't bother you? Are you sure you're not just avoiding the question because you don't have a good answer?"

Sam leaned against the counter. "This probably won't satisfy you, but think about it. Assume for a minute that God exists, and He's all powerful and created the universe and everything in it. Can you do that for a minute?"

"For a minute," Jillian said lightly.

"Okay. So He created the universe and everything in it. Have you really thought about that and let it sink in? That's incredible, and if He did it, He's incredible. We refer to Him as if He's sort of like us, but He isn't," Sam said, her eyes bright and her gestures growing more animated. "He's beyond our comprehension, and He's obviously intelligent beyond what we can imagine. He can juggle a ton more variables then we or any computer can, and that won't change in the future, no matter how powerful computers become. So, is it possible that He can be loving *and* have valid reasons for allowing suffering that we aren't in a position to understand? I think it is." She raised a finger. "I'm not saying we can't possibly understand because I want to avoid the question or shut you up. I'm saying we don't know because we don't, and we can't, and I think it's human arrogance to think that we can. All we can do—"

"Maybe it's human arrogance that makes you refuse to see that this is all there is," Jillian suggested. "That when you die, you'll cease to exist."

"All we can do is trust that He has good reasons for allowing it," Sam said, ignoring her.

Jillian folded her arms. "Sure, don't question it. What did Jesus say? Be like a child. I get it."

Sam's face tightened. "Did I say that? Do you think I haven't thought about it? You really believe that thoughtful theists have never thought about this stuff? That we're all drooling idiots who just believe what we're told?"

"No, I—"

"We have free will. We can decide to do things that cause suffering, but that's been covered so many times I'm sure you know the argument, so what about when someone suffers and it's nobody's fault? I'm sure you can think of instances where someone willingly suffers when they understand the why. Chemotherapy, for example. The only difference between that and the larger question of suffering is that we don't understand why, but that doesn't mean there isn't a why, at least for me." Sam pointed at Jillian. "You don't believe in Him. I accept that. At the same time, the loving God and suffering problem, or whatever you want to call it, isn't a problem for me and many other theists. If you want to convince someone there isn't a God or take pot shots at their faith, I'd take another approach."

"That's not what I want to do," Jillian mumbled.

"Really? Then why do you keep bringing this stuff up?"

Because . . . she'd pass for now; she hated the answer. "According to you, then, Isabel has pretty much been in prison all these years for some reason we don't understand."

"I don't have the big picture that He does. I don't know what His ultimate purpose is. Maybe Isabel's suffering will mean some scientific advancement will take place in the year 2400 that will save millions from suffering. We don't know."

"The same applies to that merchant that you brought up. Maybe he did something that eventually led to a scientific breakthrough hundreds of years later. Maybe that's what his life meant. It doesn't matter that he's gone, dead—permanently, and nobody knows he ever existed at this point. His life counted for something."

"That feels wrong to me," Sam said, pressing her hand against her chest. "I'll admit that's not a logical argument, but that's my reaction. I feel as if his suffering, his striving, his growth, should count, for *him*. And I believe it will, because I believe this life isn't it, another reason the," she formed air-quotes with her fingers, "suffering problem, while hard to deal with emotionally at times, doesn't tie me up in knots. When I suffer, I trust that it will somehow benefit me down the road. And that can be tough when it seems senseless, it really can. But I prefer my world to yours, because in yours, all suffering will ultimately be for nothing. Nothing at all."

"You prefer your world? You make it sound like a choice."

"Sometimes it is. I don't understand why any rational human being would rather live in your meaningless world. I prefer a world with meaning."

Frustration made Jillian's hands clench. "My world isn't meaningless."

"Because you inject delusionary, or is that illusory, meaning. But let's not go in circles."

"No, let's not," Jillian snapped. *Damn.* If it were anyone else, she'd change the subject, but she always felt compelled to be honest with Sam. "You don't like it when people assume you're an idiot because you're a believer, right? Well, you're assuming I haven't thought about the meaning of life. I have. I've wondered why anybody should give a shit. I get how absurd it is for us to get so wrapped up in our struggles and dramas when we'll all end up dead and forgotten in the end. Those problems that kept us up at night, the betrayals that made us wonder how we'd ever trust again, the gossip that stung . . . it's all absurd. In a hundred years, it'll be as if nobody now alive was ever here, unless we did something remarkable, and most of us don't. I get it. Without a Creator, is there a reason we're here? No. It just happened. There's no reason. Nothing has a reason. Life is absurd. I get it."

Jillian's heart was racing. She slowly exhaled, then forged ahead. "But the stuff I do while I'm here . . . it has meaning. It can matter to someone else. It matters in that moment. It's real in that moment. It makes a difference in that moment. And, hey, if this is it, it's even more important that we make life as pleasant as we possibly can for everyone. *We* have to right the wrongs. *We* have to administer justice. *We* have to protect the weak. *We* have to make sure that those who spoil it for someone else get exactly what they deserve. Because this is it. There's no pot of gold at the end of the freaking rainbow."

Even though the air was heavy, the ensuing silence didn't worry Jillian. She knew Sam well enough to know that she wasn't offended or angry. She was thinking.

"I understand that," Sam finally said. "I agree that what we do matters to others. But without God, all the striving and growth and development are for nothing. They have no meaning. Having said that, there's a lot of common ground between us. If I thought we should sit back here and let Him handle everything in the afterlife, I would have told Brian to go jump in a lake. God will handle everything, but that doesn't mean I can't pitch in and help," Sam said, chuckling. "And if you didn't see things the same way I do, you would have told me and Roberta to go away and leave you alone. We both willingly joined the Fellowship because we want to make a difference here, in this life."

"I agree," Jillian said, feeling the tension drain from her and the room.

"So perhaps we can respect each other's views? I don't pick at your views. Why do you pick at mine? Are you trying to convert me to atheism?"

"No." As far as Jillian was concerned, trying to sway someone to atheism was as bad as trying to sway someone to Christianity or any other religious belief system. She didn't want their views shoved down her throat, so why would she turn around and do the same to them? Sam's beliefs didn't bother her. Being in love with someone who held Sam's beliefs . . . Jillian poked and prodded because she wanted to understand why a thoughtful, intelligent person—why Sam—believed in God. The last person she would have expected to fall for was a devout Christian. It wasn't as if she'd seen herself skipping arm in arm with her beloved to atheist rallies. She hadn't seen herself with anyone. But if she'd given any thought to who she'd like to be with, a Christian who took it seriously wouldn't have been on her list.

Sam would feel the same, in reverse. If she was going to be in a relationship—a big if, for Sam—she'd want a Christian. She'd want someone whose number one priority was God. She'd never consider walking through life with an atheist. If only Jillian could get through to her heart what her head had always understood. Her feelings were an exercise in futility. She'd have to learn to accept Sam's friendship. She *did* accept it. She valued it. It would have to be enough.

A relationship with Sam wouldn't be the best idea, anyway. What would happen if things turned sour? They couldn't get away from each other. Plus, Jillian was used to being on her own—meaning single. After Amy, which hadn't been a grand love affair, but an infatuation, she hadn't felt compelled to meet someone else, hadn't hung out in clubs or cruised online. She'd gone too far, isolated herself, but that didn't mean she needed a romantic relationship. She and Sam *were* linked. They shared a unique bond: the joint gifts. They'd be close friends, look out for each other, and not have to deal with relationship bullshit.

"What are you trying to do, then?" Sam asked, jerking Jillian back to their conversation.

She lifted her hands and dropped them to her lap. "I don't know, I'm just curious. It's part of getting to know you, I guess."

"By attacking my beliefs?"

"I don't mean to." But she couldn't stop herself from getting in one last point. "Have you ever thought that believing in things like an afterlife and God righting all wrongs is a way of coping with life being unfair?"

"For those of us who actually try to follow what we say we believe?" Sam shook her head. "There are much easier ways to cope, especially in this world." She scowled. "Come on, you can do better than that. Look, I accept that you're an atheist. I don't preach to you. Why can't you just accept that I'm not an atheist?"

"You don't care that I'm an atheist," Jillian said, wanting to hear Sam say it again, even though she knew it didn't change anything.

"I didn't say I don't care. I said I accept it."

And there it was, along with the tension they'd previously diffused.

Sam scratched her cheek, her eyes on Jillian. "I'm not dogmatic when it comes to beliefs. You know actions matter more to me. Some people who say they believe in God do terrible things. Some atheists do wonderful things. Behaviour always trumps words and professed beliefs. Having said that, I believe that having faith in God, serving Him, is better for the soul. I'm not going to pretend I don't. That doesn't mean we can't work together, okay? I'm tempted to tell you that if you don't want to work with me, just turn off the joint gifts. After all, they come from within you, right?"

Jillian bit back a retort. She should have quit a minute ago, rather than throwing another punch. "The joint gifts are useful, and I don't mind having you around." Understatement of the freaking year.

"Well, that's good."

Jillian couldn't tell whether Sam was being sarcastic.

"I'd say it would have been better for you to be linked to someone else, but I'm afraid you're in the minority in the Fellowship, and not everyone places the emphasis on behaviour, like I do."

"I guess it's fortuitous that I share the joint gifts with you, then," Jillian said.

Sam's eyes narrowed. "Yeah. What a coincidence!" she drawled. Then her brow furrowed. "Thanks."

Jillian gaped at her. "For what?"

"I've struggled with why He chose to link me to you. Now I understand."

"Why, because nobody else would tolerate me?"

"No, because they'd only tolerate you." She pushed away from the counter. "This conversation wasn't a total waste, after all. I get it now." She walked out of the kitchen.

Jillian stared after her. *Well, I'm so glad I could be of service.* Hey, if any other theists needed to know why God had done something, she'd be glad to help them out! Her flash of amusement didn't alleviate her dismay at some of what Sam had said, or her disappointment with herself. Seriously, what was she trying to do? Make Sam hate her? If she couldn't have Sam, she'd tear her down?

I'm an idiot. Sam valued behaviour over words. Jillian said she wanted to get to know her, wanted to be her friend, respected her beliefs. Could she blame Sam for thinking, *Uh-huh*? If Jillian wanted to be her friend, she'd better start acting like one. If she respected Sam's beliefs, she had to stop picking at them. If she had to bite her tongue until it bled, so be it. They knew where they both stood on the God question, and they had to work together. Jillian wanted to earn Sam's trust and be a good friend to her, damn it.

She kicked back her chair, squared her shoulders, and went to find Sam. They had a trafficking ring to take down.

With one eye on the restaurant's entrance, Sam spooned soup into her mouth and waited for Seaman to arrive for his lunch date with 7445. When the hostess had led her to a table in the middle of the dining room, Sam had asked if it would be possible to move to one near the kitchen. She'd wanted as wide a view of the room as possible. Fortunately she wasn't the only one eating alone. Numerous tables at the popular lunch spot had only one occupant. Many by themselves were focused on their phones or reading newspapers. Sam could have asked for a Supporter to come along, but that would have meant making conversation. The obvious lunch mate would have been Jillian, but they didn't want her in Seaman's sights.

Sam hadn't voiced the other reason she'd wanted Jillian to remain at the condo: she didn't want another conversation about her beliefs. She wanted a break before the inevitable next time Jillian wanted to go at it about God. No matter how much she tried,

Jillian wasn't going to stop pointing out what she considered hard pills to swallow when it came to God and faith. The nature of their work and lives meant that she couldn't let it go. When Sam had told Jillian they had a lot of common ground, when she'd assured her that she wouldn't feel out of place in the Fellowship, she'd been sincere. But it had to be difficult, being surrounded by people who not only disagreed with you on a fundamental question about life, but reminded you of a father who'd ripped your life apart. *Why did You choose her, of all people, to be a Deiform? You must know something I don't.* Sam chuckled. *I'm sure You know lots of things I don't.*

A woman strolled into the dining room and surveyed those seated. Not Seaman, but maybe his lunch date? Nope, the woman threaded her way to a table where another woman sat. Sam checked her watch. Seaman was five minutes overdue. Had his plans changed? A minute later, Seaman answered the question by striding into the restaurant. The hostess led him to an unoccupied table.

Sam pushed her soup away and waited for her pasta dish. Not wanting to risk taking photos inside, she'd eat quickly, then wait across the street and snap 7445 coming out of the restaurant.

Two minutes later, shock stabbed through her when a tall man with graying temples entered the restaurant and scanned the dining room. She watched him walk to Seaman's table and pull out the chair across from him. *Now I understand why You called us here.* She'd still take photos, but she wouldn't need Jeremy to identify 7445. She knew exactly who he was.

Chapter Seventeen

JILLIAN SHOOK HER head at the screaming match taking place between two business partners on a reality show. Despite knowing it was contrived and the two men probably weren't as hot-headed when there were no cameras in the room, she still watched, open-mouthed. The condo's front door thumped shut. She quickly muted the show and looked toward the hallway. Sam strolled in with a camera slung over her shoulder. "Did you get photos of the contact?" Jillian asked.

"Yeah." Sam turned on the camera and flipped through the photos.

"Now we just have to wait for Jeremy to figure out who it is."

"No need." Sam shrugged off the camera strap and turned the camera's viewer toward Jillian.

She peered at the face on the display. "Can I buy a vowel?"

"You'd know who he is if you read the church magazine."

"I'm too busy talking to people."

"Which I appreciate. It's John Barker. Bishop John Barker."

A memory stirred. "Patrice has mentioned him a couple of times. He works with immigrants."

"Yes, he does."

Great, another clergyman taking advantage of immigrants. Why the hell had she joined the Fellowship, anyway?

"We don't know if he's involved with the Olmos situation."

"What? Why not, because he's a bishop?" Jillian shook her head. "He's 7445. Why refer to him by a number?"

"It could be an account number."

"Or it could be because they're being super careful not to tie him to trafficking. Think about it. Given his connections, he'd be the perfect person for a trafficking ring to recruit. You just don't want him to be guilty because he's a bishop."

"And you assume he's guilty because he is," Sam snapped. Then she raised her hand. "Let's start again. We obviously need to investigate him. Barker is involved with the church's work with immigrants, so he could have been meeting with Seaman for innocent reasons. I doubt it, but we have to keep an open mind."

"Why do you doubt it?" Jillian asked, surprised.

"Because clergy mixed up in criminal activity is exactly the sort of thing we usually investigate."

Like Dad? At least he hadn't claimed to be immigrants' second coming of Christ. More had come back to her about Barker. The guy had spearheaded a joint program with the city that aided immigrants, was involved with several church initiatives related to immigrants, and seemed pretty popular with immigrants and natives, alike.

Sam set the camera on the coffee table and slumped into a chair. "We weren't going to go to the cops, anyway, at least not until we know more."

Since Sam was bending over backward to consider all the options, Jillian would too. "Okay, Seaman had 7445 penciled in for lunch, but maybe his plans changed since you were in his office. Or maybe Barker is like Rodale. He thinks he's doing good, when he's not."

"Or maybe he's a fraud. Maybe he tells himself he's giving these people a better life. Maybe that's how he sleeps at night."

"But he does give people a better life. He's involved with legit organizations and programs." Of course, that would be the perfect front, but Jillian was trying! "I wonder if Max and Maria have ever met him. Was he here fourteen years ago, when Isabel came in? Maybe he doesn't know that Seaman is involved with a trafficking operation, and maybe Max and Maria don't know that Isabel feels trapped, that she's in debt to some trafficking ring."

Sam's face conveyed her incredulity loud and clear. "How could they not know?"

"They might not have realized the ring was going to saddle Isabel with an exorbitant debt that would take her years to pay off and keep climbing with interest. They might not know how terrified she is."

Sam raised her brows. "We're talking about a couple who took her son."

"Isabel might have agreed to it. And, yes, I do realize I'm grasping at straws," Jillian quickly added. "I guess I'm a little pissed off at myself for being taken in by Maria. Of course she must know. I ran across enough wolves in sheep's clothing during my agency days."

"She told herself a story about Isabel that made the medicine go down," Sam said. "With Barker potentially involved, and who knows who else, this is one of those cases where we'll need solid proof, or people will drag their feet. After all, who will they want to save? People like Isabel? Or their image of John Barker—the story he's told them all these years?" She stood. "I've already called Jeremy. He's digging into Barker. He mentioned that the bugs I planted in Seaman's office haven't produced anything interesting. He'll check for Barker's voice, though."

"What's our next move?"

"We need Barker under surveillance. We should be able to handle it with two Supporters. Hopefully that and Jeremy will help us figure out how Barker fits in. I'll put a surveillance schedule together, but our next real move is yours, doing something you're good at."

Jillian gave her a puzzled look. "What?"

"Being sociable."

JILLIAN LOWERED HER menu and smiled across the table at Maria. "I'm glad we're finally doing this. I kept meaning to suggest lunch." She'd done so on Sunday, when she'd spotted Maria heading for the church's exit, rather than for the hall where coffee hour would take place.

"I'm glad you did." Maria watched two people stroll by on the sidewalk outside, then turned away from the window. "I was hoping we'd keep in touch when you were finished with Dylan."

"I can't believe we only have a few tutoring sessions left. I'll miss him."

"You can tutor him next school year."

No, she couldn't. By the fall, they should have completed this case, or be very close to doing so. Jillian would be somewhere else, playing someone else, investigating something else. What excuse would they use for leaving? "I'm not sure he'll need me. He's improved a lot."

"Thanks to you." Maria leaned forward, so she could stretch her arm across the table and touch Jillian's hand. "You were a godsend. We'd given up on tutoring. We didn't know what to do. I know you're busy with your own business, so I'm grateful you found the time for my son. I really am."

Guilt battled with indignation. Her son? Dylan wasn't Maria's son—in the biological sense. Maria was the only mother Dylan knew. She'd brought him up, loved him, comforted him, read him bedtime stories. How would a court rule when everything came out and Isabel wanted him back? Did she have a legal leg to stand on? Maria and Max had definitely falsified a birth certificate, but had they done so with Isabel's permission, or had they coerced her? At this point, would it be more important to right a past wrong, or to do what was best for Dylan, assuming that his best interest would be to remain with the only parents he'd ever known? Either way, Dylan's world would be shattered. Another innocent caught in the crossfire. Life sucked.

"If you ever need anything from me, let me know," Maria said, dragging Jillian back to their polite conversation.

"You don't owe me anything. You've been paying me," Jillian said with a smile.

Maria waved a dismissive hand. "A pittance compared to what we've received in return."

Jillian could almost like her. Hell, she did like her. She'd love to see Max as a tyrant who'd taken advantage of Isabel and forced his wife to claim his love child as her own, but that would be too convenient. She didn't know Max well, but he didn't come across as a controlling husband who ruled the roost. When he was around, Maria spoke her mind, and she'd also stood up to him during the argument Jillian had overheard. They seemed to be an average couple, which made the situation with Isabel all the worse. Jillian took a deep breath. "Actually, you might be able to help me out, or rather, a friend of mine."

Maria's gaze sharpened. "How? What do you need?"

"One of my friends from high school just moved into Hamlin Court. Small world," Jillian said. "She's pregnant, and they want a live-in nanny. She's still got three months to go, but they want to get to know someone before the baby is born. They're hoping for someone long-term. Sam and I haven't needed anyone, so I didn't have an agency to suggest. Where do you get your people from?"

"Oh, uh . . ." Maria sipped her water. "We haven't hired anyone in years." She folded her arms, stared out the window. "I wish I could suggest someone, but . . . tell them not to use the Reynolds Agency. I've heard bad things about them."

"The Reynolds Agency?"

Still gazing out the window, Maria nodded. "I know someone who had a bad experience with them," she said, so softly that Jillian had to lean forward to hear her. "Tell your friends to avoid them."

"I will."

Maria shifted in her chair and avoided Jillian's eyes. "I wish I could be more helpful."

"No, that's great. Knowing who not to use is just as important as a recommendation, right?" *"The Reynolds Agency,"* she said, hoping that Sam was loitering close by outside.

"Got it."

A waiter came to their table. "Are you ready to order?"

Jillian glanced at Maria. "Yes, we are."

Three hours later, she sat at the kitchen table with Sam and listened to Jeremy report on what he'd found out about the Reynolds Agency. In business for almost thirty years. Twenty years ago, ownership had passed to Joel Reynolds, the founder's son and—surprise, surprise—Bishop John Barker's cousin. Had the agency always been dirty, or had Barker made Joel a proposal he couldn't refuse? *You're getting ahead of yourself.* They didn't have any proof that the agency was involved in human trafficking, but they were determined to get some. A Supporter was watching Barker right now, perhaps wasting his time. Since putting Barker under surveillance, they hadn't observed the guy so much as dropping a piece of litter. He was a freaking saint, or at least appeared to be. He was 7445. He was involved in this mess.

The Olmoses had come into the picture fourteen years ago. Were they still paying the agency? If so, why, after all this time? Blackmail? To protect Isabel? To keep Dylan?

"That's it," Jeremy said.

"Thanks, it's good info. Let us know if you find anything else." Sam hung up her phone and snatched it up from the table. "I'm going to call Patrice, ask her if she's heard anything about the Reynolds Agency."

"Are you going to tell her about Barker?"

"No. I don't want her asking around about him, or worse, telling him." Sam strode toward the hallway, then turned. "Patrice would be an asset to the Fellowship."

"You're not thinking of bringing her in," Jillian said, cringing at the petulance in her voice. "We don't know enough about her, and there's no reason to." Supporters were made when someone was in danger or had expertise the Fellowship could use. Then there were cases like Andy. They'd brought him in so he wouldn't go to the police about Junior. How was he? Where was he?

"No, I'm not thinking of bringing her in," Sam said evenly. "I'm just saying she'd be an asset." She left the kitchen.

Jillian stared after her, wondering why Sam wanted to call Patrice in private. She wanted to creep into the hallway and eavesdrop on Sam's side of the conversation, but willed herself to stay in her chair. God, she hated this. She hated wondering how Sam felt, what she thought, what she was doing. Love was wonderful . . . when it was reciprocated. The unreciprocated type hurt. All those love songs could go to hell.

Sam came back into the kitchen and frowned at her. "Are you coming? I can call Patrice on the way to the agency. We'll project in now, and maybe break in later."

Jillian pushed back her chair and leaped to her feet. To think that some people wanted to connect with their inner child. She had an inner adolescent she'd like to kill right now.

A WEEK LATER, Jillian sat in the kitchen, which she'd come to regard as command central, determined not to snap at Sam. When would they get a break? Their visit to the Reynolds Agency had been a bust, surprising neither of them. The shoddy security had told them that nothing important was inside, waiting to be discovered. Patrice hadn't heard anything bad about the agency. She'd promised to keep her ear to the ground, but they weren't holding their breath.

Tailing Barker had produced nothing. Now they were watching Joel, too. They'd learned that he gambled. Whoop-de-do. They couldn't find any evidence of money flowing between him and Barker. "We're not getting anywhere. Barker's at home tucked up in bed after spending the day working his ass off and writing cheques to charity." You could set your watch by Barker's routine. The guy was home every night by ten and emerged the next day at seven on the dot. He and his wife had gone to a movie and attended several church and charity functions, but that was it. Jillian blew out a frustrated sigh. "Maybe Barker's not involved. Maybe it's Joel. Maybe Barker's meeting with Seaman was innocent."

"Or maybe Joel's name is at the top of the agency's organizational chart, but Barker operates the place. Think about it. If Barker has always been 7445 and his hands are dirty, he's been involved in this for years. He's adept at projecting a sterling public image. He—" Sam's phone rang. "Yeah," she barked. Then her face brightened. "Good. We'll check it out." She smiled at Jillian. "Joel visited a warehouse this afternoon, and it belongs to the agency. It might be nothing, but why would an employment agency need a warehouse?"

Jillian wanted to pump her fist into the air. "Let's go."

Sam held up her hand. "Patience. Let's go tonight, after dark. This could be something. We don't want to tip them off."

Jillian folded her arms. Patience wasn't her strong suit.

"Maybe they keep new arrivals there," Sam said.

Suddenly Jillian wasn't so eager to rush out.

They left the condo just after 9:00. Twenty minutes later, they slowly cruised past the warehouse. "Not many windows," Jillian said; only a few were visible from the road. The warehouse extended into the darkness. "How about you go?" she said, when Sam turned a corner and parked.

Sam didn't argue. "You can piggyback along."

Jillian wasn't sure she wanted to. She'd suggested Sam go because she didn't want to see people caged like animals. *Coward.* She had to grow up; she no longer investigated crimes that took place on paper.

She watched the vitality drain from Sam, then reluctantly rested her hand on Sam's arm. *"I'm with you."* But she couldn't see much. There was no way to turn a light on.

When Sam stirred, Jillian quickly lifted her hand. "Let's go in," Sam said. "Nobody's in there."

Outside the car, Jillian scanned the warehouse's surroundings while she waited for Sam to get her knapsack from the trunk. Her eye spotted movement. A security guard emerged from the shadows and strode toward the warehouse. "There's a security guard," Jillian hissed.

Sam stepped to her side. "Let's watch for a bit, see what his routine is."

Half an hour later, they were satisfied that there was only one security guard and that he passed by the warehouse approximately every ten minutes. "Come on," Sam said, when the guard disappeared into the shadows again.

They sprinted to the warehouse entrance. Sam plunked the knapsack onto the ground and pulled out a leather case. *"You pick it,"* Jillian said, figuring Sam intended to anyway. *"You're faster."* Through practice, Jillian was getting better, but the ticking clock hanging over her head would make her clumsy.

Sam grunted and pulled two picks from the leather case. A minute later, she pushed the door open. Jillian followed her inside, her eyes adjusting to the dimness. *"Should we risk a flashlight?"*

"We'll have to keep away from any windows." Sam pulled a flashlight from her knapsack and turned it on. The small beam cut several feet into the darkness.

Jillian could make out shapes in the nearest corner of the warehouse. They crept in that direction. Empty water bottles lay on the floor, next to a pile of blankets and a gas stove. Sam nudged Jillian's arm and pointed. Several metal barrels were stacked against the wall.

"Gas for the stove, maybe?" Jillian squinted at the label on the side of one barrel. *"I can't read it. Shine the light on it."*

"Here, you do it." Sam handed her the flashlight and moved away.

Weird. Jillian swung the flashlight up and nodded. *"Gas."*

"Be careful." Sam's voice sounded shrill in Jillian's mind. *"You don't want to ignite it."*

"It's in barrels, Sam."

"Okay, it's gas, and it's in barrels. Do you have to keep staring at it?"

"No, I suppose not." They moved on and found a couple of rolled up sleeping bags, a garbage can containing empty takeout containers, a portable toilet, and an empty wooden table surrounded by four chairs. They crept toward the door. Sam peered at her watch. "Four minutes until the guard returns. Let's wait until he's passed by. I want to lock the place on our way out."

Jillian snapped the flashlight off. As they stood in the darkness, she thought about what they'd discovered—namely, nothing. No cages or shackles. Maybe people were being kept here before they were shipped off to their owners, or maybe workmen used the warehouse to cook lunch and play cards. They weren't in an isolated location. There was a construction site halfway up the block.

"That didn't help much," Jillian said when they were safely back in the car.

"We'll put a couple of Supporters on the warehouse," Sam said.

Even if this was where the ring brought new arrivals, it could be ages before a new group arrived. Roberta and Jeremy were working on creating Jillian's friends who needed a nanny, but it could be a month or two before those friends met anyone from the ring who counted. There had to be a faster way to find out if Barker was involved and who he was working for. "We know Barker is connected to Seaman. We need to prove that Seaman's dirty."

"How? He brings them in legitimately. It's what happens afterward that's criminal." Sam paused while she changed lanes. "He knows what's going on, but it won't be easy to prove it, and it still wouldn't prove that Barker is involved."

Jillian's hands clenched. "So what are we supposed to do, then? Wait until another group of victims arrives? We don't know if Joel and this warehouse have anything to do with it."

"We're on Barker. We're on Seaman. Now we'll be on this warehouse."

"And if we see a new group arrive, then what? Will we move in?"

"Not right away. That would spook the ring. We'll watch, to see who's transporting them and where they go. Every bit of information will help us get to the ring's leadership."

"I'm sure the immigrants in the group will appreciate that when they're being beaten and raped," Jillian spat.

Sam glanced at her. "If we pounce on that group, we'll save that one group. If we break the chain, we'll stop the trafficking for good. I know it's hard, but in this case, patience will pay off."

Patience. Always freaking patience.

Chapter Eighteen

Sam leaned forward on the bench outside Barker's office building and snapped a photo of a street performer, then strolled over to the corner and dropped a loonie into his hat. Her phone vibrated. She peered at its display and opened the tracker app. Barker's car was on the move. She hustled to the underground garage where she'd parked the car and headed north—the same direction Barker was driving. They hoped to catch him meeting with someone connected to the ring. Could this be their lucky day?

As she shadowed Barker, she mulled over what she'd told Jillian about being patient. Easier said than done. When the new people arrived, sitting by as they were driven to their prisons would make Sam want to punch something. She'd tell herself that they'd get them out, but what if they didn't? Not every investigation worked out the way they'd hoped. What would she tell Jillian then? What would she tell herself?

She hung a left, then a right three blocks later. All right, she was now on the same street as Barker, but several blocks behind him. Not wanting to be pulled over, she didn't recklessly pass anyone. Barker made catching up to him easier by remaining on the same road. Who, or what, was in the north of the city?

Barker turned onto a one-way street lined with townhouses. Sam turned as well and immediately pulled over, to avoid being spotted. Intending to catch up with him when he left the narrow road, she peered at her phone, then looked up when the dot stopped moving. Barker had parked up the street. She watched him cross the road and bound up a townhouse's steps. Seconds later, the townhouse door opened. Barker slipped inside.

Sam drove past the townhouse with the stone lions sitting on either side of its path. She found a spot three cars away from Barker's, pulled a camera from the knapsack on the passenger seat, and snapped the front of the townhouse. While she waited for Barker to emerge, her mind returned to the conversation with Jillian. Should they just sit and wait? Should they let the trafficking ring put another group of people into bondage? This wasn't the first time Sam had faced tough questions and made difficult decisions, but she hadn't had someone there to raise the questions she suppressed.

Sam honestly believed that if they always gave in to their emotions and refused to ever let anyone suffer for long-term gain, they'd do less good. They'd rack up swift, small wins at the expense of the large battles. When she'd discussed God and suffering with Jillian, she'd meant what she'd said: that there was a reason for suffering, a purpose that wasn't always evident. But when it came to the next group of victims who'd arrive expecting decent jobs, Jillian was asking the same questions Sam had asked herself during her first few years with the Fellowship. She hadn't stopped asking them, but had she become desensitized? Was she too quick to offer up answers for why they had to wait, or why they couldn't save a person *and* win the battle? *Do I not trust You as much as I should?* She mustn't be complacent.

Half an hour later, she snapped pictures of Barker leaving the townhouse. Unfortunately, nobody was at the door to wave him off, but that didn't matter. She had an address. After Barker had driven past her and turned, she pulled out to follow him. He drove right back to his office. Sam dialed her phone. "I have an address for you to check," she said to Jeremy; "118A Brighton."

"Got it. Anything else?"

"Put a Supporter on it. Let's see who else visits 118A."

"I'll call you when I have something."

Sam hung up and headed back to the condo. They'd reduced their surveillance to lunch hour and a couple of hours after 5:30, when Barker usually left his office. The guy was so careful, she'd almost given up hope of seeing anything interesting. As far as the ring went, Barker either only met with Seaman, or made contact with others at the numerous events he attended. The townhouse could be a dead end, too. He could have been visiting a friend.

When Sam strode into the condo's living room, Jillian looked up from her newspaper. "Anything?"

"Maybe. He spent his lunch at a townhouse."

Jillian's brows shot up. "Really?"

"Yeah. I've put Jeremy on it."

"Did he grab lunch anywhere?"

Sam sank into a chair. "No."

"Maybe he went to a friend's for lunch." Jillian folded the newspaper and tossed it onto the coffee table. "It could be nothing."

"I know." Sam brushed her pant leg, even though there was nothing there. Should she tell Jillian about the thoughts that had run through her mind as she'd waited outside the townhouse? Why give her false hope? *Why are you being so negative?* The question was one of those mental thoughts Sam was never sure had originated with her or come from Him. Whoever was asking was right. She was assuming they'd fail to come up with a decent plan and successfully execute it. "Do you remember what you were saying about it being awful that we'd have to let a group through?" she said, trying not to sound too interested.

"Yeah."

"Maybe we can come up with a plan to, I don't know, speed things up, or at least disrupt the ring without blowing everything."

Jillian's gaze sharpened. "Do you have something in mind?"

"No," Sam admitted. "I thought we could talk about it."

"Sure!"

"If we come up with something, Roberta might not go for it, but at least we'll have tried."

"Damn right, we'll have tried." Jillian shot to her feet and paced. "We've got to be able to come up with something." She stopped in front of Sam and stared down at her. "Anything's better than standing by and letting people get sold into slavery, right?" she asked, her eyes flashing.

"Right." A burst of excitement almost drove Sam to her feet. Jillian's enthusiasm was contagious, but it was also a condemnation. In Jillian, Sam saw herself twenty years ago, when she'd believed that everything was possible, that good would always prevail. Reality had worn her down. Worse, she hadn't noticed. When had she stopped moving mountains and settled for molehills? When had *can't* rolled more easily off her tongue than *can*. She was a Deiform. She worked for an omnipotent, omniscient Being. Trying and spectacularly failing had to be better than not trying at all. The first demonstrated faith. The other . . . she felt as if a gust of wind had blasted open the shutters and blown the cobwebs from her soul.

Jillian was pacing again. Sam gripped the chair's arms and stood. "Okay, what do we know?" she said.

It took them an hour and a half of suggestions, alternatives, misgivings, and arguments to come up with a risky plan they both agreed could work. With Jillian looking on, Sam outlined the plan for Roberta. Sam didn't have her on speakerphone. Even though she was representing both of them, she'd prefer not to be publicly slapped down. "That way, we'll break the ring and save any new groups."

"You *might* break the ring and save any new groups. On the other hand, you could push the ring underground. We'd get out the people we know about, but all the key players would still be in place. We could keep an eye on them, but they'd change things up, figure a way around us, and you know we're stretched thin." Roberta lapsed into silence.

"I know it's risky, but it could work. It's not an outlandish plan." Sam looked at Jillian, and almost smiled when Jillian lifted her crossed fingers. "Both of us will find it difficult to look the other way when the next group arrives."

"Both of you." Roberta sighed. "I'm starting to wonder why He decided you two would share the joint gifts. You're too much alike. You egg each other on."

Sam walked to the window and gazed out, so Jillian wouldn't see her frown. "I'd say everyone in the Fellowship would prefer not to see people suffer, so isn't our plan worth trying? I know we need to keep the bigger picture in mind and do what's best long-term, but if there's a way for us to break the ring *and* save new arrivals, shouldn't we try? Shouldn't we believe we can do it?"

Silence. Sam didn't need to be in the same room to see Roberta's pinched mouth and the faraway look she got in her eyes when she was thinking—or asking. Still staring out the window, she waited.

"Are you sure you want to risk losing the ring?" Roberta finally said.

"Even if we let the next group through, there's no guarantee we'll get the ring. There's never a guarantee."

"That's true, but some plans have better odds than others."

"Our plan right now is sitting around on our behinds hoping that Jillian's two friends will eventually meet someone in the ring and get a nanny, or that Barker or Seaman will do something obviously stupid." Sam turned back to Jillian, and noted the tension around her mouth and eyes. "This ring has operated for a while. They're not going to slip up. And even if we do find out through our friends when a nanny will be able to start, what then? So we'll have some idea of when the next group will arrive."

"We'll also be able to make contact with whoever collects the money. You don't need Maria for that."

"It could be months."

"I suppose we'll still have the friends plan to fall back to if Maria says no," Roberta murmured thoughtfully, giving Sam a glimmer of hope. "But your way is confrontational, and she could tell someone in the ring about it."

"It'll get things moving."

Another long sigh. "All right, but only because I don't want two disgruntled Deiforms on my hands."

"And our plan could work," Sam pointed out. "If you didn't believe it could, you wouldn't agree."

"It's a risky plan, but not a hopeless one," Roberta said, her amusement coming through loud and clear.

"So we have your blessing?" Sam said, giving Jillian a thumbs-up.

"Yes, you have my blessing."

"Depending on how things go, we'll need cash. A lot of it."

"When you need it, I'll arrange it."

"Thanks." They said their good-byes and hung up.

"Yes!" Jillian said, leaping to her feet and pumping her fist.

Sam flashed her a quick smile, already thinking about what they needed to do, now that Roberta had approved the plan. "Arrange to see Maria. I'll call the church and make an appointment to see Patrice."

"Let's hope the townhouse Barker visited gives us something useful. Then we can decide who to approach."

That would be the tricky part that could blow everything. Heck, the entire plan was tricky. Roberta was right; after months of searching for a problem and then blending in with the locals, one conversation, or arousing the suspicions of a single person, could lose the ring. On the other hand, everything could go perfectly. *Have faith. And don't screw up.* He'd help them, but He had to work through them, through their actions. It was a riskier plan, but Sam believed it could work, and it would mean that no more people would be driven to prisons masquerading as homes. She peered at her phone's display and pulled up the church's number.

"Sam."

She looked up. Jillian met her eyes. "Thanks for listening to me. I know I can be a pest, and I don't have as much experience as you do with these sorts of investigations."

"There's no need to thank me. You were right." Sam swallowed. "You reminded me of what's important." She turned toward the window again.

STROLLING THROUGH A park near the church, Jillian unzipped her hoodie and shoved her hands into her pockets. What she was about to do had sounded great when she and Sam had come up with the plan. Now her nerves were screaming otherwise. She gave Maria, who was walking next to her, a sidelong glance.

"We should make this a weekly thing," Maria said. "Max and Dylan always do something together on Sundays, which can leave me at a loose end. Father-son bonding time. Sunday is a family day for my other friends, too." She patted Jillian's arm. "It would be good to have a friend I can lunch with."

Jillian struggled not to let her guilt show. She was about to blow this temporary friendship out of the water. It would be easier if she didn't like Maria and could cast her in the role of villain, but—come on, Maria had kept Isabel captive for years and stolen her son! Jillian should hold her in contempt, not feel sorry that she wasn't really her friend. In a year or two, she'd be like Sam and hold everyone at arm's length. The gifts shouldn't be called gifts; they came with a high price. *Tough.* She had to get on with it. She couldn't chicken out, especially since she'd wanted this plan. Sam and Roberta would never listen to her again.

"Next time, invite your sister. I see her at church every week, but I hardly know her. She's so quiet."

Jillian grunted, then steeled herself. Her hands balled in her pockets. "I suggested that we walk through the park because I want to talk to you about something," she began. "I didn't want anyone else to overhear us."

"Oh? What is it?"

"It's about Isabel."

"Isabel?" Maria stopped walking and turned to Jillian, her expression puzzled.

Her hands still in her pockets, Jillian faced her. "I work for a family who's looking for a missing loved one. My investigation led me here, and then to the Reynolds Agency. I know that's where Isabel came from. I know she's not allowed to leave your employment." She couldn't quash her rising indignation. "How could you keep her against her will for all these years?"

"What are you talking about?" Maria said shrilly.

"You know what I'm talking about. The Reynolds Agency brings people into the country promising them legit jobs, then places them with families who want cheap labour. Those poor people—"

"Cheap?" Maria's voice hardened. "I can assure you that working with the Reynolds Agency isn't cheap, and Isabel is free to leave any time she wants to."

"That's not what I've heard."

"I don't care what you've heard." Maria jabbed a finger at Jillian. "How dare you accuse me of mistreating Isabel! What do you know? You think I'm a bad person? What about you? You come into my home, tutor my son, and all the time it's to spy. My son liked you. So did we."

Jillian winced. "That's not why I tutored Dylan. I didn't know about Isabel when I offered to help. And I'm not here to judge." Though she couldn't help doing so. "I want you to help me stop the people behind the Reynolds Agency from bringing in more people. I want to free everyone who's already here. If you truly care about Isabel, you can—"

"I already told you, Isabel can leave any time she wants to."

"Maria—"

Maria's hand sliced through the air. "This conversation is over. I'll be looking for another church. Don't call me ever again. Don't ever talk to my son." She stomped away.

Hating herself for what she was about to do, Jillian called out, "I know about Dylan. I know he's not your biological son."

Maria stiffened and stopped short. "I don't know what you're talking about."

"Yes, you do. There's no point in denying it. I went to Vancouver and talked to the midwife. Did Isabel give him up freely, or did you just take him?"

Maria whirled and marched back to Jillian. Her eyes were moist. "We adopted him."

"Really?" Jillian was withering inside, but she had to press. "I take it you have adoption papers, then."

A tear spilled down Maria's cheek. "You're worse than the people you're chasing."

"No, I'm not. I'm hoping you're not, either. Help me."

"And lose my son?" Maria thumped her chest. *"My son."*

"I don't know what will happen with Dylan," Jillian said truthfully. "But what would he think if he knew you'd denied Isabel her freedom, just to hold onto him. Is that what he'd want you to do? He's fond of Isabel."

Maria's face crumpled. Her tears flowed freely. "I'm not a bad person," she croaked.

"Then help me," Jillian pleaded. "Help me put an end to it. It can't have been easy for you, carrying it all these years."

Maria quietly sobbed. Jillian grasped her elbow and steered her to a bench. "Look, I like you, I really do." When she motioned for Maria to sit, Maria sank onto the bench without a peep. Jillian sat next to her. "How did you get involved with this? Why do you continue to go along with it? Isabel, I mean. Not Dylan." They were two separate issues. Jillian could understand why Maria didn't want to lose Dylan.

Maria pulled a tissue from her purse and wiped her nose. "You won't believe me, but we didn't know at first," she said softly. "We only realized what was going on later. I'm sure it was the same for the other families."

"How did you clue in?"

Maria dabbed at her eyes. "When they come around every month to collect their payment, they always meet with Isabel. They say it's to pay her wages, and to make sure she's still happy and everything is working. In the beginning, we believed them. But as we got to know Isabel, we realized she was frightened by these visits. We had the advantage of speaking her language, but that didn't matter. She was too afraid to tell us anything. So we asked them, 'Why is Isabel afraid of seeing you?'"

"Is it always the same person that comes?"

Maria shook her head. "In the beginning, it was Tommy. We've had three different people over the years."

"What happened when you asked Tommy?"

"He tried to, uh . . ." Maria searched for the appropriate word.

"Reassure you?" Jillian prompted. "Tell you it was normal, or that everything was okay?"

"Yes. He said Isabel was still settling in, getting used to a new country. But she kept being afraid, and she eventually told us that Tommy was threatening her, that until she paid off her debt, she couldn't leave us. We were horrified . . . and stupid," Maria said with a shake of her head. "We asked Tommy for an explanation. That's when we were told that we were a part of it, that we were keeping her prisoner, making her work for nothing."

"Why didn't you go to the police?"

Maria snorted. "Tommy said they'd make Isabel disappear before the police had a chance to speak with her, and then they'd tell the press about us, make it seem as if we were the guilty ones. And the next time Tommy visited, he hit Isabel. He said it was punishment for breaking their confidentiality agreement. He made it sound like they're a real company." Her mouth twisted. "They're not. They're criminals. We talked about going to the police anyway, but we were too afraid. So we went along with it. We went along with it. We told ourselves that Isabel was still better off than she had been before, that we were still giving her a better life." Maria heaved her shoulders and crumpled the tissue she held. "I wonder if that's what the other families tell themselves?"

"How did Dylan happen?" Jillian asked.

Maria swallowed. "I guess once you cross one line, it's easier to cross others."

"Did Max rape her?"

"I don't know. I don't know how it started. I don't think I wanted to know. Isabel said he didn't, but I don't know how much she trusted me back then—or how much she does now," Maria added quietly. "I wanted to kill them both, but him more than her. He should have known better. Isabel . . . how much could I blame her? What chance did she have to meet someone? What chance did she have to get married?" Maria reached into her purse for another tissue.

"Did you find out about the affair because Isabel was pregnant, or before then?"

"I had no idea. If she hadn't gotten pregnant . . ." Maria blew her nose. "She didn't know what to do. She told Esme—our maid," Maria added when Jillian drew breath. "Esme came to me, not Max, which I'll admit, gave me some satisfaction. I was stupid, though." Maria shook her head. "When I first heard, I thought Isabel must have been sneaking out, or was involved with Nick."

The chauffeur? The gardener? Jillian didn't ask. "Isabel told you it was Max?"

"Not directly. I told Max that maybe this was our chance to give Isabel freedom. We could tell Tommy she was pregnant, that we'd help to find her a place to live, get her settled. But Tommy went crazy," Maria said, wide-eyed. "We even offered to pay off her remaining debt, but no. He was shouting and shaking his fist at her. We thought he was going to kill her. He got the father out of her. That's how I found out. In front of him, Max, everyone." She lowered her head.

Jillian let her have a moment to deal with the humiliation, yet again.

"I love Max, but he can be a hard man," Maria said. "When Tommy was threatening her, he didn't step forward and say it was him. She had to do it. I've wondered what would have happened if Tommy had hit her. Would Max have stood there and still said nothing?"

"He didn't want to hurt you," Jillian said. Ripping apart Maria's husband wouldn't help. "He was probably embarrassed."

"Embarrassed? Upset that he was found out, more like!" Maria inhaled deeply and slowly exhaled. "I'm sure he didn't want me to know, but not hurt me? He still carried on with her. I looked the other way."

"Because of Dylan?"

Maria closed her eyes and nodded. "We're a family held together by secrets."

"So Tommy came up with the plan that you and Max would claim Dylan as your own," Jillian said.

"No! He insisted that Isabel get an abortion. He said if Isabel had a baby, she'd be useless to them. We were afraid for her, so we said we'd adopt the baby, and Isabel would stay with us, and things would carry on as usual. He said no way, until we offered him money. Then he called someone." Maria picked apart the tissue in her hand. "When he got off the phone, he told us we couldn't adopt the child. To go through the courts . . . there would be questions about Isabel, questions about how we treat her. And Max had raped Isabel."

"But Isabel said—"

"It didn't matter what actually happened. If they told her to cry rape, she'd cry rape. It wasn't only her life on the line now. Tommy said no, if we want the baby, we take the baby. We were stupid, and eager. We'd tried to get pregnant. We had IVF. It didn't work. It was easy to talk ourselves into it, to believe we were doing the right thing. I saw it as something good coming out of Max's . . . indiscretion. But we were stupid." Anguished eyes met Jillian's. "They knew it would mean we were more involved, more tied to Tommy and his gang than ever before. Now there were three prisoners, not just one. We did it to ourselves."

"Help me break you out of prison," Jillian said.

"What about Dylan?"

"I don't know what will happen. I can't promise anything. I know you love him."

Maria bit her lip and nodded.

"Then do the right thing."

"You'll get yourself killed, and us. These people . . . they're ruthless."

"I work with some powerful people. I won't be doing it alone. We'll protect you."

Maria drew a shaky breath. "What would we have to do?"

Jillian outlined the role the Olmoses would play in the larger plan. "Will you help us?" she said. "Will you help Isabel and all the others? Will you help yourselves?"

"I'll have to talk to Max and Isabel," Maria said.

"Does that mean you want to do it?"

"Yes. I'm tired. I'm tired."

Jillian gave Maria's arm a sympathetic pat. "Thank you."

"Max and Dylan won't be home for a while."

"I'm still up for lunch, if you are," Jillian said, rising.

"Why not?" Maria stood and fell into step with Jillian, but the air between them was awkward, and Maria's shoulders were hunched. Jillian had mixed feelings about the woman walking next to her. She saw her as a victim and a villain. Gray. Rarely black and white. Had the Olmoses believed they were doing the right thing, or had they been protecting themselves? Would Dylan end up suffering the most? What would happen to everyone if the plan failed? Jillian forced the distressing questions from her mind and wondered how Sam was doing.

Rocking on her heels with her hands clasped behind her back, Sam gazed out the window and waited for Patrice to speak. When the silence stretched into minutes, she turned around. Patrice sat in thought, her steepled fingers touching her chin. She might be praying, if not for her open, wary eyes.

"I know someone who might be able to help." Patrice motioned for Sam to sit. Sam wanted to remain on her feet, but she sank into a chair and studied Patrice's troubled face. "Who are you, really?" Patrice asked.

Sam crossed her legs. "What do you mean?" she said evenly.

Patrice slid open her drawer and lifted out a business card. She frowned at it. "Private investigator," she murmured. "Private investigators usually gather information. Private investigators report to someone. They uncover dirt that will help someone resolve a situation. They don't usually resolve the situation themselves. They might gather intelligence on a trafficking ring. They wouldn't break it." She set the card on her desk with a snap.

"I do work for someone. I'm carrying out their instructions. You're right, PIs normally don't get into the trenches. Sometimes Jillian and I do."

"Who do you work for?"

The question evoked flashes of TV shows and movies Sam had watched. "Are you going to slap me around until I tell you?"

Patrice almost smiled. "No. But . . ." She heaved a sigh. "I feel like I'm dealing with a Jekyll and Hyde. You seem sincere in your faith, but you initially lied about your occupation, and I have the feeling you're still hiding something."

"I am. I can't tell you who I work for."

"Can you give me some idea? Is it the government? A corporation? An individual?"

Sam pondered how she could honestly answer the question. "Does it matter? You spoke to Isabel. You know I'm not making the situation up. We want to help her and everyone else this ring has trapped."

"It matters." Patrice lifted the business card and eyed it again. "I don't even know if this is true." She tossed the card down.

"Our intentions are good. We want to rescue these people and stop the ring from replacing them. We won't be eradicating human trafficking, but we'll deal a severe blow to it in this area."

"You're avoiding my question."

Yes, I am. Maybe she should shake Patrice's hand and leave. The Fellowship could, and would, ease the transition of those like Isabel into new lives, but Roberta preferred that it work with existing organizations, rather than going it alone. Isabel and the others would have to be provided with housing, job training, support. The more that was done through regular channels, the easier. Sam was starting with Patrice because she already knew about the situation, had kept quiet about it, had connections in the city, and would know who to trust. If Sam were to approach an organization out of the blue, there would be questions, and she could inadvertently involve someone who'd tip off the ring.

Still, her need wasn't urgent enough to reveal her Deiformic nature to Patrice. She'd only had to do that once, when securing someone's aid had been critical and the only course of action. That person now belonged to the Fellowship. Sam wouldn't do the same to Patrice. "I'm sorry I had to lie to you. I could try to figure out how to get these people the help they're going to need, but I don't know who's connected to the ring. I don't know who to trust. Just like you don't know whether to trust me."

"It's not that I don't trust you. My instincts say I should. I just know I'm not getting the whole story." Patrice rubbed the back of her neck. "I want to help these people, but I only know about Isabel for sure, and I know you're hiding something. I believe what you're telling me. At the same time, I have to be sure I won't be getting involved in something illegal."

Sam chewed her lip. This was one of those times she'd have to trust her gut, but it would mean going against what she and Jillian had agreed upon. *So be it.* If she were working alone, she wouldn't hesitate, and she was certain that Jillian would change up a plan at some point. Things didn't always go as expected. "I work for the church," Sam said.

Patrice's brow furrowed. "What?"

"The church." Sam pulled out her phone. "I didn't want to tell you this, because I didn't want to put you into an awkward position, but you've left me no choice." She pulled up a photo of Barker and Seaman and handed her phone to Patrice. "Recognize him?"

"Of course I recognize him," Patrice said.

"He's with Ben Seaman, an immigration lawyer who works with the ring. Bishop Barker has been meeting with him for years. Seaman refers to him using a number. Barker's cousin also owns an agency that provides wealthy families with foreign workers."

Patrice stared at the photo and swallowed.

"We're still working out exactly what Barker does for the ring, in addition to providing them with a front they can use when dealing with their, uh, clients. But he's definitely involved."

"I don't believe it," Patrice murmured. "I mean, I do. I'm not naive. But I should know better than to be disappointed."

"You have to keep this to yourself. If he gets wind of anything, we won't be able to help anyone. I was hoping not to put you into a position of divided loyalties."

"My loyalty is to God and the integrity of His church," Patrice said indignantly.

Sam nodded, pleased that her instincts had been right.

Patrice held out Sam's phone. "He has to be brought to justice."

"He will be. But let us handle that." Sam took her phone back. "We don't know if anyone else from the church is involved, and it's possible that someone who helps immigrants has also helped the ring. I came to you because I hoped you'd know who to contact—who to trust."

"I know someone who should be able to help. He's rock solid."

"Good." Patrice was on board. "When we know how many people we'll free, I'll let you know. Tell him the church will help him get everyone settled."

Patrice quirked a brow. "Through you."

"Yes. Through me."

Patrice plucked a pencil from a mug filled with them and rolled it between her fingers. "All right. Will I see you in church next week?"

"Yes."

Patrice's eyes narrowed. "Until it's time to move on to the next church?"

Sam could tell from Patrice's tone that the question was rhetorical. She turned to leave.

"Be careful, both of you. I don't have to be familiar with all this to know that these people won't go away easily. They have too much to lose."

Sam glanced over her shoulder. "We'll be careful." As she strode down the corridor to the church's side exit, she reflected that there wouldn't be a funeral for her, but if there was, she wouldn't mind Patrice presiding. She was the genuine article.

JILLIAN ZIPPED UP her hoodie and hugged herself when a sudden breeze provoked goosebumps. She glanced at Sam. This walk through the park was a hell of a lot more comfortable than the one with Maria a few hours ago. They could be having this conversation in the condo, but they'd both felt antsy. The plan was in motion. So far, so good. She shoved her hands into her hoodie's pockets. "I felt guilty talking to Maria."

"She's not innocent."

"I know, but she's not a bad person. They didn't know they were agreeing to take in a slave."

Sam's mouth tightened. "They didn't ask enough questions."

"They were just regular people, Sam. Who thinks they're dealing with a trafficking ring when they go to an agency to hire live-in help? When they suspected something was wrong, they started asking questions."

"And did nothing. Max slept with Isabel. They took her child. They've had years to help her escape her situation, but they've done nothing."

"They were afraid. They *are* afraid."

"Of what? The ring, or losing Dylan and getting into trouble?"

"I don't know," Jillian reluctantly admitted. "Probably both."

Sam was silent for a moment. "The Olmoses aren't evil, but I'm having trouble seeing them as the victims, here."

"They're trapped as much as Isabel is."

"Through their own doing."

Jillian knew that, so why was she compelled to defend the Olmoses? "They made stupid decisions. They didn't set out to deny Isabel her freedom and take her son." Jesus, why *was* she defending them? "It could have been anyone. Most people would have done what they did. Well, I'm not sure about the Dylan part, or maybe I am. It was all about fear."

"I'm sure their problems getting pregnant helped," Sam said dryly. "Look, you'll probably think I'm being hard and judgemental, but they're responsible for a lot. I agree that in the beginning they were just ignorant, but once they knew the truth, they chose to go along with it." When Jillian opened her mouth to speak, Sam held up her hand. "Yeah, I know, it would have been hard, and risky, to go to the police. But that's what good people, truly good people, would have done. Do I see them as bad people to their core? No. But I'm sorry, I can't excuse them for this."

"I'm not excusing them!" Jillian shouted. A couple sitting on the grass nearby looked their way. She lowered her voice. "Maybe it's because I sat on the bench next to Maria while she wept, but I can have some sympathy for them. I can understand why they didn't go to the police."

"That doesn't mean you have to condone it," Sam said evenly.

"No, and I don't. I'm just saying that I can't cast them in the role of selfish, evil villains who only cared about themselves and what they wanted."

"They're slavers, Jillian. Don't feel sorry for them."

"Choices aren't always black and white. You've been in the Fellowship for twenty years. It's easy to make the right choices when you have a powerful organization backing you. You have no idea what it's like to live in the real world."

Sam's face tightened.

"I have a hell of a lot of sympathy for Isabel, too, not just for the Olmoses," Jillian continued. "There's no shortage of victims, here."

Sam didn't reply. Her eyes were on the path in front of her. Jillian didn't know why, but she'd hurt her. Somehow she'd hurt her. She wanted to apologize, but she didn't want to inadvertently wound Sam further. Best to keep her mouth shut. They walked in silence, the air between them now as awkward as it had been on her walk with Maria.

"We both want to free Isabel and the others and shut down the ring, right?" Sam finally said, her voice lacking its usual vigour.

"Absolutely. We both want the same thing," Jillian said, wishing the gifts would allow her to rewind the last five minutes.

"That's what counts." Sam flashed a quick smile, but it didn't reach her eyes. "You're right, there are a lot of victims."

Including Dylan. Nobody could argue that he wasn't innocent in all this and didn't deserve all the sympathy in the world. "Assuming everything goes okay, what will happen to Dylan? Roberta said we'd deal with him and the Olmoses later, but what do you think? Will Max and Maria go to prison? Are we going to help Isabel get custody of Dylan? Will he have a say in what happens?"

Sam's phone rang. Still fretting about Dylan, Jillian tuned out Sam's side of the conversation. The only way of preserving Dylan's world would be to continue the lie that Maria was his biological mother. What about Isabel? What about the truth? Did Dylan have to be the sacrificial lamb that would free everyone else?

Sam whistled, bringing Jillian back to her surroundings. "That's the ammunition we need," Sam was saying. "Thanks." She raised her brows at Jillian. "It turns out the townhouse Barker visited is also visited by many other men. We have the photos to prove it. Jeremy looked into the owner. The guy has a record . . . for prostitution."

"Seriously?"

"Yeah. The fact that Barker is gay, or at least bisexual, wouldn't get him fired. The fact that he's married and visiting a prostitute . . ."

"That'll be difficult to spin." Jillian's heart raced. Good, they had the bastard by the throat. Her elation fizzled. Was that how the investigators had felt when they'd obtained proof of Dad's sins? Had they pumped their fists in the air, clapped each other on the back, rushed to come up with a plan to bring down the hypocritical pastor? Barker was scum, but he had a wife and two children who'd share in his punishment. More worlds blown away. Would breaking the ring further the good in the world, or would they just trade one set of victims for another? She could almost understand people who looked the other way to preserve the status quo. Almost.

"What about Dylan?" she said, returning to the one true victim who was more than a piece of data at this point. She liked the kid. It had been easier when she'd dealt with numbers, not people—or rather, not people she cared about.

Sam looked at her. "I don't know. But don't worry, we'll do what's best for him."

Would they? It wouldn't matter. His life would be shattered anyway. Jesus, what a screwed up world! She didn't believe in heaven, but she had no problem believing in hell.

Chapter Nineteen

Jillian shut the passenger door and waited while Patrice slipped from the backseat. Sam rounded the car and fell into step with them as they walked to the Olmoses' front door. Patrice slowed halfway up the wide path; her eyes swept the length of the house. "Have you ever been here before?" Sam asked.

"No. I try to make a point of visiting everyone at least once a year, but Maria has always been busy." Patrice grimaced. "I suppose she didn't want me to run into Isabel."

Or maybe she'd felt guilty. It was one thing to show up at church every week; another to have someone in a collar sipping tea in your house, while a slave laboured nearby and the son you'd stolen played in his room. If Patrice had shown up without her collar, as she was doing today, it wouldn't have mattered. Clergy was clergy.

They'd brought Patrice along with them not to intimidate or condemn, but because they'd figured Isabel would be more at ease with her than with a Fellowship translator.

"Reverend Dougherty might have visited when they first joined the church, but that was before my time," Patrice said. They reached the front door. "Are you both speaking to Isabel with me?"

"No," Sam said. "Jillian will go with you. I'll stay with the Olmoses. Hopefully they've rounded up whatever paperwork they have." She rang the doorbell. Someone had been watching for them, because the door instantly opened.

Maria, not Esme, motioned them inside. Her wan smile faded as soon as her eyes settled on Patrice. She clasped her hands in front of her. "I could have translated for you," she said to Jillian, "but I understand why you don't trust me."

"It's not that," Jillian said, only half lying. "We want Isabel to feel that she can speak freely."

"Thank you for letting us speak to her," Patrice said. "You're doing the right thing."

Maria swallowed and nodded. "She's in the study," she said quietly. "Max is in the living room. He has everything you asked for. We don't know if it will help." She stood awkwardly.

"I know the way to the study, so if it's all right with you, I'll go there with Reverend Patrice," Jillian said. "You can take Sam to the living room."

"Yes. It's this way," she said to Sam.

Jillian half expected to see Dylan waiting for them, but it was Isabel who sat hunched at the table. She lifted her head, and looked resigned, not afraid. She was trapped—again—but hopefully freedom was just around the corner this time. After closing the door, Jillian nodded to Isabel and took the chair across from her. Patrice rolled a chair around the table and sat right next to Isabel. In the car, they'd discussed what to cover.

"Tell us everything you remember about when you travelled to this country," Patrice said to Isabel.

"I don't remember much. It was such a long time ago now, and we were in a truck. There weren't any windows."

"Do you have any idea where you crossed the border?"

"No."

"Where did you go? When did you get out of the truck?"

Isabel took a moment to think. "I'm sorry, but it was a church," she said.

Patrice remained expressionless. "There's no need to be sorry. You didn't do anything wrong. Do you know which church?"

Isabel shook her head. "We were taken down into a hall. That's where we slept. There were sleeping bags."

"Who let you in?"

"I don't know. We were told to get out of the truck and went through a door and right downstairs. We didn't go anywhere else. I didn't see anything to help you know where it was."

"Did you see anyone who belonged to the church?" Patrice asked, as Jillian bit her tongue. She'd wanted to ask the same question.

Isabel slowly shook her head again. "No."

"Did anyone say a name of a person, or town?"

"No. They didn't talk to us except to tell us what to do and where to go. We stopped there one night. Except for that room and the bathroom, we didn't go anywhere else inside."

"Where did you go after that?"

"We drove for a while. When we stopped, we were taken into a warehouse. They had beds there. Over the next week, they took us out, one by one. That's when I came here." Isabel leaned forward and gripped Patrice's wrist. "I know another woman was taken to a family not far from here."

"How do you know that?"

"I saw her in the store. The same store where she saw me." Isabel jutted her chin toward Jillian.

"Is that the only place you ever go?"

Isabel's face slackened. "I haven't been anywhere else for a long time."

Since Vancouver, Jillian guessed.

"Do you ever see a doctor or dentist?" Patrice asked.

"When I had my son."

"Apart from that."

Isabel's brow furrowed. "Just once. I had the flu or something. A doctor came here. I think he worked for the same people who brought me here."

"But you've never seen a doctor outside this house?"

"No."

Patrice shook her head in disgust. Okay, Jillian thought, so it was getting more difficult to be sympathetic to the Olmoses. Then again, they might have been afraid of angering the ring.

"Is there anything else you can tell me about when you came here, or since you've been here, that can help us identify who's involved?"

"No. Mr. Max and Mrs. Maria would know more than me." Isabel spoke the words without venom. Was she a fount of forgiveness and sympathy, or had the years beaten her down? Jillian would want to kill the Olmoses. She'd hate them.

Patrice grasped Isabel's hand and squeezed it. "Thank you. We're going to help. Let me tell Jillian what you just told me."

Doing her best not to look impatient, Jillian periodically nodded as Patrice relayed her conversation with Isabel. It would be easier if the gift allowed her to speak all languages, but Sam would say it would mean they had the same ability as God, which the gifts didn't allow. Jillian hadn't thought much about the reason for this particular gift's limitations. Was it more difficult to speak a foreign language, than it was to understand it? Did the source of the gifts within her have more control over comprehension than it did over speech? She was sure she could come up with several reasons that had nothing to do with God, but now wasn't the time. She pulled out her phone, found a photo of Barker, and showed the image to Isabel. "Ask her if she's ever seen him, either when she was brought here, or since then."

Patrice translated the question. Isabel studied the photo, then shook her head.

"Can you ask her about the circumstances around Dylan's conception and birth? Was it a consensual affair? Did she agree to hand him over to the Olmoses? Was she pressured?"

Patrice squared her shoulders and said to Isabel, "I want to ask you some questions about Mr. Olmos—Mr. Max—and Dylan. Did Mr. Max rape you?"

Isabel's eyes widened. She vigorously shook her head. "No. No. I'm not proud of it. I respect Mrs. Maria. But I was a younger woman, and I had no one, and no chance to meet anyone. Mr. Max . . . he's handsome. He always treated me well. When he showed interest . . . I'm not proud of it."

Based on the argument Jillian had overheard and what Maria had told her, she suspected the affair had gone on for a while, until Max's interest had waned. Did Isabel feel abandoned? Was that why she wanted to escape the Olmoses? Jillian kept the questions to herself. The answers wouldn't help them shut down the trafficking ring.

"What about Dylan? Whose idea was it to let Mrs. Maria be his mother?" Patrice asked Isabel.

Isabel's eyes grew moist. "It was the only way. They were going to force me to get rid of him. It was the only way to save him."

"So you agreed to it. You weren't forced."

"I said yes." Isabel squeezed her eyes shut and slowly shook her head. "It was the only way. It was the only way," she whispered.

Patrice patted Isabel's hand and turned to Jillian. "At least we don't have rape and child stealing on our hands. Isabel says it was all consensual, though given the circumstances with Dylan, I don't think she had a choice. Not a real one."

"Maria says the ring would have terminated the pregnancy one way or another if she and Max hadn't offered to take the child, so . . . yeah."

"Do you have any other questions?"

"Not right now. Please thank her. Tell her she's a brave woman."

Patrice nodded and translated Jillian's words. When they left the study, Isabel was as they'd found her, hunched over, lost in her thoughts, and perhaps her regrets.

Sam was waiting with Maria in the foyer, a folder tucked under her arm. "Did Isabel help you?"

"A little." Jillian glanced at Maria. "We can discuss it in the car."

Maria stepped forward. "I know you think we're terrible," she said, gazing at Patrice. "We did what we thought was best for everyone. We were trying to protect her."

Patrice's eyes narrowed. "Helping us now is a good first step, but there's much to forgive."

Maria lowered her head. "I'll pray to God for forgiveness."

"I'd start by asking Isabel for forgiveness," Patrice said, making Jillian warm to her. "I understand you can't free her now, but when she no longer needs protecting, you have to let her go."

"And Dylan?" Maria whispered.

Patrice looked to Jillian and Sam. "We'll talk about Dylan soon," Sam said.

"Will we? I'd like to know what's going to happen to Dylan." Jillian was tired of not getting an answer. In fact . . . *"Who gets to decide? Will I get a say? I actually care about him."* Shit, that hadn't come out the way she'd wanted it to. *"You know what I mean."*

"We'll talk about it with Roberta after we've dealt with the ring."

"Don't leave me out."

"I won't." Aloud, Sam said, "We should go. Thanks for your help. We'll be in touch."

They walked silently to the car. When Sam turned onto the road, Jillian could sense the tension draining from everyone. "After Isabel's group crossed the border, it stopped at a church," she told Sam.

"I'll try to find the church she mentioned," Patrice said.

Sam looked into the rearview mirror. "That will help. They could still be using the same church. We need to know whether or not the minister is involved."

"I hope not," Patrice breathed. "Are you going to speak to Bishop Barker?"

"Probably."

Silence from the backseat, then, "Do you really work for the church?"

Jillian resisted the urge to glance at Sam. "Yes," Sam said.

"It's just that I did a little asking around, and—"

"We don't want to tip off Barker," Sam snapped.

"I was discreet. I—when someone's being investigated for wrongdoing, the church is usually upfront about it—within the church. People working for the Diocese don't go undercover."

"How would you know?" Sam asked. Jillian was happy to stay out of it.

"Well, I suppose I wouldn't." Patrice paused. "Look, I know the trafficking situation is real. I assume your intentions are good. You say you want to free everyone and stop the inflow."

"Why else would we get involved?"

"You could be a rival group that wants to take over the trade, so to speak."

"Let me give you a little bit of advice," Sam said. "It's best to have this type of conversation when you're not alone in a car with the people you think might be thugs. If we *were* a rival group, what you just said would probably get you killed." Jillian pressed her lips together to stop a chuckle from escaping. "We're not thugs. We work for the church," Sam continued.

"Then you won't need my help getting an appointment with Bishop Barker?"

"No, we won't, and you should leave things to us now. We don't know for sure that Barker's involved, but if he is, he's in with a ruthless gang that won't hesitate to kill anyone who gets in their way. Don't bring yourself to his attention."

"The same applies to both of you, surely."

"Don't worry about us," Sam said after a moment.

"I'll pray for you."

"Thank you." Sam smiled into the rearview mirror. "We never turn down prayers."

Jillian didn't have to bite her tongue, but she wouldn't echo Sam's thanks. Hey, if Patrice wanted to pray for them, let her pray. It would make her feel better. *Isn't that what prayer is all about?*

SAM SAT IN the lobby of the church's administrative building and restrained herself from glancing at her watch, not wanting to appear impatient. The receptionist had already cast several curious looks Sam's way, wondering who she was and why she was there. The Fellowship had worked its connections to get her a speedy appointment, and Sam had deliberately offered vague answers when the receptionist had tried to glean information regarding the purpose of her visit. If the woman could see the contents of the satchel at Sam's feet, she wouldn't wonder. Inside: the photographs taken outside the townhouse and paperwork linking Barker to numerous organizations, including government services, that worked with immigrants. Barker had legitimate reasons for liaising with many of them, but the Fellowship suspected he was using relationships he'd forged on behalf of the church for his own extracurricular activities.

Unfortunately Jillian couldn't be here. She was associated with the Olmoses, whom they wanted to protect. Also, this situation was too reminiscent of her father's fall from grace. Sam loathed Barker's involvement as much as Jillian did, but they needed to push him, not cut him to pieces. Maybe Jillian would have kept her cool, but Sam was glad her connection to the Olmoses had offered the perfect reason to avoid a potential meltdown.

Sam didn't have any family scandals haunting her. Was that still true? Had anything terrible happened since she'd left them? She always imagined Dad at his office, Mom doing her usual volunteer work, and Alex . . . she was the only family member who wasn't completely frozen in time. Sam saw her ministering to a sick dog lying on an examining table, but the image couldn't resemble reality, because she saw the sixteen-year-old Alex examining the dog, not a thirty-something woman. Was Alex married? Did she have children? Did she tell them about their Aunt Sam, or was her sister a distant memory? It would be best if she was. Sam liked to tell herself that she'd left them for the purest reason, but when she was sitting on the island gazing out at the water, or playing the organ as the morning sun filtered through the stained glass, or feeling satisfied at a job well done, "selfish" came to mind.

The receptionist rose and beckoned to Sam. "I'll take you to the bishop's office. It's just around the corner." Half a minute later, she tapped on Barker's door and opened it. "You can go in now," she said to Sam.

"Thank you." She strode into his office and extended her hand. "Sam Davis," she said, using the temporary identity Jeremy had thrown together for her. "Westwood" would link her to Jillian.

Barker stood. His handshake was firm, confident. He nodded to the receptionist, who quietly closed the door. "Please take a seat, Ms. Davis." He settled into his own chair and clasped his hands on his desk. "What can I do for you?"

Sam gave him a cool look. "I work for a group within the church that deals with potential improprieties. It's come to our attention that you're involved with bringing immigrants into the country and exploiting them."

Barker's face flushed. "Everyone knows I work with immigrants. I help them. I don't exploit them. There must be some type of mix-up."

"Do you know Ben Seaman?"

"Yes, he's an immigration lawyer. We work with him all the time."

Ah, so it was "we" now.

"What I mean is, the church does. I don't personally work with him."

"Our information says otherwise." Sam had proof in her satchel. She leaned back in the chair and crossed her legs, trying to look relaxed, in control. "I'm here to give you the opportunity to explain yourself, Bishop Barker. We know you've used several churches along the border to shelter immigrants, immigrants you then force to work for wealthy families, so they can pay off a debt that never clears." Patrice had tracked down the church Isabel had mentioned. The pastor had acted in good faith, believing that he was providing immigrants with a place to rest their heads as they travelled the road to better lives. He'd told her about two other churches in Barker's underground prison transport. "You cut them off from society and treat them like slaves. Everyone thinks you champion immigrants, but we know better."

Barker moistened his lips. "What group did you say you work for?"

"We keep the church in line. We work behind the scenes."

Barker snorted. "I'm a bishop. I don't know of any such group, and I'm not stupid. Who do you really work for? Do you work for a group that makes up lies about the church? Am I being recorded? Will I see myself on YouTube? Get out of my office, or I'll call the police." When Sam didn't move, Barker lifted the phone receiver.

Sam flipped open her knapsack, pulled out a stack of photos, and tossed several onto his desk, one by one. His eyes on the images before him, Barker slowly set down the receiver. "We have more," Sam said. "Plenty to send to your colleagues, the media, and your wife."

"My wife," Barker said hoarsely. He continued to stare at the photos, but didn't touch them. "What do you want?"

"We want it to stop, and you're going to help us."

"Or you'll send these photos to my wife." Barker raised his head. "You don't work for the church."

"We want a meeting with whoever you work for," Sam said.

Surprise flitted across Barker's face. "Who I work for," he echoed.

Sam nodded. She could sense Barker's wheels turning.

"You don't know who you're dealing with," Barker said. "Do you think I wanted to work for these people? I was forced. Do you think you're the only ones who can take photos?" His eyes flicked to the gallery laid across his desk. "They came to me when I'd been married for two years, had a baby on the way, and was laying the groundwork for several of the key immigration services the church has today. I was doing good," he roared. "Until then. You know how different it was twenty-five years ago. I had no choice."

"You always have a choice," Sam said flatly.

"Not a real one. The alternative was destroy my wife, never see my child, lose the respect of my peers, and not be able to do any good at all." His mouth twisted. "My only real choice was to work with those people."

"Why you? What brought you to their attention?"

"I work with immigrants."

"Lots of people work with immigrants, and you were a minister at the time."

"A minister in compromising photographs."

Something was missing. "But why would they target you?"

Barker slowly exhaled. "I suppose there's no point protecting him," he murmured. "I have a cousin who gambles. He ran up debt and borrowed money from the wrong people. They wanted their money back, money he didn't have. He'd heard rumours about their other . . . business activities. My name came up. It was either cooperate with them, or lose my cousin."

"What about the police?"

He barked a laugh. "Don't be so naive." He suddenly rolled back his chair and shot to his feet. "I'm understating the situation Joel put me in. If I'd declined their proposal, I suspect they would have killed both of us. In fact, that's still true. I've tried to help Joel, but . . ." Barker shook his head. "His demons have him by the throat."

Sam gripped the arms of her chair. "You use your position in the church, and the trust people have in you because of who you are, to move people you know will be enslaved into the country. You do it so your secret life won't be revealed and your cousin can gamble with money he doesn't have. How can you live with yourself? How can you step into a pulpit and preach?"

Barker wearily ran his hand through his thinning hair. "I've helped countless immigrants since then. The programs I created are used across the country." He turned his back to Sam, gazed at a bookcase filled with religious books. "I know it doesn't make up for it, but I had no choice."

"You have one now."

"Do I? I have to choose between being seen as an informant, which will probably mean a bullet to the head, or having my life and family destroyed. They'll kill Joel, too."

"We just want a meeting. You didn't come to us. We came to you."

"They might believe that. They might not." He blew out a sigh. "Maybe I should have said no, all those years ago. I've always wondered if the hell I would have lived through by turning them down would have been more bearable than the hell I've lived since then." He turned to face Sam. Sympathy stirred at the sight of his red eyes.

"If you do this, we'll protect you."

"You honestly think you can protect me?"

"We can."

Barker blinked at her. "A rival group, then? Because only a stronger group that's as ruthless as them can protect me." Sam didn't move a muscle. Barker's shoulders slumped. "I'll do what I can. I'll be putting myself out on a limb. I can't guarantee they'll agree to a meeting. If they don't . . ." His eyes went to the photos again.

"Let's take it one step at a time. Tell them we want a meeting." Sam slipped a business card from her back pocket and laid it on Barker's desk. "You can call me at that number. If I don't hear from you within a week, I'll assume you've changed your mind." She pointed at the photos. "I'll leave those with you." She left his office and nodded to the receptionist on the way out. Had Barker told the truth about the ring blackmailing him, or had he willingly joined its ranks? There was a lot of money to be made by selling human beings like cattle.

"So?" Jillian said, the moment Sam climbed into the passenger seat of the car.

She pulled on her seatbelt. "He'll try to get us a meeting with someone in authority. Hopefully that'll get us closer to the top." As Jillian drove from the public parking lot, the sun hit Sam full blast in the face. She pulled down the passenger side's visor. "He thinks we're a rival group wanting to muscle in on their business."

"Did he explain what the hell a bishop is doing mixed up with human trafficking?"

"He said they also have photos of him that they threatened to make public. Also, his cousin got himself into trouble with them. Gambling debt. Barker's cooperation is part of the arrangement that allows both of them to keep breathing."

"His cousin being Joel Reynolds, and we already knew about the gambling."

"Yeah."

Jillian was silent for a moment. "He's bullshitting you."

Sam wanted to groan. "You weren't even there."

"He caved way too easily. The guy's been doing this for how long? He's been lying to everyone, using the church, putting people into slavery. You show him a few photos and he confesses everything? Come on."

"He's also a man who values his reputation and the image he's so carefully crafted. You've heard the sound bites and seen the videos. Family man, devout clergy, awards coming out of his ears for his public service." Sam glanced at her. "I'm not sure it's about the photos alone. It's all of it. He knows we know all of it."

"Still, we're not dealing with a nice guy here. Something about this doesn't feel right."

"I'm not saying he's innocent, but I'm not ready to declare him guilty of more than he's telling us," Sam said.

"I'm going to look at his financial records."

Sam turned to her. "We've already had someone look at them."

Jillian shook her head. "No offense to the someone, but I'm better than whoever it was. I'm looking at his records."

"Okay." If Jillian could show that Barker's involvement went deeper than he claimed, Sam would welcome the information. If Jillian couldn't find anything suspicious in Barker's records, she'd hopefully give him the benefit of the doubt until they had more to go on. It was a win-win situation, either way.

Jillian slowed to stop at a traffic light. "I know, shades of my father. Maybe I'm being too quick to convict Barker." Her voice grew wistful. "Maybe someday I'll be able to work cases like this without my father's ghost haunting me."

Sam wished that for her, too.

Chapter Twenty

JILLIAN LOOKED AWAY from the laptop and rubbed her eyes. *Got you, you son of a bitch.* At the agency, she would have leaned back and celebrated her triumphant discovery. This time, the stakes were higher. Her role in the investigation wasn't over. Instead of picking up the phone, calling Keller, and arranging her exit, she and Sam would have to deal with Barker.

She picked up the cup of tea Sam had placed at her elbow, took a sip, and grimaced. It was cold. Since receiving Barker's records and the donation list yesterday afternoon, eating, drinking, and sleeping had been irritating interruptions. She pushed back her chair and stretched. The condo was quiet. Sam must be reading.

Jillian found her in the living room. "I was right," she said, without sounding smug. "Barker has been laundering money through several avenues. For someone who was apparently blackmailed into the criminal life, he's sure raking it in, and his accountant is good." But she was better. "Two entries." She held up her fingers. "Two, in the past six months. They were all that tipped me off to a few dummy corporations, and if I hadn't been looking, I would have easily overlooked them. Come see."

Without waiting for Sam to follow, she bounded into the kitchen and plopped back into the chair. Sam leaned over Jillian's shoulder a moment later. "What am I looking for?"

Jillian swallowed. Sam's cheek was almost touching hers, and the hand Sam was resting on the back of the chair was pressed against Jillian's back. Warmth spread through her, and it wasn't due to empathysense. She cleared her throat. "How much do you know about accounting?"

"Nothing."

Considering Sam didn't have to worry about money, Jillian wasn't surprised. "I'll keep it simple, then." She picked up her pencil and pointed at the spreadsheet on the screen. "You see this value here, and the one here. Add them up, and the sum appears," she brought up another spreadsheet, "here. This is a company that supposedly sold Barker a home entertainment system. The amount isn't huge—we're not talking tens of thousands of dollars here—but he regularly does business with this company. I took a look at its records, and it doesn't have a ton of clients. It was enough to get me going. I found more companies, and more money." She reluctantly leaned forward and twisted toward Sam. "He's not being blackmailed into working for them. He's one of them."

Sam straightened and chewed her lip. "Maybe we have it completely wrong."

Jillian thrust her hand toward the screen. "I'm not making this up! It's right here in—"

"I mean that maybe the trafficking ring isn't being run by organized crime. Maybe it's a local operation headed up by Barker and cousin Joel." She leaned against the kitchen counter. "We know Joel isn't an upstanding citizen. We know he's always had a gambling addiction to feed. He could have approached Barker with a proposal that would leverage his agency and Barker's connections."

"He'd know Barker isn't the Christian he claims to be."

"It's a real possibility," Sam admitted.

"Then if he sets up a meeting, it'll be a sham. There is no moving up the ladder. We've already found the top dog," Jillian said.

"*If* he's in charge. It's a possibility."

Yeah, well, her gut had told her Barker wasn't the victim he claimed to be, and that same gut was telling her that Barker was running the trafficking operation. "Take me with you to the meeting," Jillian said.

"We need to keep you out of it. They'll connect you to the Olmoses."

"I'll use another name. They're not going to take my photo and compare it to photos of people who've had contact with the Olmoses. You've had contact with Maria at the church."

"True."

"If Barker's in charge and he arranges this meeting with whomever, he'll be doing it to find out more about you, or to get rid of you. Isabel says people have disappeared."

Sam folded her arms. "We haven't confirmed that. So far, it's only gossip. We have that one body Jeremy found, but we can't connect it to Barker. The pathologist didn't consider the death suspicious."

"Look, I know you're used to doing this stuff on your own, but I really think—" A phone rang.

"It's mine." Sam left the kitchen. Jillian trailed after her, and swore under her breath when Sam looked at her phone's display and said, "It's him. Hello." A pause. "Have you arranged a meeting?" Silence, then, "I'd prefer to meet somewhere public." With the phone to her ear, Sam walked back into the kitchen with Jillian on her heels. "If that's the only way, then I guess I'll have to agree, but I'm bringing someone with me."

Jillian gave her a thumbs-up. She could hear Barker's tinny voice responding.

"That's fine." Sam picked up Jillian's pencil and wrote down an address on the pad Jillian had used to scribble notes as she'd followed Barker's money. "I agree, but I'd like to see how the meeting goes first." After uttering several more one-word responses, she hung up. "He's set up a meeting. He says it's with someone who has the authority to make decisions, or at least has a direct line to the boss."

Jillian looked at the address. "I don't recognize the street."

"It's in a new subdivision that's being built on the outskirts of town." Sam tapped away on her phone and turned it around, so Jillian could see the map of the area. "We're meeting at 4:00 p.m. tomorrow."

"Let's go check it out now."

Sam nodded her agreement. A couple of hours later, they drove away from the house where they'd meet Barker's associates. "It's just a house, and we're not in the middle of nowhere," Sam said.

"No, but the lots are big, and most of the houses are empty." Their astral tour of the meeting place hadn't reassured Jillian that they wouldn't be walking into an ambush. A suburban house that had the feel of a safe house. Neighbours, but far away enough that they might not hear any shots. "They could walk in tomorrow and shoot us in the head."

Sam frowned. "Why? What would it accomplish? All it would do is piss off our organization. They have no idea who we are or how powerful we are. Barker, or whoever is in charge, has agreed to the meeting because he wants to find out what I have to say. He doesn't know what we want, or how much of a threat we are."

"Call me crazy, but I think psychopathic criminals can be unpredictable. They might shoot us for kicks."

Sam snorted. "They're running a business. They don't do things for kicks."

"I hope you're right," Jillian murmured. Why had she agreed to this plan again? Hell, she'd helped come up with the damn thing. "There could be a whole welcoming committee inside when we arrive tomorrow."

"We'll have projected inside to make sure that's not the case." Sam's mouth turned up at the corners. "We do have certain advantages, here."

She still didn't like it, but she was being jumpy. Why would Barker's people walk in there and shoot them dead tomorrow? Barker had assumed that Sam represented a rival group that wanted to squeeze out the ring, but a savvy businessman didn't work on assumptions. He'd want to gather information, then make a decision. Still, that gut of hers . . . She wanted to take down the ring as much as Sam did, but tomorrow, her priority would be keeping them alive.

JILLIAN OPENED HER eyes and watched the blood return to Sam's face. They'd just projected into the house where they'd meet Barker's associates. Nobody was inside. They wouldn't be jumped the moment they stepped into the foyer. She checked her watch. "They could arrive any minute."

"We'd better get going," Sam said, turning the key in the ignition. A minute later, she pulled up to the curb outside the house, rather than into the house's gravelled driveway. "Let's stay in the car until they arrive."

Anything suspicious and they'd drive away. The house wasn't isolated, but the nearest neighbours were several hundred feet away and hidden behind fir trees. Jillian patted the holstered gun at her side, reassuring herself that it was still there, underneath her hoodie.

In the distance, a dust cloud announced an approaching car. A blue SUV careened into the driveway, kicking up more dust. "It's Joel," Jillian said, when the cloud had settled. "And he's alone."

Joel leaped from the SUV and waved at them, appearing way more relaxed than he should be. Jillian couldn't tell whether he was carrying a firearm, but she'd be surprised if he wasn't. Neither side had agreed to show up unarmed. When Sam opened the driver's door and got out of the car, Jillian followed her lead.

Joel grinned at them. "Joel Reynolds," he said, sticking out his hand.

Sam hesitated, then shook it. "I'm Sam Davis," she said, as Jillian gritted her teeth and pumped Joel's hand. "This is Jillian Jones. I thought we were going to meet someone in authority."

Joel's grin faded. "He'll be here." He pulled the SUV's back door open. Jillian tensed and slipped her hand inside her hoodie, then moved it away when Joel drew out a paper bag. "I just stopped at a market and bought some apples. You want one?"

"No, thanks," Jillian said, as Sam mumbled the same.

"Suit yourself." Joel plucked a red apple from the bag and bit into it. He motioned toward the house. "Let's go inside."

They followed him up the driveway, gravel crunching underfoot. Joel didn't seem worried that they'd jump him. Jillian let out her pent breath. Maybe she was anxious for nothing. They just wanted to talk. While Joel unlocked the front door, she looked back at the road. Nope, she still couldn't shake the feeling that something wasn't right. *"We should wait outside until the other guy shows up."*

"We can't guarantee others won't arrive after him. If we're ambushed, we can shift. We can stop hearts."

"I can only stop one or two."

"I can stop more. Unless they bring an army, we'll be okay."

"Come on in," Joel said.

"Is this your place?" Jillian asked, knowing it wasn't. According to the municipality's records, someone named Michael Bergeron owned the place. A background check hadn't turned up anything sinister, but the Fellowship wasn't the only organization capable of creating identities.

"It's a friend's. I'm taking care of it for him. He lives out west. This is an investment. We're looking for tenants."

Jillian stepped into the living room she'd seen through Sam's eyes ten minutes ago. The lack of personal items—photos, knickknacks, books—hadn't escaped their attention, but if Joel was telling the truth, it would make sense.

"Let's go through to the kitchen," Joel suggested. "It's roomier."

It would also mean they couldn't use the living room window to see who was arriving. "I'd prefer to stay here," Jillian said.

"Suit yourself." He plunked into a chair, then rolled his eyes when they both remained on their feet. "Hey, we're just having a little chat today, right? You want to keep an eye out, be my guest, but I hope you'll loosen up a little. I hate tense conversations."

"Let's sit," Sam said. *"Even if we see something outside we don't like, there's not much we can do about it now."*

"We should have brought Supporters."

"We agreed to meet alone."

True. Jillian sat stiffly on the sofa. Her view of the driveway was obstructed, but she'd see any new arrivals a few seconds before they entered the house. She watched Joel devour his apple, thankful that he didn't want to make polite conversation. He'd almost finished eating it when a man crossed in front of the window. The front door opened.

The man stepped inside. "Good, everyone is here."

"Do you recognize him?" Jillian asked.

"No." Sam stood. "I'm Sam Davis, and this is my associate, Jillian Jones. Who are you?"

"For today, I'm John Smith," the man said. Joel snickered. "Let's get down to business, shall we? You wanted to speak to someone who represents our interests."

"Can you do that?" Sam asked.

"I wouldn't be here if I couldn't, but I'm afraid I have nothing to say to you."

Then why—this *was* a trap! Jillian didn't need to tell Sam; Sam's pistol was already in her hand. Jillian pulled hers and levelled it at Joel. "What is this?" Sam said.

"You wanted a meeting, you got your meeting," Smith, or whoever the hell he was, said. Joel set his apple core on an end table and wiped his mouth with his hand. Smith's relaxed posture and Joel's nonchalance alarmed Jillian even more.

"We're walking out that door," Sam said.

Smith shook his head. "I have a gift for you. It would be rude for you to leave without receiving it."

Jillian's heart leaped into her mouth when several more people walked by the window. *"Tell me when to stop hearts,"* Jillian said, not wanting to play their hand too soon. Then she struggled not to gape. A hooded figure stumbled into the living room, followed by two men. One had a gun pointed at the captive's head.

"For you," Smith said, nodding.

The man without the gun whipped off the hood. A pale Patrice stared at them. There went shifting, stopping hearts, and whatever else they could do. One move or finger spasm and a bullet could rip through Patrice's brain. *"What now?"*

"I don't know," Sam said.

In different circumstances, Jillian would have chuckled at her blunt honesty. Sam was never one to sugar-coat.

"If we have to, we'll sacrifice her, but that'll be a last resort."

Jesus. Jillian understood that two Deiforms were more valuable than one life, but a life was a life. "What's she doing here?" she said, jutting her chin toward Patrice.

"Oh, don't play coy," Smith said. "We know the good reverend has been asking a lot of questions about the good Bishop Barker, our valued associate."

Joel snorted. "Valued associate?"

Smith shot him a warning look. "Now, would you be so kind as to lower your pistols and place them on the floor."

Jillian didn't have to communicate telepathically with Sam. They had no choice. She slowly crouched and set her pistol on the hardwood.

"Now lift your hands, so one of my associates can make sure you don't have any nasty surprises hidden anywhere."

Jillian straightened and lifted her hands. She met Patrice's eyes. She wanted to give her a reassuring smile, but she couldn't muster one. Patrice must be frightened, but she wasn't crying or begging for her life. Jillian admired her nerve.

She kept still while one of the men patted her down and lifted her phone from her pocket. Okay, they were disarmed and cut off, but they had the gifts. They just had to figure out how to use them without getting Patrice killed. They hadn't considered a hostage. Bastards.

"I'm sorry," Patrice murmured.

"Quiet!" Smith snapped. "You're to be seen, not heard."

Sam glared at him. "Now what?"

"You made a mistake, poking your noses into our affairs," Smith said. "We're here to send a message. Come with me. I have something to show you." He brushed past them. The man who'd patted down Jillian waved his gun. "Put your hands behind your head and follow him."

Flashing back to being arrested in the agency's parking garage, Jillian did as she was told. With a gun still at Patrice's head and another one pointed at her and Sam, she didn't have any options that wouldn't threaten Patrice. Smith—ha!—led them down a hallway and flung open a door. "Go," he barked, motioning for his captives to pass him. Jillian's sense of foreboding became stifling as she descended the stairs leading to the basement, carpet muffling her footsteps. Except for a floral sofa sitting against one wall, the finished room was empty.

"Against the back wall," Smith snapped. Jillian staggered forward when someone shoved her from behind. Sam stood at her side. They turned around and faced their captors. Smith, Joel, and the other two men stared back at them. So did Patrice, a muzzle still pressed to her skull. Was she resigned? Praying? Paralyzed with fear?

"What do you want to show us?" Sam asked.

Smith smiled smugly and swept his arm in front of him. "Your grave."

"We might have to sacrifice Patrice. Be ready."

"Shift or hearts?" Jillian said.

"Don't you want to know who we represent?" Sam asked. "You'll be upsetting some very powerful people." *"I don't know yet."* Sam paused. *"She'll probably die, either way. Just be ready."*

Smith shrugged. "We know you're not cops. So what are you? Part of a two-bit gang nobody has ever heard of? You think you're the first group who's tried to muscle in on our business? I don't give a flying fuck who you are."

"Let Reverend Patrice go. She's not involved."

"Oh, it's a little too late to let her go." Smith clapped his hands together. "Including her will send a much stronger message. She stays."

"My people won't like this," Sam said.

Smith's jaw tightened. "Screw your people. When they have to sweep you off the floor, they'll look for other business opportunities."

"Sweep us off the floor?"

Smith nodded. "A bullet to the heads will be too good for you. No, we'll give you a few minutes to contemplate your imminent deaths." He nodded to the thug who wasn't focused on Patrice. "Go with him," he said to Joel. The two men clumped up the stairs.

"Project and find out what's going on," Sam said. *"I'll stay with Patrice."*

Jillian bit her lip. "Can I sit down?" she whimpered.

A smile played on Smith's lips. "Be my guest."

Jillian sat against the wall, hugged her legs to her chest, and lowered her head. She floated upstairs, caught up with Joel and the other guy as they were opening the front door and going outside. "I should have brought those records I've been meaning to lose," Joel said. "I could have added them to the bonfire."

Bonfire?

They went to a van parked behind Joel's SUV. Joel swung open its back doors. "She shouldn't have fucked with John in his office."

"Which one?" his companion asked. "The reverend?"

"No, one of the other two. The stockier one. She really put John's nose out of joint. You don't bring it into his office. Never his office."

"Is that why he told Mike to drag it out?"

"Yeah. I'd just shoot them, but John wants it to hurt." Joel reached into the van and pulled out a gas can.

Oh, shit.

"What about the reverend, though?" Joel's companion asked. "Killing a minister..."

"A minister who was asking too many questions and knows what we look like. Just do as you're told, or you'll join her." Joel handed the gas can to him, then pulled one out for himself. "Come on. It's disco inferno time."

Jillian had heard and seen enough. Wanting time to relay the information to Sam before Joel and company returned to the basement, Jillian willed herself back into her body. She lifted her head. The room spun. She choked back bile. *"They're coming back with gas. I think they're going to set us on fire. Barker ordered this and he wants it to hurt. Apparently you really pissed him off by mentioning his extracurricular activities in his lofty office. We need to do something. Now."*

"Let's see exactly what they intend to do."

Jillian couldn't help but look at her. *"What? Are we going to wait until they light the match?"*

"We have to be absolutely sure we can't save Patrice."

Joel and his sidekick came down the stairs. Patrice shrank into her captor at the sight of the gas cans. She closed her eyes. Her mouth moved. She had no way out. She'd burn, like the Christian martyrs.

"Should I pour it over them?" Joel asked.

Smith shook his head. "They'd be in too much pain to appreciate what's happening to them. Start pouring about here." He pointed at a spot halfway between Jillian and the stairs. "And pour all the way up the stairs and into the hallway." His lips curled. "I want them to understand how tantalizingly close salvation is, if only they could walk through the fire. Imagine, their lungs burned, their bodies charred, because they can't get to the stairs. So close, but oh, so far."

Jillian wanted to smack his mouth shut.

Smith pointed at the other guy with the gas can. "You'll come with me and do the kitchen," he said, referring to the room right over where Jillian stood. He turned to the man holding Patrice's life in his hands. "Don't release her until I tell you to." Then he faced Jillian and Sam. "It's been a pleasure. Joel, if they so much as twitch before you're finished, light them up." Smith hurried up the stairs with his underling.

Joel soaked the area Smith had indicated and slowly backed toward the steps. Jillian swallowed. *"I don't see many options, especially any that will help Patrice. If only he'd push her over here. We could stop the guy's heart."*

"Which is why she won't join us until the last minute. They don't know we can stop hearts, but they do know that once that gun isn't pointed at Patrice's head, we'll make a move. But that's fine. I have a plan."

"You do? What?"

"We have different gifts, according to the grace given to each of us. Romans 12:6."

Sam wasn't quoting scripture to comfort herself. She appeared calm, serene. "I'm not following," Jillian said.

"The gifts will shine today." Sam paused. "I can run through fire."

Jillian blinked at her. "What?"

"It's my boon, Jillian. It protects me from fire."

It took a minute for Sam's words to sink in. "Okay, let's say I accept that, because we don't have a lot of time to discuss it, here. I don't see how that saves Patrice. I can shift, but—"

"I'll get out. You and Patrice will translocate to me."

"Whoa, whoa, whoa! I might be able to translocate to you, but we only practised over short distances, and not through fire, and not with another person. Can Patrice translocate with me? We can't shift people with us."

"True, but we agreed that translocating doesn't involve stepping outside time."

"What about the fire?"

"You can pass through walls, remember? Somehow the physical world doesn't affect us when we're translocating. The fire won't touch you."

They hoped. "What about distance?"

"We know it works the length of the condo. I'm betting we can go farther. I've got to be in telepathic range, though, to let you know when it's safe."

"Use empathysense."

"How? I'll feel cooler when I'm out, but you'll still be right next to a raging fire. You might not pick up on it." Sam paused. "I'll run to the side of the house. That should get me close enough for telepathy."

"Okay, let's say it does work. How will we explain it to Patrice?"

"You'll stop her heart before I run outside. It shouldn't take me longer than ten seconds to get into position. That'll leave you enough time to translocate before she comes around. And if she comes around early, we'll deal with it. I'd rather bring her into the Fellowship than let her die."

Jillian could agree with that.

Joel reached the top of the stairs. Jillian's heart pounded. They were running out of time. "So we're not only going to try to translocate her, and me, through fire, but her heart will be stopped while we're doing it?" Jesus.

"It might not work. Patrice could die. So could you. So I won't blame you at all, if you don't want to do it. I'll understand. It's your call."

Her call. She wished she had Sam's unwavering belief in the gifts. Stopping Patrice's heart would be easy, but the rest . . . Could Sam really run through fire? There were too many ifs and assumptions in their plan. *"If we shift, Patrice . . . Patrice will burn."*

"Yeah. But we'll stop her heart before we go and put her into the fire." Sam's voice dropped to a whisper in Jillian's mind. *"Hopefully she won't feel anything."*

Christ.

"Push her toward them now," Smith roared down. "Make sure she's clear of the gas."

The man with the gun sneered. "Over you go." He pushed Patrice so hard that she tripped and fell next to Sam. "I'm coming up," the man yelled, then his eyes widened when he heard the same *whoosh!* that set Jillian's heart racing. Flame raced down the stairs and engulfed him. Screams of agony set her teeth on edge. Her nails dug into her palms.

Patrice sank to her knees. She clapped her hands over her ears. "Sweet Jesus," she breathed.

Those bastards. Jillian stared at the wall of flame between her and safety. Her nose stung. She coughed. She wasn't sure if the air she was trying to breathe stank of burning flesh, or she was imagining it.

"Whatever we're going to do, we need to do it now." Sam crouched and covered her nose with her arm. *"Shift or translocate?"*

Sweat trickled down Jillian's temple. Patrice murmured next to her, probably praying for their souls and preparing to meet God. Jillian looked Sam in the eye. She wouldn't ask Sam to tell her how strong she was, that she could do it. She had to believe in herself. *"Translocate."* Patrice's heavenly welcoming party would have to wait.

Sam straightened. *"Get ready."*

Jillian moved closer to Patrice and put her arm around her shoulders. Sam faced the wall of fire, her head lowered. A lump rose in Jillian's throat. *"Sam, if we're wrong, and translocating through fire kills me, I need to tell you—"*

"*You have to believe that you'll survive.*" Sam lifted her head. "*Do it now.*"

Patrice slumped into Jillian. "*Go.*" Jillian cringed when Sam stepped into the fire. She waited for Sam's screams to join those still echoing in her mind, but all she heard was the roar of the approaching fiery wall. She pressed her body against Patrice's and wrapped her arms tightly around her. Her eyes watered. She coughed into Patrice's shoulder. If translocation failed, she'd have to—no, it would work. What use were the gifts if she could only use them to save herself? She believed they came from the good within her, the unselfish part, the person who wanted to save Patrice's life. She was going to translocate right to Sam, damn it, and Patrice was coming along for the ride.

The fire roared. Sweat blinded her. The choking air irritated her nostrils and throat, making it difficult to breathe. She clung to Patrice and waited for Sam's word. Had she made it through the fire? How long should Jillian wait before she shifted and condemned Patrice to death?

"*Now!*" Sam barked.

Jillian closed her eyes and visualized Sam, reached for her— A loud crack broke her focus. Was the ceiling coming down? Shit. Shit, shit, shit!

"*Now, Jillian!*"

"*I'm trying!*" *Shut everything out.* See Sam, only Sam, who was waiting for her, for them, and nothing would prevent them from reaching—

She shivered in the sudden chill and sucked down the clean, refreshing air. Patrice? She was there, in Jillian's arms, but had she survived? Jillian loosened her hold, then let Patrice go when Sam said, "I've got her." Her eyes burned. A coughing fit racked her body. She lay down and closed her eyes.

"Try to stay still for a minute."

Light pressure on her chest, followed by the familiar pain. She welcomed it. She needed it. She could breathe easily again. "Patrice," she croaked.

"Alive."

She opened her eyes and blinked at the clear blue sky. A pale Sam peered down at her. She nodded at Jillian. "You did good."

"So did you," Jillian whispered. She closed her eyes again.

"Let me tend to Patrice," Sam said.

Jillian lay quietly for a minute, then pushed herself into a sitting position. They were near the side of the house. She could see the glow of the fire through a window.

Sam pointed to the road. "We need to move away."

The short rest and Sam's healing had restored Jillian's vitality. She got to her feet and flexed her fingers. It was good to be alive.

Appearing dazed, Patrice looked at Jillian, then at Sam. "I don't understand how we got here."

"You passed out," Sam said. "We'll tell you about it later. Right now, we need to get away."

They hurried down the empty driveway and to the car. *"Do you want me to drive?"* Jillian asked Sam.

"No, I'm okay."

"Shouldn't we call someone about the fire?" Patrice said as she slid into the backseat.

"We'll stop at the first pay phone we see." Sam fired up the engine and sped away from the curb.

"I'm surprised they didn't take the car," Jillian said.

"I think they wanted the authorities to blame our murders on the poor guy they burned, so they wanted to leave the car outside and the keys in my pocket. It would have been a murder-suicide situation." *"They left our phones and guns in the house. I noticed them on my way out, but I wasn't going to stop to get them."*

"Good call," Jillian said, wondering if Sam would notice her dry tone.

"I'll tell Jeremy to wipe the phones." "Do you have someone you can stay with for a night?" Sam asked Patrice. "It'll take a while for the authorities to figure out there's only one body. I want to get to Barker before he knows any of us are alive."

"I can go to my brother's." Patrice blew out a sigh. "I can't believe Bishop Barker ordered those men to kill us. I *wouldn't* believe it, if I hadn't heard it with my own ears."

"What happened?" Jillian asked. "Where did they pick you up?"

"Near the church. I'd just left for the day and was walking to my car when a van pulled up. You know the rest. But never mind that. How did we get out?"

Jillian gave Sam a sidelong glance. *"Go ahead,"* Sam said.

Great. "You passed out. We managed to beat a path through the fire. I kept it clear while Sam carried you."

"Using what?" Patrice asked. "I didn't see anything that would beat back the fire."

Good point. She and Sam still wore their hoodies. "Um, there was a blanket on the floor."

"We didn't notice it at first. It was the same colour as the carpet," Sam added.

"We were very lucky," Jillian said.

"Oh, look, a gas station. I bet they have a phone." Sam pulled into the station. "Let's go ask."

Fortunately Patrice dropped the subject of their miraculous escape. *"When I projected to see what Joel and the other guy were up to, he mentioned records he wanted to get rid of,"* she said to Sam.

"Maybe they implicate Barker. Right now, we don't have anything we can give to the authorities about the trafficking situation. Do you feel up to a break-in tonight?"

"Yes," Jillian said emphatically. She'd uncovered enough to convict the guy for money laundering, but she wanted everyone to know that the bastard also imported slaves. The more charges, the merrier. Barker was going to sit in prison for the rest of his pathetic life.

Chapter Twenty-One

Sam strode into the building that housed the church's administrative offices and approached the receptionist's desk. "I'd like to see Bishop Barker, please."

The receptionist tore her gaze away from her computer screen. "Do you have an appointment?"

"No, but he'll want to see me. Tell him it's Sam Davis."

"Please, sit down."

"No, I'll wait here."

The receptionist lifted her phone receiver and pressed a button. "There's a Sam Davis here to see you. She doesn't have an appointment." The receptionist frowned and covered the receiver with her hand. "Sam Davis, right?" she whispered.

Sam nodded.

"Yes, Sam Davis." Silence, then, "I'll send her in." She hung up and smiled at Sam. "You can go in. You've seen the bishop before, right? His office is just around the corner."

Not for long. Sam had considered breaking into his office and greeting him when he arrived, but had rejected the idle fantasy. Since the receptionist has alerted him to her arrival, Sam wouldn't have the satisfaction of seeing surprise on Barker's face, but that was a small loss.

"Ms. Davis," Barker boomed when she entered his office. "How nice to see you again!"

Sam snorted and pushed the door shut. "Let's not play games. Sorry I had to leave your fiery party early."

Barker's brow furrowed. "I have no idea what you're talking about."

She plopped into a guest chair and dropped her satchel to the floor. "Don't you want to know how my meeting with your superior went yesterday?"

"Once I arranged the meeting, I was out of it. I have no interest in what your two organizations discussed."

Sam wanted to roll her eyes. "Before you entered the seminary, did you ever consider going into acting? You're pretty good, but unfortunately for you, your men were chatty. They figured we wouldn't be alive to tell any tales, like the one that features you as the leader of the trafficking operation."

Barker's expression remained neutral. "I still have no idea what you're talking about. What men?"

"Joel, for one."

"I told you that Joel's mixed up with some unsavoury people, and by choice, not because he doesn't have any other options."

Sam stared at him. "If you want to play dumb, that's fine. We have enough to send you to prison for a long time. We don't need to pin the fire on you." She flipped open her satchel and pulled out the account statements Jillian had marked up. "It seems you have more money than you can possibly make from your position here, and you've used rather illegal ways to conceal that fact." She tossed the papers onto his desk.

Barker's eyes flicked to them. "I'll have an accountant look this over."

"I doubt you'll want your accountant to look over these." Sam pulled out the records she and Jillian had taken from Joel's home office the previous evening and added them to the papers on Barker's desk. "There's ample proof in those records to tie you to immigrants that entered the country and then disappeared. Nobody has ever heard from them again."

The air grew tense. Barker kept his eyes on Sam.

"You probably thought Joel had destroyed the records, or at least locked them away, but Joel's not as good at hiding things as you are. He's not a criminal mastermind. He must disappoint you." She leaned forward and tapped the top sheet that tied Barker to a "shipment," as Barker's sick little group called them. "Take this, for example. It clearly states that you've located—what do you call them? Owners? Yes, owners for the people you've deceived, and the amounts you'll collect every month from that point forward."

She drew back when Barker leaped to his feet and violently shoved the papers off his desk. "That idiot," he snarled. "You're in the same business I'm in. Surely we can come to some arrangement. You've proven you're quite capable. I'll cut you in."

"No deal. When I said that I represent the church, I meant it." Sam moved her hand closer to the pistol a Supporter had delivered to her that morning. "This is how it's going to work. You're going to resign your position. Then you're going to turn yourself in, and you're going to make it very clear that the church knew nothing about your trafficking operation, because it didn't. You're also going to give me the name of every person you brought in and where they are now." She jerked her head toward the papers now lying on the floor. "Those records only go back seven years. You've been at it a lot longer than that."

"And then what?" Barker asked mildly. "I rot in prison? What if I told you that I have knowledge of other trafficking operations, that I can give you the names of hundreds of immigrants across the country trapped in slavery, including sexual slavery, and identify the people involved in those operations? What would that be worth to you?"

Sam's immediate reaction was to tell him to shove it. Twenty years ago, she would have said the words. The world had grown grayer since then.

"I'll give you everything. I'll resign, but you'll keep me out of it. No prison. No grand revelations about my money, or my involvement in trafficking." He pointed to the papers scattered on the floor. "Those records are the only evidence tying me to anything. You'll have them as insurance that I'll keep my end of the bargain."

"Your people will talk. They'll give you up."

"Not if you only take them down for the trafficking operation. I have proof of other . . . activities they've participated in. I'll also make sure their families are taken care of while they're sitting in prison. That'll be my insurance. I'll explain that to them when I tell them it's over." Barker leaned forward and splayed his hands on top of his desk. "I suppose you could insist that we all go to prison and I turn that proof over to you, but I won't. If you send me to prison, all those innocent immigrants will remain in prison, too. Because you'll never find them without my help. To sweeten the pot even further, I'll give you what I have on my idiot cousin and his agency. You'll be able to shut it down."

"Your agency, you mean," Sam said. "If you give us everything on Joel, why would he keep quiet about you?"

"I didn't say I'd give you everything on Joel. I said I'd give you enough to shut down the agency."

Considering Joel hadn't flinched at setting one of his own colleagues on fire and leaving three people to die, Sam didn't doubt that he'd participated in more than gambling and using his agency to front a trafficking operation. "Let me recap what you're proposing. You'll resign your position and retire. You'll give us what we need to send everyone involved in your trafficking operation to prison. You'll also give us details about other trafficking operations across the country, and you'll hang Joel. Your people will stay in line because you have proof that would keep them in prison until they die, and you'll take care of their families.

"In return, we don't touch you. We'll have the proof of your money laundering and your involvement in the trafficking operation to ensure that you keep your end of the bargain," she held up a finger, "which will include never standing in a pulpit again, never engaging in any criminal activity again, and staying away from Karen Patrice."

Barker inclined his head to indicate agreement. "That sums it up."

Discussing a deal with the likes of Barker felt dirty. In an ideal world, there would be no need for such a bargain. In a close to ideal world, Sam would turn it down. But she lived in the real, messy world. When she'd first joined the Fellowship—when she was innocent and naive—she would have stood her ground. The desire to punish Barker and bring him to justice would have blinded her.

She'd witnessed too many horrors since then. Sometimes punishment, justice, the righteous anger, was best left to the Lord, especially when it meant saving people here. She wouldn't condemn innocents to shackled lives because she wanted to see a handful of people get what they deserved. *I'll leave it to You.* He'd take care of them. Still . . . "We can find those people. We found you."

"You can try. It'll take months, maybe years, without my help, and that's if you find them at all. In the meantime, all those people they brought here will languish. You don't want that. You want to save them. Of course, when you round up those responsible, you'll keep my name out of it. That's part of the deal, too. But go ahead and prosecute them all. I don't care."

Sam leaned back and pretended to think about it, hoping Barker would wilt under the prospect that he'd be disgraced and imprisoned. He didn't oblige her. There was no point dragging it out. "You have a deal. I want everything you've promised, and you'll resign by the end of the week."

"Of course." Barker extended his hand, then let it drop when Sam didn't move. "I have your word, then?"

"Yes, you have my word, and my word is solid."

"You can make this decision on behalf of the church?"

"Yes." *Not this church. The Church.*

"Very well." Barker sank into his chair. "You'd better pull out something you can use to take notes." He leaned back and laced his fingers behind his head. "Where should I start?"

Jillian drove onto the Olmos estate and pulled into a free guest spot. Patrice was waiting for her. She pushed away from her car and smiled. "What a wonderful morning to be alive!"

"It's beautiful, isn't it," Jillian said with a grin. It faded when she looked at the Olmos house and remembered why she was here.

Patrice held her hands in front of her, palms down. "You can't see it, but they're still shaking. Did you sleep last night?"

"A little." She'd only crawled into bed around 3:00. They'd had to pore over Joel's records and plan for today. "Sam's with Barker now." The bastard was facing years in prison. She hoped Sam was enjoying tearing him down. "I don't know how long it will take the authorities to round everyone up once they've received our information, but it doesn't matter. Nobody will be collecting from the Olmoses anymore." She gazed toward the house again. "When I called Maria last night, she said they've been discussing what to do ever since we spoke to Isabel. I hope they've come to an agreement."

Patrice grimaced. "Me too. Let's find out."

They strode to the front door. The maid swung it open and led them into the living room, where Max, Maria, and a visibly nervous Isabel sat. After exchanging polite greetings, Jillian accepted Maria's invitation to sit. Max leaped to his feet and offered Patrice his place on the sofa, even though there were two other empty chairs. Patrice ignored his offer and settled into one of the chairs, probably wanting to sit where she could see everyone. Max went to the fireplace. He tried to strike a casual pose, but he couldn't keep his hands still.

"On the phone, you said you won't have to meet with the one who collects our money," Maria said.

Jillian nodded. "Things moved faster than we expected. It's over. Nobody will bother you again." It was time to discuss Dylan and Isabel. Hoping Patrice would take the lead, Jillian looked at her.

Patrice met her eyes, then shifted her attention to the Olmoses. "Because you helped us, we promised we wouldn't give your names to the authorities, but there was a condition."

Maria nodded gravely.

"Have you decided what to do?"

Maria turned to Isabel before responding, which Jillian took to be a good sign. "Isabel is part of our family. We've always wanted her to be free."

"We were protecting her," Max said.

Jillian shifted in her chair but kept her mouth shut. She wasn't here to berate the Olmoses for their complicity and excuses.

"Let's talk about the future, rather than the past," Patrice said mildly. "Where do we go from here?"

"Isabel wants to continue living with us," Max said. "She wants to go to school, to get a certificate. As Maria said, she's part of our family. She doesn't owe us anything. We owe her." His eyes flicked to Isabel, then back to Patrice. "We can't repay her for the years she's lost, but we can make sure she wants for nothing from this point forward. When she's ready, she'll have her own home, her own life."

"What about Dylan?" Patrice asked.

"She wants us to keep him." Maria's lips trembled. "At some point, we'll tell him the truth. Isabel will always be in his life. Always."

Patrice repeated Max and Maria's words in Spanish. "Is that what you want?" she asked Isabel. "Do you want to continue living with the Olmoses?"

"I do," Isabel said, nodding.

"And you want them to continue to raise Dylan and be his legal parents?"

"Yes. This is the best place for him. It's what he knows, and Mrs. Maria and Mr. Max, they love him."

Maria's eyes moistened. She grasped Isabel's hand and squeezed it. "Thank you," she murmured. "He loves you, Isabel. You will always be special to him, and to us."

"Are you sure this is what you want?" Patrice asked Isabel. "You don't feel pressured? This is truly what you want for yourself and Dylan?"

"This is what I want. I wanted to be free, and I am. The Olmoses are my family. I want to stay with them, and this is Dylan's home, his family."

Patrice turned to Jillian. "It's what Isabel wants." She turned back to the Olmoses. "I'll be visiting you frequently to make sure she's not a prisoner here. Do you understand?"

"Yes, we understand," Max said.

Maria's head bobbed in agreement. "What happens now?"

"As Reverend Patrice said, she'll be keeping an eye on the situation," Jillian said. "If she sees anything that worries her, she'll let me know, and I'll be back. In a week or two, she'll come by with Isabel's legal papers. A passport, a health card, everything she needs."

Maria pulled a tissue from a nearby box and dabbed at her eyes. "Thank you."

"The authorities shouldn't come knocking on your door." The Fellowship would hold back any evidence that mentioned Isabel or the Olmoses. "If they do, call Reverend Patrice. She'll let us know." Patrice had a number that would connect her to Jeremy or Emma, depending on the time. "We'll take care of it."

"So you're leaving, then," Maria said.

"Yes, I am. I want you to know that I didn't offer to tutor Dylan to get to you. I had no idea about your situation. I just wanted to help him pass math." Jillian wanted to say good-bye to him, but an aunt had taken him out for the morning, so he wouldn't overhear this conversation and wonder why Jillian and the reverend were visiting. She had the feeling she'd leave a trail of unsaid good-byes behind her in the coming years. "He's a great kid. Don't screw this up, okay? Think of him."

"We will." Maria swallowed. "He has three people who love him very much."

They lapsed into silence. "I think that's all we need to say for now," Patrice said. "I'll be by next Monday to see how things are going." She gazed at Isabel. "I'd like to hear what you're thinking of doing at school. "Perhaps we can go out for a coffee or tea and discuss it."

When Isabel looked to Maria, Maria shook her head. "You don't have to ask me. You're free now. You can come and go as you like."

"Can I learn how to drive?"

Maria smiled through her tears. "Yes, you can."

"That settles it, then. I'll pick you up on Monday around 10:00," Patrice said to Isabel, then repeated everything they'd said in English, for Jillian's benefit.

"Sounds like we're off to a good start." Eager to bring the awkward meeting to a close, Jillian rose. "Good luck."

"You, too," Maria said. "If you're ever in town, call me. We can do lunch."

"I'll do that," Jillian said, knowing she wouldn't. She might be back here someday, but to investigate someone else. There was nothing else to be said. "We can show ourselves out."

When they left the living room, she didn't look back, and she and Patrice didn't speak until they were outside. "I feel a lot better knowing you'll be monitoring them," she said to Patrice, meaning it.

"I'm optimistic." Patrice stopped near her car and squinted into the morning sun. "I know the situation was abominable, but I see them as well-intentioned people who couldn't figure out how to get out of a frightening predicament."

"I waffle between seeing them that way, and being angry with them for not trying to get help. I don't know what I would have done in their position." Notifying the authorities could have freed Isabel and the others much sooner. On the other hand, it could have had dire consequences. Barker was a ruthless, vindictive, son of a bitch. He would have retaliated. "I do believe they have regrets and they'll spend the rest of their lives trying to make it up to Isabel."

Patrice grunted. "You know, I was thinking about yesterday," she said slowly. "You're right, I must have passed out. I remember you comforting me. Then I was outside."

Comforting her? Oh yeah, she'd put her arm around Patrice in preparation to hang onto her while they translocated. Plus, she hadn't wanted Patrice's head to hit the carpet when her heart stopped. "Sam spotted a way through the fire. We were lucky."

"Oh, I don't think it was luck," Patrice said firmly.

Jillian shoved her hands into her pockets. She might as well get used to it. In the crowd she now hung out with, she'd always be outnumbered.

"Are you sure you and Sam don't have time for lunch?"

"I wish we did, but we have a flight to catch. Don't worry, Sam will call and let you know what's happened with Barker." They could have stayed and had lunch with Patrice, but Sam had said no, it was time for them to leave. Jillian could see the sense in it. They'd never see Patrice again.

"What about the poor man they burned alive? Did you see the news this morning? They mentioned the fire, but not the body."

"They're either still sifting through the rubble, or they haven't released the information to the media yet."

"Are you sure we shouldn't go to the police?"

"Yes. We'll make sure the authorities know about Joel's connection to the house."

"We could just tell them Joel was there," Patrice said.

"No. We don't want to get caught up in the investigation."

"You and Sam, you mean."

Jillian shook her head. "All of us." She wouldn't tell Patrice that if she went to the police, she'd do it alone, and good luck finding the two women who'd supposedly been in the basement with her. They'd be long gone. "Don't worry. They won't get away with murder."

Patrice clasped her hands in front of her. "I don't like it, but I'll go along with it. What you told me about the Olmoses and Maria turned out to be true. The same goes for Bishop Barker. I'll believe you again."

"It really is for the best." Jillian checked the time. "I should get going."

"I guess this is it, then." When Patrice extended her hand, Jillian warmly shook it. She agreed with Sam. Patrice was one of the good guys. Patrice shielded her eyes from the sun and peered at Jillian. "I know I don't have the full story about you two, but I suppose prying won't get me anywhere." Jillian gave her a small smile, which Patrice returned. "I'll pray for both of you." She opened her car door.

"Deliver Isabel's papers to her," Jillian said.

"I will." Patrice slammed her door shut and lowered the window. "I'll make sure the Olmoses do everything they said they'd do."

"If there's a problem—"

"I have the number." Patrice fired up her engine. "May God go with you." She pulled out of the spot and waved good-bye.

Jillian didn't stop waving until she could no longer see Patrice's car. Had Sam avoided caring about people for the last twenty years, or did pretending she didn't care help her to leave one group of people behind for the next? So far, Jillian preferred the shorter cases. No ties. Fewer lies. When they'd had to endure a long, involved investigation like this one, she wouldn't pretend she didn't care, that the people she'd encountered hadn't left a mark. As far as she was concerned, she'd already used up her allotted numb time for this life. Pain was part of the package now. It meant she was alive.

She'd remember why it had been worth it when Sam recounted her meeting with Barker. Too bad she couldn't have been there to see the smirk wiped off his face. She'd have to settle for hearing about it second-hand. She'd savour every luscious detail.

JILLIAN COULD HARDLY believe her ears. She pushed away from the back of the sofa and looked up at Sam. "You did *what?*"

"I made a deal with him that keeps him out of it," Sam said.

"Let me get this straight," she said, hoping she had it wrong. "Barker won't be going to prison. He gets to waltz off into the sunset with his reputation and his money. Why? Why the hell would you make a deal with the devil?"

Sam sank into a chair, opened her satchel, and pulled out a pad. "It's all here," she said, turning the pad toward Jillian. The top page was filled with her small, neat script. "We can rescue hundreds more. He gave us everything, not only about his operation, but others across the country."

"Everything except him." Jillian blew out an exasperated sigh.

Sam lowered the pad. "In a perfect world . . ." She shook her head and tossed the pad onto the coffee table, then leaned forward. "Look, I went in there intending to nail him and his entire operation, but when he said he could help us rescue others, I had to listen. We didn't even know there were others. Don't you agree that letting one get away is worth saving a bunch of innocent people from their hells and shutting down more trafficking rings?"

Sacrifice one for the many. The ends justified the means. Why couldn't the world be fair?

"Let's say I'd turned down his offer and turned him over to the authorities," Sam said. "The church would have become embroiled in a scandal it had nothing to do with."

"Who cares about the church?" Jillian snapped.

"I do. But that's not the main reason I made the deal. I wanted to save those people."

"We would have found them."

"I hate that I'm echoing Barker, but when? We wouldn't even know where to start."

"Roberta might."

Sam shook her head. "It doesn't work like that."

Nope, Roberta didn't have a crystal ball or Ouija board to give her answers. She relied on an invisible, omnipotent being, and Jillian trusted her. Maybe they should all be committed to the funny farm. "What about Patrice? She's expecting him to go to prison."

"I'll explain it to her the same way I'm explaining it to you."

"She won't like it," Jillian murmured.

Sam's voice rose. "What would you have done in my shoes? Would you have turned him down, told him that you cared more about sending him to prison than freeing all those other victims?"

"I would have wanted it all," Jillian said petulantly. She regretted her words when Sam looked down at her hands. She was being too hard on her. If she imagined herself in Sam's shoes, sitting across from that smug bastard, she might not have had the wisdom to weigh the options, consider the consequences, come down on the side of the innocent, even though it would have made her want to puke. Did she honestly believe Sam was happy that Barker would get off scot-free? Could she have slept at night, knowing there were others out there they could have saved, but they'd chosen to give Barker what he deserved, instead? Would imagining him in prison have chased away the images of those still in chains? "I understand why you did what you did," she said quietly. "It sticks in my throat, though."

Sam lifted her head. "Mine, too. The deal doesn't come without a price, and I'm not talking about what we gave Barker. I'm talking about us. We'll always know. If we ever hear his name again, it'll set our teeth on edge. At least I believe he'll ultimately pay for his crimes."

"I'd say I believe in karma, but too many people get away with being assholes, so frankly, I don't. I think we live in a chaotic, brutal world that we kid ourselves is civilized." She could feel a stint on a soapbox coming on, which neither of them needed right now. "I get it. I'm behind you. Did you tell Roberta?"

Sam nodded. "I've already given Jeremy the key names. I'll give him my notes when we get back to the island."

"Why did you write them? Why didn't you just type them into your phone?"

Sam's shoulders heaved. "I don't know. I guess . . . I think I wanted to put it all down on something real, that I can touch. I wanted it to flow through me, the horror of it. Seeing it as a bunch of pixels wouldn't have been the same."

Jillian stared at her. If she ever thought she had Sam all figured out, she'd remind herself of this conversation. She'd also better change the subject before she made a fool of herself. They'd hardly had a chance to catch their breath since escaping the fire yesterday. Sam owed her a story. "How did you get your boon? Now that I know about it, I figure there's no harm in your telling me."

"You're right, I should tell you."

A pang of guilt quickly dissipated Jillian's surprise. She'd caught Sam at a vulnerable moment.

"It's not something I'm proud of," Sam said.

Guilt be damned. She *had* to hear the story now. "Why? What happened?"

Sam was quiet for a moment, then said, "It was only my second solo investigation. The town I was in didn't have a safe house, so I rented an apartment over an electronics store, near the church I was investigating."

"Did the Beguilers find you?"

Sam shook her head. "I almost wish they had. Then it wouldn't be so embarrassing. No, I'd rented an apartment right over a fencing operation. If I'd done my homework properly, I would have known that. I guess someone didn't get paid, because one night they chucked a few Molotov cocktails through the store's window. The place was a tinderbox. By the time I woke up, my apartment was burning. I'd say I was lucky that I didn't die in my sleep of smoke inhalation, but it wasn't luck." She paused, maybe waiting for Jillian to toss in her usual two cents about the number of possible explanations for waking up that didn't involve God, but Jillian held her tongue. It was Sam's story, and Jillian wanted to hear more.

"It was similar to what happened yesterday. Fire roaring, heat, smoke . . . I'd tell you there was no way to get out, but I'm not sure that was true." She lifted her hands in an apologetic gesture. "I panicked. Everything I'd learned went straight out of my head. I could have shifted, but I didn't even think about it. My mind froze. All I could think was that I was going to die, but that's not what upset me. It was letting everyone down. Ruth, Brian, Roberta . . . they'd gone through the trouble of bringing me in and training me, and it would all go to waste. So I called out. I called out to Him . . . and He answered."

"But how did you know? How did you know the fire wouldn't burn you?"

"I just knew. I just knew that if I walked through the fire in the hallway, I'd survive."

"But how did you know?" Jillian repeated.

Sam touched her temples. "It was as if I'd always known. And I knew about boons. Not about the one I received specifically, but that He usually bestows them when things are looking grim. I guess He knew I wasn't going to figure out how to get out of there on my own. I'm fortunate He decided to help me, rather than to punish me."

"Punish you for what, exactly?" Jillian said, unable to bite her tongue this time. "Being human? Being frightened? Not being perfect? You were half asleep and confused. Anyone would be, waking up to a freaking inferno. Your flight and fight response kicked in. When the adrenaline is pumping, we don't always think straight. It was only your second investigation, too."

"I told myself the same excuses."

"They're not excuses. What did Ruth and everyone else say when you told them?"

"That the Lord had blessed me. That they were relieved and grateful I was alive. Oh, yeah, and not to worry about all the equipment that went up in smoke. I don't know what they said privately, though."

Jillian smiled. "Probably the same things."

"I should have shifted." Sam rolled her eyes. "That's one time I'd have liked to have done it involuntarily."

"You did what you had to do to survive, and I'm absolutely positive that given the choice between you not asking for help," hey, it was Sam's story, "and dying in the fire, they were all happy that you asked for help and got it. You didn't let anyone down."

"I let myself down." She lowered her eyes. "I let Him down."

Bite tongue, bite tongue! "You need to be more sympathetic toward yourself. If someone else told you the same story, you'd say, 'Don't be so hard on yourself.' Because I've heard you say that to people. 'Don't blame yourself. Don't be so hard on yourself.' So cut yourself some slack. You survived, and you've spent twenty years since then making a difference. You have nothing to be embarrassed about. And you know what? This is why I want to hear about you from you, rather than reading it in a file. I bet your file says something like," Jillian lowered her voice, "'Sam received her boon when she was trapped in a fire.'" She cleared her throat. "I bet it doesn't go into all this."

"All what? How stupid I felt?" Sam held up her hand when Jillian drew breath. "I'm sure it also doesn't say how fire has frightened me since then. It makes me shake. I don't even like gas ovens. Kind of silly, considering how fire can't touch me."

"You didn't shake yesterday. You faced the damn fire, told me you were going to run through it, and did."

Sam's brows drew together. "You're right, I didn't break into a sweat—not because I was petrified, anyway." She met Jillian's eyes. "I couldn't let myself be afraid. I knew I had two people to save."

Blood pounded in Jillian's ears. "Excuse me," she sputtered. "*Two* people?" Her hand went to her chest. "I could have shifted. The only reason I didn't was because *we* had to save Patrice, something you couldn't have done without . . ." She trailed off when she noticed the glint in Sam's eyes and her twitching mouth. "You're terrible. I should throw this cushion at you, but I promised myself I wouldn't throw anything else at you."

Sam chuckled. "We should go." She stood and placed her hands on her hips. "It's been a while since I've spent so much time in the same place. I'm looking forward to going back to the island, but it'll seem weird moving on."

Jillian nodded. "Life almost felt normal there for a while."

"Yeah, it did," Sam said, surprise tinging her voice. "I have to admit, I'm starting to see the value of the joint gifts. I couldn't have saved Patrice by myself."

"No, you couldn't have," Jillian said with a grin. "We made a good team. We *are* a good team."

"I'm still getting used to being part of a team." Sam lifted the pad from the coffee table and slid it back into the satchel.

"Is it that bad?"

She flipped the satchel shut and walked to the front door, where their packed bags waited. "You don't insist on being in my face twenty-four hours a day," she said over her shoulder. "That helps."

Jillian had followed her. "I'm glad I'm not getting on your nerves. I don't want to do that. At the same time . . ." She took a deep breath. "I can't help but care about you. I mean, we're like family now, you know." Jesus, how lame could she get?

Sam turned to her. "We're sisters on paper, and in the Fellowship."

Ugh. She didn't want them to be sisters.

"I'd be upset if you got yourself killed," Sam said, making Jillian's heart soar. "The joint gifts are too valuable, and so are Deiforms. Plus, I trained you."

Now her heart was lying flattened on the ground after being run over by a steamroller. She struggled to keep her expression neutral. Why the hell had she steered the conversation in this direction?

"And you keep me on my toes." Sam's mouth turned up at the corners. "I like that about you."

Okay, now she was orbiting the moon again. Could someone please stop the roller coaster? She wanted to get off.

"I know I'm not the best roommate. I'm trying not to be too anti-social. I appreciate that you give me my space. If you keep doing that, I think things will be all right."

Crushed, Jillian grunted. She understood Sam's need for space, but that hardly sounded encouraging, no matter how many ways she tried to spin it.

Sam picked up her bag with her free hand and slung it over her shoulder. "I was thinking that maybe we could try playing something together, you on guitar, and me on keyboards. I'd say piano, but I can't take one with me when we're on the road."

"Seriously?" Jillian said, failing to mask her surprise.

"Yeah, seriously. I usually play Christian music, but—"

"That's fine. I've never minded the music."

"We'll start with something easy, see if we enjoy playing together."

Her throat tight, Jillian could only nod. Forget about getting off the rollercoaster; she'd hang onto the safety bar a while longer. After years of protecting herself, Sam was cracking the door open. Jillian wouldn't rush her. If Sam even suspected that Jillian liked her in that way, she'd tuck right back into her shell, and awkward wouldn't begin to describe the air between them. Jillian would have to be patient.

Patience. Always freaking patience.

BREAKING NEWS: A new development today in relation to the human trafficking rings police departments across the country moved against last month. Operation Safe Passage freed hundreds of people, including thirty-two in our community. Joel Reynolds, one of the men accused of being involved in the local ring, was fatally stabbed in prison while awaiting trial. Officials aren't saying anything beyond that they're investigating the incident.

Reynolds was the cousin of former bishop John Barker, who resigned from his position two months ago for health reasons. Barker was supposed to be present at the naming ceremony held this afternoon for a new resource centre for immigrants. City council voted to name the building the Bishop John Barker Immigration Centre, in recognition of Barker's dedication to aiding immigrants and their children. The ceremony had to go ahead without its guest of honour. Our condolences to the former bishop.

Author's Note

Thanks for reading *Unseen Bonds*. I hope you enjoyed it. There's a short poll at my website about your reaction to certain parts of the story. I'd appreciate it if you'd hop over and express your opinion. There are only two multiple-choice questions, so it'll be quick.

www.sarahettritch.com/unseen-bonds-poll

Thanks,
Sarah.

Other Titles by Sarah Ettritch

Threaded Through Time
The Salbine Sisters
The Rymellan Series
The Missing Comatose Woman

If you'd like to be notified when the next Deiform Fellowship book is released, sign up for the notification list at Sarah's website: www.sarahettritch.com

Thanks for reading!

www.ingramcontent.com/pod-product-compliance
Lightning Source LLC
LaVergne TN
LVHW040140080526
838202LV00042B/2967